WARCRAFT

DUROTAN

Also available from Titan Books and Christie Golden

WARCRAFT

THE OFFICIAL MOVIE NOVELIZATION

THE OFFICIAL PREQUEL NOVEL

DUROTAN

by CHRISTIE GOLDEN

Warcraft: Durotan
ISBN: 9781785653834

Published by Titan Books
A division of Titan Publishing Group Ltd
144 Southwark St, London SE1 0UP

First edition: May 2016
10 9 8 7 6 5 4 3 2 1

A CIP catalogue record for this title is available from the British Library.

Printed and bound in the USA.

LEGENDARY.COM **TITAN**BOOKS.COM

This book is dedicated to Chris Metzen, my Blizzard brother who, back in the year 2000, first entrusted me with Durotan and gave me the chance to create Draka. It is a true and then-unimaginable honor, fifteen years on, to be able to revisit them and help introduce them to a new audience.

WARCRAFT

DUROTAN

PROLOGUE

The crimson trail steamed in the snow, and Durotan, son of Garad, son of Durkosh, shouted in triumph. This was his first hunt—the first time he had hurled a weapon at a living creature with the intent to kill it—and the blood proved his spear had found its mark. Expecting praise, he turned to his father, his narrow chest swelling with pride, and was confused by the expression on the Frostwolf chieftain's face.

Garad shook his head. His long, glossy black hair fell loose and wild about his broad, powerful shoulders. He sat atop his great white wolf Ice, and his small, dark eyes were grim as he spoke.

"You missed its heart, Durotan. Frostwolves strike true the first time."

Disappointment and shame brought hot blood to the young orc's face. "I… I regret that I failed you,

Father," he stated, sitting up as straight as he could atop his own wolf, Sharptooth.

Using his knees and hands in Ice's thick ruff to direct him, Garad brought the beast alongside Sharptooth and regarded his son. "You failed to kill with your first blow," he said. "You did not fail *me*."

Durotan glanced up at his father, uncertain. "My task is to teach you, Durotan," Garad continued. "Eventually you will be chieftain, if the Spirits will it so, and I would not have you offending them unnecessarily."

Garad gestured toward the direction of the blood trail. "Dismount and walk with me, and I will explain. Drek'Thar, you and Wise-ear come with us. The rest of you will wait for my summons."

Durotan was still ashamed, but also confused and curious. He obeyed his father without question, slipping from Sharptooth's back and giving the huge wolf a pat. Whether the frost wolves were adopted as mounts because of their color, or whether the clan had named themselves after their snow-hued fur, no one knew; the answer had been swallowed by time. Sharptooth whuffed and licked his young master's face.

Drek'Thar was the Frostwolves' elder shaman—an orc who had a close connection with the Spirits of Earth, Air, Fire, Water, and Life. According to Frostwolf lore, the Spirits dwelt in the far north—at the Edge of the World, in the Seat of the Spirits. Older than Durotan, but not ancient, Drek'Thar had been blinded in battle years before Durotan's birth.

A wolf ridden by the attacking clan had snapped at Drek'Thar's face. It was only a partial bite, but it had done enough. A single tooth had punctured one eye, and the other eye lost its vision shortly thereafter. Durotan could still see thin, pale scars snaking out from under the cloth Drek'Thar always wore to hide his ruined eyes.

But if something had been taken from Drek'Thar, something also had been given. Soon after losing his sight he had developed extra senses to compensate, perceiving the Spirits with keenness unrivaled by the younger shaman he trained. From time to time, the Spirits even sent him visions from their seat at the Edge of the World, as far north as north could be.

Far from helpless, as long as he could ride Wise-ear, his beloved and well-trained wolf, Drek'Thar could travel where any other orc could go.

Father, son, and shaman pressed through the deep snow, following the blood. Durotan had been born in a snowstorm, which was supposed to augur well for a Frostwolf's future. His home was Frostfire Ridge. While the snow sullenly retreated before the brightness of the summer months, it merely bided its time until its inevitable return. No one could say how long the Frostwolf orc clan had made this inhospitable place their home; they had been here as long as any could remember. "Always," one of the older Frostwolves had said simply to Durotan when he was old enough to wonder.

But night was coming, and the cold increased. Durotan's dense, warm boots of clefthoof hide struggled to resist saturation, and his feet began to grow numb. The wind picked up, knifing like a dagger through his thick fur cloak. Durotan shivered as he trudged on, waiting for his father to speak while the blood in the snow stopped steaming and began to freeze.

The red trail led over a broad, windswept expanse of snow and toward a gray-green smudge of trees clustered at the feet of Greatfather Mountain, the tallest peak in a chain that extended for hundreds of miles to the south. Greatfather Mountain, so the lore scrolls told, was the clan's guardian, stretching his stone arms out to create a protective barrier between Frostfire Ridge and the southlands. The scent of clean snow and fresh pine filled Durotan's nostrils. The world was silent.

"It is not pleasant, is it? This long walk in the snow," Garad said at last.

Durotan wondered what the correct response was. "A Frostwolf does not complain."

"No, he does not. But... it is still unpleasant." Garad smiled down at his son, his lips curving around his tusks. Durotan found himself smiling back and nodded slightly, relaxing.

Garad reached to touch his son's cloak, fingering the fur. "The clefthoof. He is a strong creature. The Spirit of Life has given him heavy fur, a thick hide, layers of fat below his skin, so he may survive in this land. But when he is injured, he moves too slowly to keep himself warm. He falls behind the herd, so they cannot warm him, either. The cold sets in."

Garad pointed to the tracks; Durotan could see that the beast had been stumbling as it moved forward.

"He is confused. In pain. Frightened. He is but a creature, Durotan. He did not deserve to feel thus. To suffer." Garad's face hardened. "Some orc clans are cruel. They enjoy tormenting and torturing their prey… and their enemies. A Frostwolf takes no joy in suffering. Not even in the suffering of our enemies, and certainly not in that of a simple beast which provides us with nourishment."

Durotan felt his cheeks grow hot with another flush of shame. Not for himself this time, or because of his poor aim, but because this idea had not occurred to him. His failure to strike true was indeed wrong—but *not* because it meant he wasn't the best hunter. It was wrong because it had made the clefthoof suffer needlessly.

"I… understand," he said. "I am sorry."

"Do not apologize to me," Garad said. "I am not the one who is in pain."

The bloodstains were fresher now, great, scarlet puddles in the hollows made by the clefthoof's erratic gait. They led on, past a few lone pines, around a cluster of boulders topped with snow.

And there they found him.

Durotan had wounded a bull calf. It had seemed so enormous to the young orc then, gripped as he had been in the throes of his first true bloodlust. But now, Durotan could see that it—he—was not fully grown. Even so, the calf was as big as any three orcs, his thick hide covered with shaggy hair. His breath rose in rapid white puffs, and his tongue lolled between blunt yellow teeth. Small, recessed eyes opened as he scented them. He struggled to rise, succeeding only in forcing Durotan's ill-cast spear deeper and churning up slushy red snow. The calf's grunts of agony and defiance made Durotan's gut clench.

The young orc knew what he had to do. His father had prepared him for the hunt by describing the inner organs of the clefthoof and how best to slay it. Durotan did not hesitate. He ran as fast as the snow would permit toward the calf, seized the spear, yanked it out, and drove it directly, cleanly, into the animal's heart, leaning his full weight on the weapon.

The clefthoof shuddered as he died, relaxing into a limp stillness as fresh, hot blood drenched his coat and the snow. Garad had hung back and was joined now by Drek'Thar. The shaman tilted his head, listening, while Garad looked at Durotan expectantly.

Durotan glanced at them, then back at the beast he had slain. Then he looked into his heart, as his father had always taught him, and crouched in the bloody snow beside the beast. He pulled the fur-covered glove from his hand and placed his bare fingers on the calf's side. It was still warm.

He felt awkward as he spoke, and hoped the words were acceptable. "Spirit of the clefthoof, I, Durotan, son of Garad, son of Durkosh, thank you for your life. Your flesh will help my people live through the winter. Your hide and fur will keep us warm. We—I am grateful."

He paused and swallowed. "I am sorry that your

last moments were filled with pain and fear. I will be better next time. I will strike as my father has taught me—straight and true." As he spoke, he felt a fresh awareness and appreciation of the cloak's life-saving weight on his back, the feel of the boots on his feet. He looked up at his father and Drek'Thar. They nodded approvingly.

"A Frostwolf is a skillful hunter, and a mighty warrior," Garad said. "But he is never cruel for sport."

"I am a Frostwolf," Durotan said proudly.

Garad smiled and placed a hand on his son's shoulder. "Yes," he said. "You are."

1

The ululating cries of orcs on the hunt rent the icy air. Durotan had tasted battle with other clans, but few challenged the Frostwolves here, in their northern homeland. Bloodlust and the thirst for honor were most often quenched as they were now, with howls and victory songs as mounted orcs ran down strong prey that fled before them.

The earth trembled beneath the thundering feet of a herd of clefthooves, shaggy and lean in the last moments of a winter that had seemed as if it would never slacken its grip on the land. The Frostwolves harried them gleefully, their delight at finding meat infusing them with fresh energy after two days of tracking the herd.

Garad, his long black hair threaded with silver but his body still straight and strong, led the group.

Beside him on his right, her body more slender than her mate's but her movements as swift and her blows as lethal, rode Durotan's mother, Geyah. Garad did not always command, often stepping back to allow Durotan to take the role, but the younger orc never felt as alive as he did when hunting at his father's left side.

Finally, riding on Durotan's left, was Orgrim Doomhammer, Durotan's best friend. The two had gravitated toward one another ever since they could walk, indulging in all manner of competitions and challenges that always ended not with anger, but with laughter. Orgrim's mother claimed her little warrior had been so eager to fight that he struck the midwife's hand with his head as he entered the world, and the Spirits left him with a bruise in the form of a reddish splotch on his otherwise brown skull. Orgrim was fond of this story, and therefore always shaved his pate, even in winter, which most Frostwolves thought foolish. The four of them had often ridden in this formation, and their moves were as familiar to one another as their own heartbeats.

Durotan glanced over at Garad as they pursued the clefthooves. His father grinned and nodded. The clan had been hungry for some time; tonight, they would feast. Geyah, her long legs gripping the sides of her wolf, Singer, nocked her bow and waited for her mate's signal.

Garad lifted his spear, Thunderstrike, carved with runes and adorned with leather wraps and notches of two different styles. A horizontal slash represented a beast's life; a vertical one, an orc. Thunderstrike was cluttered with both vertical and horizontal markings, but the vertical ones were not few. Every one, Durotan knew, had been made when a foe fought well and died cleanly. Such was the way of the Frostwolves.

The orc chieftain pointed Thunderstrike at one clefthoof in particular. Words would not carry well over the steady pounding, so Garad looked around as the other Frostwolves raised their own weapons, indicating they had seen the designated target.

The herd's cluster formation as they stampeded meant life for those in the center—provided they did not stumble. The targeted cow's steady gait veered slightly away from the tight grouping. Her belly did not swell with a calf; no Frostwolf would slay a pregnant clefthoof, not when their numbers dwindled with each of the increasingly bitter winters. Nor would the hunters slaughter more than they could carry back to Frostfire Ridge, or feed to their wolf companions as thanks for their aid in the hunt.

"Let the wild wolves work for their own suppers," Garad had said once, as he scratched Ice behind the ears. "We Frostwolves will take care of our own."

Such had not always been the case. Garad had told Durotan that in his youth, the clan sacrificed at least one and often several animals as thanks to the Spirits. The creatures lay where they had fallen, food for wild beasts and carrion crows. Such wastefulness had not occurred often in Durotan's time. Food was too precious to squander.

Garad leaned forward. Knowing this as sign to charge, Ice lowered his head and sprang.

"Hurry up!" The good-natured jibe came from Orgrim, whose own wolf, Biter, raced past Durotan like an arrow fired from a bow. Durotan called his friend a scathing name and Sharptooth, anxious to feed, also sprang forward.

The wave of wolves and riders descended upon the hapless cow. Had she been but a few strides closer to the herd, she might have been protected by their sheer number, but although she bellowed plaintively, the herd merely increased its speed. The lead bull had abandoned her, too intent on driving the rest far enough out of range of the terrifying orcs so that no more of his herd would fall. The clefthooves were not stupid, and the cow realized soon enough that this was a fight she would have to win—or lose—on her own.

She wheeled with a speed belying her enormous size and turned to face her would-be killers. Clefthooves were prey animals, but that did not mean they did not have personalities, nor did it mean they were not dangerous. The cow that stood to face them, her cleft hooves churning up the snow as she snorted, was a fighter, as they were—and she clearly intended to take more than a few orcs and wolves down with her.

Durotan grinned. This one was worthy prey! There was no honor, only the sense of a need fulfilled, in hunting beasts that did not stand and fight. He was glad of the clefthoof's courageous choice. The rest of the party saw her defiance, too, and their cries increased in delight. The cow snorted, lowered her head crowned with massive, sharp horns, and charged directly at Garad.

The orc chieftain and his wolf moved as one, springing out of danger long enough for Garad to hurl Thunderstrike. The spear caught the great beast in her side. Ice gathered himself to attack. As he and other white wolves leaped for the clefthoof's throat, Garad, Durotan, Orgrim, Geyah, and the rest of the hunting party hurled spears, arrows, and shouts of challenge at the clefthoof.

The fight was a frenzy of motion, a cacophony of snarls, grunts, and war cries. Wolves darted in and out, their teeth ripping and tearing, while their riders struggled to get close enough to land blows of their own. Memories of his first hunt flashed in Durotan's mind, as they always did. He shoved his way to the forefront of the fight. Ever since that long-ago trek following the train of bloody snow, Durotan had been driven to be the one who struck the killing blow. To be the one to end the torment. It never mattered if, in the thick of the fight, others witnessed him strike and credited him the kill. It only mattered that he dealt the blow.

He wove his way around the white blurs of the wolves and the fur-clad bodies of his clanspeople, until the smell of blood and rank animal hide almost made his head swim. Abruptly, he found an opening. Durotan dropped into himself, gripping his spear tightly and letting his focus narrow to this single purpose. All that existed for him now was the spot just behind the cow's left foreleg. The clefthooves were large, and so were their hearts.

His spear found its mark, and the great beast shuddered. Bright blood stained its hide. Durotan had struck clean and true, and though she struggled for a few more moments, at last, she collapsed.

A huge cry went up and Durotan's ears rang. He smiled, breathing heavily. Tonight, the clan would eat.

They always brought more hunters than were needed to take a beast down. The joy of the hunt was in the tracking, the fighting, and the slaying, but many hands were also needed to butcher the animal and prepare it for the trek back to the village. From Garad himself to the youngest member of the party, everyone joined in. At one point Durotan straightened, stretching arms bloody to the elbow from hacking at the carcass. Motion caught his eye, and he frowned, peering into the distance.

"Father!" he called. "*Rider!*"

Everyone stopped what they were doing at the word. Worried glances were exchanged, but all knew better than to speak. Riders never came after a hunting party, which could mean frightening the prey, unless the party had been gone for too long and there was concern for their safety. The only time a single rider would be sent out would be if Garad were suddenly needed back at the village—and that meant bad news.

Garad looked at Geyah in silence, then stood and waited for the rider to approach. Kurg'nal, an older, grizzled orc whose hair was white as the snow, slipped off his wolf and saluted his chieftain, thumping one huge hand to his broad chest.

He wasted no words. "Great chieftain—an orc has come to speak to you under the banner of parley."

Garad's brow knitted. "Parley?" The word sounded odd on his tongue, and there was confusion in his voice.

"What is 'parley'?" Orgrim was one of the largest orcs in the clan, but he could move with great silence when he so chose. Durotan, intent on the conversation, had never even noticed his friend step beside him.

"Parley means..." Durotan fumbled for the words. To an orc, they were so strange. "The stranger comes only to speak. He comes in peace."

"What?" Orgrim looked almost comical, his tusked jaw hanging open slightly. "This must be some kind of trick. Orcs do not *parley*."

Durotan didn't reply. He watched as Geyah stepped beside her mate, speaking to him quietly. Like Drek'Thar, Geyah was a shaman, but she had a very specific task. She was the Lorekeeper, one who tended the scrolls that had been passed down for generations and ensured the ancient traditions and rituals of the Frostwolves were not lost. If anyone understood how to properly respond to an orc coming under the banner of parley, it would be her.

Garad turned to face the silent orcs patiently awaiting his response. "An orc named Gul'dan has come to speak," he told them. "He invokes the ancient ritual of parley, which means he is our… our guest. We will treat him with respect and honor. If he is hungry, we will feed him the choicest food. If he is cold, he may have our warmest cloak. I will listen to what he has come to say, and behave in all ways in accordance with our traditions."

"What if he does not respond in kind?" asked one orc.

"What if he shows the Frostwolf clan disrespect?" another shouted.

Garad looked to Geyah, who answered the questions. "Then it is shame upon his head. The Spirits will not favor him for scorning the very tradition he invokes. The dishonor is his, not ours. We are Frostwolves," she stated, her voice rising with her conviction. Shouts of agreement went up in response.

Kurg'nal still looked uncomfortable. He tugged at his beard and murmured something to his chieftain. Durotan and Orgrim were close enough to catch the softly spoken words.

"My chieftain," Kurg'nal said, "there is more."

"Speak," Garad ordered.

"This Gul'dan… he comes with a slave."

Durotan stiffened with instant dislike. Some of the clans enslaved others, he knew. Orcs fought amongst themselves on occasion. He himself had been part of these battles, when other clans trespassed on Frostfire Ridge and hunted Frostwolf food. The Frostwolves fought well and fully, not hesitating to kill if necessary, but never doing so out of rage or merely because an opportunity presented itself. They did not take prisoners, let alone slaves; the fight was over when one side yielded. Beside him, Orgrim snarled softly at the words as well.

But Kurg'nal was not done. "And..." he shook his head, as he couldn't himself believe what he was about to say, then tried again. "My lord chieftain... both the slave and her master... are *green!*"

2

Garad asked Durotan and Orgrim to return to Frostfire Ridge with him and Geyah. He ordered the rest of the party—a male orc in his prime, Nokrar; his fierce-eyed mate, Kagra; and a barrel-chested orc called Grukag—to stay behind, to finish preparing the meat and hides for the trip back to the village.

Durotan burned with questions he knew better than to ask. Besides, what could Garad even tell him? The idea of "parley" was something the chieftain had doubtless heard about as a youth, but likely had not thought about for years.

They rode in tense silence toward their village. Once, the lore scrolls said, the Frostwolves had been nomads. They followed the game all over Draenor, wherever the beasts would wander. Their homes could be broken down quickly, tied into bundles, and slung upon the backs of their wolves. But all that, if it was even true, had changed long ago.

The clan had settled in Frostfire Ridge, with Greatfather Mountain and his protection to the south, the Spirits safely in their Seat in the north, and meadows stretching toward forests to the east and west. As most orcs did, Frostwolves marked the boundaries of their territories with banners—a white wolf's head against a blue background. They built sturdy huts of stone, mud, and wood. In the past, most family units took care of themselves, calling upon the might of the clan only in rare times of famine or attack.

But now, many of the outlying huts were empty skeletons and had been for years, cannibalized for their timber as their inhabitants, family by family, moved closer to the center of the settlement. Food, rituals, and work were shared. And now, curiosity was shared as well.

While smaller cooking fires burned throughout the village as needed, there was a large pit in the center that was always fueled. In the winter, it provided necessary warmth. Even in the summer a smaller fire was kindled for gathering together, for storytelling, and for meals. A place of honor was reserved for Garad—a boulder that, long ago, had been carved into a chair.

Every Frostwolf knew the story of the Stone Seat. It went back to the time when the clan was supposedly nomadic. One chieftain, though, felt so tied to Frostfire Ridge when he led his clan there that he did not wish to leave it. The clan was anxious. What would happen to them if they did not follow their prey?

The chieftain did not want to force his people to stay against their will, so he asked the shaman for an audience with the Spirits. He made a pilgrimage as north as north could be, to the Edge of the World. There, in the Seat of the Spirits, a sacred cave deep within the heart of the earth, he sat for three days and three nights, with no food or water, alone in the darkness.

He was, finally, granted a vision that told him this: if he was so stubborn as not to leave, the Spirits would make of his stubbornness a virtue. "You are as immovable as stone," they told him. "You have come all this way to find the Seat of the Spirits. Go back to your people, and see what we have given you."

Upon his return, the chieftain found that a boulder had rolled to the very center of the Frostwolf encampment. He declared it would forever be the Stone Seat, won for his trial in the Seat of the Spirits—the chair of the Frostwolf chieftain until time crumbled the stone to dust.

Dusk had fallen when Durotan and the others reached the village. A fire blazed in the communal pit, and its flames were ringed by every member of the Frostwolf tribe. As Garad, Geyah, Durotan, and Orgrim approached, the crowd parted.

Durotan stared at the Stone Seat.

It was occupied by the orc who had come under parley.

And in the flickering orange light, Durotan saw that the stranger, and the female who crouched beside him with a heavy metal circlet about her slender throat, were indeed the color of moss.

The male was hunched, perhaps because of the age that colored his beard gray. He was bulky in his cloak and clothing. The spikes of some creature jutted from his cloak. In the dim light, Durotan could not have said how they had been fastened to the fabric. He was staring in horrified fascination at two of the spikes upon which had been impaled tiny skulls. Were they once the heads of draenei babies... or, Spirits save him, those of infant *orcs*? They seemed wrong, deformed, if so. Perhaps some creature he had never heard tell of.

He desperately hoped so.

The newcomer leaned on a staff as adorned with bone and skulls as his cloak. Symbols had been carved upon it, and those same symbols were repeated around the opening of the stranger's cowl. In the shadow of that cowl, his eyes gleamed—not with reflected firelight, but with a glowing green luminescence of their own.

Less visually interesting, but perhaps even more puzzling, was the female. She looked like an orc—but it was clear her blood was tainted. How, Durotan could not possibly begin to guess, and the thought repulsed him. She was part orc and part... something *else*. Something weaker. Whereas Geyah and other females were not as laden with muscle or bulk as orc males, they were obviously strong. This female looked as slender as a twig to him. But then, when he looked into her eyes, she held his gaze steadily. Perhaps her body was frail, but not her spirit.

"Not a very slave-like slave, is she?" Orgrim said quietly, for Durotan's ears alone.

Durotan shook his head. "Not with that fire in her eyes."

"Does she even have a name?"

"Someone said Gul'dan called her…'Garona.'"

Orgrim raised his eyebrows at the word. "She is named 'cursed'? What sort of… *thing*… is she? And why are she and her master…" Orgrim shook his head, looking almost comically bemused. "What is wrong with their skin?"

"I do not know, and will not ask," Durotan said, though he, too, was burning with curiosity. "My mother will think it disrespectful, and I have no wish to rouse her anger."

"Nor does anyone in the clan, which is perhaps the sole reason he yet lives, after settling his green rear in the Stone Seat," said Orgrim. "One does not cross the Lorekeeper, but she does not look happy that this—this *mongrel* is to be permitted to speak."

Durotan glanced at his mother. Geyah was busily braiding some bright beads into her hair. Obviously, they were part of the parley ritual, and she was hastening to finish her preparation. The look she gave the newcomer could have shattered the stone seat he occupied.

"She doesn't look happy about any of this. But remember what she told us," Durotan replied, his gaze traveling back to the fragile but not frail slave, to the arrogant stranger sitting in his father's chair. "All of this is Gul'dan's dishonor, not ours."

What he did not say to Orgrim was that the female before him reminded him of another, one who had been banished from the safety of the Frostwolf clan. Her name had been Draka, and she had a similar attitude to this slave, even when she faced Exile and almost certain death.

As his father had drummed into him, the Frostwolves did not indulge in killing or tormenting without purpose, and therefore scorned the practice of taking slaves or prisoners for ransom. But neither did they condone weakness, and those born fragile were believed to undermine the clan as a whole.

They were permitted to reach young adulthood, as it was known that sometimes what seemed like a frailty was outgrown with the passing of years. But once they entered adolescence, the frail and the fragile were turned out to survive on their own. If they were somehow able to do so, once a year, they were permitted to return and display their prowess: at Midsummer, when food was the most plentiful, and spirits at their highest. Most Exiles never returned to Frostfire Ridge. Fewer still had done so in recent years, as survival became more difficult in the changing land.

Draka was Durotan's age, and when she faced her Exile, he had felt a twinge of sorrow. He was not alone. There had been murmurs of admiration from others as the clan gathered to watch her depart. Draka took with her only enough food for a week, and tools with which to hunt and make her own clothing and shelter. Death was almost certain, and she must have known it. Yet her narrow back was straight, though her thin arms quivered with the weight of the clan's "gifts" that could mean life or death.

"It is important, to face death well," one of the adults had said.

"In this, at least, she is a Frostwolf," another had replied.

Draka had not looked back. The last Durotan saw of her, she was striding off on skinny legs, the blue and white Frostwolf banner tied around her waist fluttering in the wind.

Durotan often found himself thinking about Draka, wondering what had happened to her in the end. He hoped that the other orcs were right, and that she had faced her final moments well.

But such honor would forever be denied to the slave before them. Durotan turned his gaze from the bold, green-skinned slave named "Cursed" to her master.

"I mislike this," said a deep, rumbling voice by Durotan's ear. The speaker was Drek'Thar, his hair almost completely white now, but his body still muscular, as straight and tall as the newcomer's was stooped. "Shadows cling to this orc. Death follows him."

Durotan took in the skulls dangling from Gul'dan's staff and impaled on his spiked cloak. An onlooker might have made the same comment, but he or she would have done so while regarding the celebration of bones that adorned the newcomer. The blind shaman saw death, too, but not as others did.

Durotan tried not to shudder at Drek'Thar's words. "Shadows lie long on the hills in winter, and I myself brought death today. These things do not bad omens make, Drek'Thar. You might as well say life follows him, since he is green."

"Green is the color of spring, yes," said Drek'Thar. "But I sense nothing of renewal about him."

"Let us listen to what he has to say before we decide he has come as a harbinger of death, life, or nothing at all."

Drek'Thar chuckled. "Your eyes are too dazzled by the banner of parley to truly see, young one. But you will, in time. Let us hope your father does."

As if hearing his name, Garad stepped into the ring of firelight. The murmuring hushed. The stranger, Gul'dan, seemed to be enjoying the stir he was causing. His thick lips curled around his tusks in a smile that was close to a sneer, and he made no move to rise from his place. Another chair had been brought for the clan chieftain; wooden, simple, functional. Garad settled into it and placed his hands on his thighs. Geyah, dressed now in her most formal clothing of tanned talbuk hide painstakingly embroidered with bead- and bone-work, stood behind her mate.

"The ancient banner of parley has come to the Frostwolves, borne by Gul'dan, son of..." Garad paused. A look of confusion flitted over his strong face, and he turned to Gul'dan in query.

"The name of my father is unimportant, as is the name of my clan." Gul'dan's voice made the hairs along Durotan's forearms bristle. It was raspy, and unpleasant, and the arrogant tone set his teeth on edge. But worse to any orc's ears than the voice were the words. The names of one's parents and clan were vitally important to orcs, and the Frostwolves were shocked to hear the question so quickly and indifferently dismissed. "What is important is what I have to say."

"Gul'dan, son of No Orc and of No Clan," said Geyah in a voice so pleasant only those who knew her well could recognize the barely leashed anger, "you rush the rituals and thus dishonor the very banner under which you have requested parley. This might make my chieftain believe you no longer wish for its protection."

Durotan smiled, not bothering to hide it. His mother was as dangerous as his father, as the clan well knew. This green orc only now seemed to be aware that perhaps he might have misstepped.

Gul'dan inclined his head. "So I have. And no, I have no wish to abandon the benefits of the banner. Continue, Garad."

Garad spoke the formal words. They were long and complex, some so archaic Durotan didn't even recognize them, and he began to grow restless. Orgrim looked even more impatient. The general tone was that of safety and a fair hearing for the one who requested parley. Finally, it was over, and

Garad turned expectantly to Gul'dan.

The other orc got to his feet, leaning on his staff. The tiny skulls on his back seemed to protest silently with open mouths. "Custom and the ancient rites that stay your hand compel me to tell you three things: Who I am. What I offer. And what I ask." He looked at the gathered Frostwolves with his glowing green eyes, almost appraisingly. "I am Gul'dan, and while, as I have said, I claim no clan of origin, I do have a clan… of a sort." He chuckled slightly, the sound doing nothing to mitigate his unsettling appearance. "But I will speak more on this later.

"Next… What do I offer? It is simple, but the dearest thing in the world." He lifted his arms, and the skulls clanked hollowly against one another. "I offer *life*."

Durotan and Orgrim exchanged frowns. Was Gul'dan making a veiled—or perhaps not-so-veiled—threat?

"This world is in jeopardy. And thus, so are we. I have traveled far to offer you life in the form of a *new* homeland—one that is verdant, rich in game and fruit and the grain of the fields. And what I ask is that you accept this offer and join me in it, Garad of the Frostwolves."

As if he had heaved a mammoth stone into a placid lake, he took his seat and gazed at Garad expectantly. Indeed, all eyes were on Garad. What Gul'dan was proposing was not just offensive and arrogant—it was *madness*!

Wasn't it?

For a moment, it seemed the Frostwolf leader didn't know what to say, but finally, he spoke.

"It is well that you come under the protection of a banner, Gul'dan of No Clan," Garad rumbled. "Otherwise, I would rip out your lying throat with my own teeth!"

Gul'dan did not seem either surprised or offended. "So others before you have said," he replied, "and yet, they are part of my clan now. I am sure your shaman can see things that ordinary orcs cannot, and this world, while troubled, is wide. I ask you to accept the possibility that you may not know all things, and that I may indeed offer something the Frostwolves need. Perhaps tales have reached your ears over the last few seasons of… a warlock?"

They had. Two years ago, a Frostwolf hunting party had allied with a group of orcs from the Warsong clan. The Warsongs had been tracking a talbuk herd. Unfamiliar with the ways of the beautiful, graceful creatures, they did not know that it was impossible to cull a single animal from the herd. The striped talbuks were much smaller and more delicately boned than the clefthooves. While an adult clefthoof could be forced away from the herd, its size meant it could more than adequately defend itself. Talbuks relied on one another for protection. When attacked, initially they would not flee. Instead, they defended their targeted brother or sister as a group, presenting predators with myriad curved horns and hooves. The Frostwolves knew how to frighten the talbuks, heroic as they were, into surrendering the lives of a few. By choosing to hunt together, the Frostwolves and the Warsong were able to feed both hunting parties and their mounts, with much meat left over.

As they feasted together, one of the Warsongs mentioned an orc with strange powers, like a shaman but different. *Warlock*, was the term they had used; a word Durotan had not heard before or since—until tonight.

Garad's face hardened. "So, it was you they spoke of," he said. "Warlock. I should have known the moment I saw you. You deal in death, but you hope to convince me to join you with talk of life. An odd juxtaposition."

Durotan glanced over at Drek'Thar, mindful of the old shaman's words: *Shadows cling to this orc. Death follows him.* And his own response: *Shadows lie long on the hills in winter, and I myself brought death today. These things do not bad omens make, Drek'Thar... Let us listen to what he has to say before we decide he has come as a harbinger of death, life, or nothing at all.*

He, Garad, and the rest of the clan were still listening.

Gul'dan gestured with one hand to his green-tinted skin. "I have been endowed with strong magic. It has permeated me, and turned my skin this color. It has marked me for its own. And yes, the magic grows strong when it is fed with life. But look me in the eye, Garad, son of Durkosh, and tell me true: have you never left a life bleeding on the snow to thank the Spirits for their blessing? Slain a clefthoof in exchange for a new child safely delivered into the world, perhaps, or left one creature to lie where it fell when a dozen talbuks succumbed to your spears?"

The listening clan shifted uneasily, though Garad appeared unmoved. All knew that what Gul'dan said was true.

"We are nourished by that kind of sacrifice," Garad confirmed. "We are fed by that life so ended."

"And so am I fed, but in a different way," said Gul'dan. "You are fed with the creature's flesh, clothed with its hide. I am fed with strength and knowledge, and clothed… in green."

Durotan found his gaze drawn to the slave. She, too, was green, however it was obvious that she was not only a slave, but a roughly treated one. He desperately wanted to ask questions—*Why was she green? Why had Gul'dan brought her with him?*—but this was his father's meeting, not his, so he bit his tongue.

So too, it seemed, did his father. Garad made no further comment, and his silence was an invitation for Gul'dan to continue.

"Draenor is not as it was. Life flees it. The winters are longer, the springs and summers briefer and less bountiful. There is little game to hunt. There—"

Garad waved an impatient hand. The firelight danced on his features, revealing a scowl of impatience. "Orc of No Clan, you tell me nothing I do not already know. Such things are not unheard of. Legends tell of cycles in our world. All is ebb and flow, darkness and light, death and rebirth. The summers and springs will again lengthen once this cycle has run its course."

"Will they?" The green fire in Gul'dan's eyes flickered. "You know of the north. I come from the south. For us, this so-called cycle is more than longer winters and fewer beasts. Our rivers and lakes run low. The trees that yield the fruits we feast on in summer have ceased to put forth new shoots, and bear small, bitter fruit if they bear any at all. When we burn wood, it does not smell wholesome. The grain rots on the stalk, or lies dormant when we seed it in soil that does not nourish it. Our children are born sickly—and sometimes not at all. *This* is what we have seen in the south!"

"I care not for the suffering of the south."

An ugly, crafty smile twisted Gul'dan's lips around his tusks. "No, not yet. But what has happened there will happen here. This is more than a bad season, or ten bad seasons. I tell you, this world is dying. Frostfire Ridge may not have seen what we have, but time knows no distance."

He extended a hand to the slave without even looking at her. Her movements obedient even as her eyes glittered, she handed him a small wrapped bundle.

He unfolded the fabric. A spherical red object was nestled within. "A blood apple," he said, holding it up. It was indeed small and sickly-looking. Its skin was mottled, not the bold crimson that had given it its name, but neither was it dry or rotting, as it would have been had it been harvested much earlier. With all eyes on him, Gul'dan extended a sharp-nailed finger and sliced it open. It fell apart into to two halves, and the watching orcs gasped softly.

The apple was dead inside. Not rotten; not eaten by worms or disease. Just dead—desiccated and brown.

There were no seeds.

3

There was stunned silence for a moment, but Garad broke it. "Let us play a game," he said. "Let us pretend that you are right, and Draenor—our entire world—is dying. And yet somehow, you and you alone have been granted the ability to lead us to a special new land where this death does not happen. If such a tale were true, it seems to me that you would be better served by simply traveling to this new land with fewer, rather than greater, numbers. Why do you trek to the north, when winter is barely past, to make such a generous offer to the Frostwolves?" Garad's voice dripped cynicism.

Gul'dan slid his sleeve up, displaying peculiar bracelets and more of his disconcertingly green skin. "I bear the mark of magic," he said simply. "I speak the truth."

And somehow, Durotan knew that he did not lie. His gaze again wandered to Garona, the warlock's slave. Was she, too, magical? Did Gul'dan keep her chained not because she was subservient, but because she might be dangerous?

"I spoke earlier of a clan," Gul'dan continued. "It is not a clan into which I was born, but a clan I have founded. I have created it, my Horde, and those who have joined it have done so freely and gladly."

"I do not believe any orc chieftain, no matter how desperate, would order his clan to follow you and forsake his true allegiance!"

"I do not ask that of them," Gul'dan said, his calm voice a contrast to Garad's rising one. "They keep their chieftains, their customs, even their names. But whereas the clans answer to the chieftains, those chieftains answer to *me*. We are part of a great whole."

"And everyone you have spoken with has swallowed this tale down like mother's milk." Garad sneered openly now. Durotan wondered how long it would be before he violated the parley banner and tore out Gul'dan's green throat, as he had threatened earlier.

"Not all, but many," Gul'dan said. "Many other clans, who are suffering and whose numbers are dwindling. They will follow me to this verdant new land and they do so without surrendering their clan affiliations, but merely taking on an additional one. They are still Warsong, or Laughing Skull, or Bleeding Hollow, but are also now members of the Horde. *My* Horde. They follow me, and will go where I lead them.

And I will lead them to a world that teems with life."

"More than one clan follows you? Warsong, Bleeding Hollow, Laughing Skull?" Garad seemed incredulous, as well he might. Durotan knew that while orcs sometimes cooperated for a single goal such as a hunt, they always disbanded when it was accomplished. What Gul'dan was telling them all seemed improbable at best, if not as fanciful as a child's story.

"All but a few," Gul'dan replied. "Some stubborn clans still choose to cling to a world that no longer succors them. Some seem to be barely orcs at all, anointing themselves with the blood of their prey and reveling in decay. We shun these, the Red Walkers, and they will die at some point, mad and in despair. All I ask of you is your loyalty as we travel together to leave behind a dying husk. Your knowledge, your skills, your strength."

Durotan tried to imagine a huge sea of brown skin, weapons in hand, used not against one another but against beasts for food to share, against the land to hew shelters and homes. All this in a world of green-leafed trees heavy with ripe fruit, animals strong and fat and healthy, and water fresh and clean. Impulsively, he leaned forward and asked, "Tell me more of this land."

"*Durotan!*"

Garad's voice cracked like lightning. Blood rose hot in Durotan's face, but after the one outburst, his father's attention was focused not on his presumptuous son, but on the stranger in their camp, even as that stranger smiled slowly at Durotan.

"So you have come to rescue us, have you?" Garad said. "We are *Frostwolves*, Gul'dan. We do not need your rescue, your Horde, your land which is only a promise. Frostfire Ridge has been the home of the Frostwolves for as long as any tale can tell, and it will stay that way!"

"We honor our traditions," said Geyah, her voice and mien hard. "We do not forsake who we are when times grow difficult."

"Others may run to you like mewling children, but we will not. We are made of sterner stuff than those who dwell in the softer south."

Gul'dan did not take umbrage at Garad's contemptuous words. Rather, he regarded Garad with an expression that was almost sad.

"I spoke earlier of orc clans that did not join the Horde," he said. "They, too, told me when I approached them that they needed no aid. But the loss of food, of water, of shelter—all that is required to exist—has taken a dreadful toll on them. They have become nomads, roaming from place to place, forced in the end to abandon their homelands. They are shadows of orcs, and they have become so, and suffer, needlessly."

"We do not 'suffer,'" said Garad. "We *endure*." He sat back slightly, straightening his large, powerful frame. Durotan knew what that gesture meant.

The parley was over.

"We will not follow you, green orc."

Gul'dan did not strike Durotan as one who

was accustomed to refusal. He wondered if the warlock would summon these mysterious magics he claimed to have at his disposal and break the parley protection by challenging Garad to the mak'gora—a battle to the death between two individual orcs. His mother might know the proper way to respond to that; Durotan did not.

He had witnessed the mak'gora only once before. An orc from the Thunderlord clan decided not to cede his prey to the Frostwolves as had been agreed upon. Instead, he had challenged Grukag, who had claimed the beast in question. It had struck Durotan as odd and disruptive; until that point, the Thunderlords and Frostwolves had been cooperating well for several days. Durotan had even made a friend, of sorts. His name was Kovogor, and the two were of an age. Kovogor was funny, pleasant, and very good with a throwing axe. When the merged hunting party camped at night, Kovogor taught Durotan how to properly throw the weapon so it would embed itself in the flesh of its target.

Grukag had won that battle. Durotan recalled his heart slamming against his chest, his blood pumping. He had never felt more alive. There was no time to think, to wonder, when he was in combat himself. But to watch another was to experience something else entirely.

Yet when it was done, and Grukag had bellowed a Frostwolf victory while standing in blood-soaked snow, Durotan had felt a strange emotion along with the shared euphoria. He had later recognized that it was a sense of loss. The other orc had been strong and proud, but in the end, his pride had been deeper than his strength, and the Thunderlords returned with one less warrior to provide their clan with food. And there was now a coldness between the clans, one that made it impossible for Durotan to even say farewell to Kovogor.

But it seemed there would be no mak'gora today. Gul'dan merely sighed and shook his head.

"Perhaps you do not believe this, Garad, son of Durkosh, but I sorrow at what I know will come to pass. The Frostwolves are proud and noble, but not even you can stand against what is to come. Your people will discover that pride and nobility mean little when there is no food to eat, or water fit to drink, or air good to breathe."

He reached into the folds of his robe—and drew out a knife.

Roars of fury tore from every orc's throat at the betrayal.

"*Hold!*"

Geyah's voice was strong as she leaped to position herself between Gul'dan, who wisely froze in mid-motion, and anyone who would do him harm.

What is she doing? Durotan wondered, but like the others, he stayed where he was, although his body cried out to leap atop Gul'dan.

Geyah's eyes scanned the crowed. "Gul'dan came under the banner of parley," she shouted. "What he is doing is part of the rite. We will let him continue... whatever we think of him."

Her lip curled and she took a step back, allowing Gul'dan to finish drawing the wicked-looking blade. Garad had obviously been prepared for this moment, and watched as Gul'dan inclined his head and extended his hand, palm upward, the knife balanced atop it.

"I offer the test of the blade to you, who hold my life in your hand," Gul'dan said. "It is as sharp as the wolf's tooth, and I abide by its decision."

Durotan watched with rapt attention as his father's enormous fingers—fingers that had once throttled a talbuk whose charge had knocked Garad's spear from his hand—closed over the knife. Firelight glittered on the long blade. Garad held it up for all to see, then drew it across the back of his lower arm. Dark brown blood welled up in its wake. Garad let it drip to the earth.

"You came with a blade that was sharp and keen, a blade that could take my life, yet you did not use it," he said. "This is true parley. I accept this blade as an acknowledgement of this, and I have shed my own blood as a sign that you will have safe passage from this place."

His voice had been strong, carrying clearly on the cold night air, heavy with import. He let the words linger there for a moment.

"Now get out."

Durotan again tensed, as did Orgrim beside him. That Garad had behaved with such open contempt told his son how deeply offended the Frostwolf chieftain had been by Gul'dan's proposal. Surely

Gul'dan would demand a chance to repudiate such discourtesy.

But again, the green orc merely inclined his head in acceptance. Planting his grisly staff firmly, he got to his feet, his unnaturally glowing eyes regarding the silent, hostile gathering for a moment before he moved forward. He tugged at the chain that ended at the female orc-thing's neck and she rose with supple grace. As she passed Durotan, she met his gaze openly.

Her eyes were fierce and beautiful.

What are you... and what are you to Gul'dan? Durotan supposed he would never know.

The Frostwolves parted for the warlock—not out of respect, Durotan realized, but out of a desire to avoid physical contact with him in any manner, as if touching someone who was so aligned with death could harm them.

"Well, well," Orgrim said with a grunt as the pair went to their waiting wolves. "And to think we had expected a boring feast to celebrate the hunt."

"I think my mother would have been happy to make a feast of *him*," Durotan said. He watched as the darkness swallowed up the green orc and his slave, then turned to look at Drek'Thar. His skin crawled.

The blind shaman was still as a stone. His head was cocked to one side as if he was straining to listen to something. Everyone else's attention was still fixed on the departing interloper, and so Durotan was certain that he was the only one who saw tears dampen the fold of fabric that covered Drek'Thar's sightless eyes.

4

"We are three entire suns on from the parley, yet it seems as though no one can speak of anything else," Orgrim lamented as he sat, face long and disgruntled, atop Biter.

"Including you, it would seem," Durotan said. Orgrim scowled and fell silent, looking slightly embarrassed. The two had ranged a league from the village in search of firewood. It was not the worst task one could have, but it was not as exciting as a hunt, though necessary. Firewood kept the clan alive in winter, and it took time to age and dry properly.

But Orgrim was right. Garad, certainly, had been thinking about the visit. He had not emerged from his hut the following morning, though Geyah had. At Durotan's curious look when she passed him, his mother said, "Your father was disturbed by what

Gul'dan said. He has asked me to find Drek'Thar, that the three of us might discuss how what the green stranger said will affect the Spirits and how our traditions might best be used."

It was a lengthy response to a question offered only by a raised eyebrow, and Durotan was instantly alert. "I will come to the meeting as well," he said. Her hair, braided with bones and feathers, flew as she shook her head.

"No. There are other duties you must attend to."

"I thought Father had no interest in Gul'dan," Durotan said. "Now you tell me there is a meeting. As son and heir, I should be present."

Again, she waved him away. "This is a conversation, nothing more. We will bring you in as needed, my son. And as I said, you have other duties."

Gathering firewood. Granted, no duty that even the lowest member of the clan performed was considered beneath a chieftain, as Frostwolves believed that everyone had a voice and a value. But still. Something was going on. Durotan was being excluded, and he didn't like it.

His mind went back to a time when, as a boy, he had been told to gather fuel for the cooking fire. He had complained loudly, wanting instead to practice sword-fighting with Orgrim. Drek'Thar had chastised him. "It is both careless and dangerous to cut down trees when we do not need large timber for dwellings," the shaman had told him. "The Spirit of Earth does not like it. It provides enough branches for our needs, and the needles are dry and catch fire quickly. Only lazy little orcs would whimper like wolf pups at having to take a few extra steps to honor the Spirit."

Durotan, of course, was the son of a chieftain, and did not like to be called a lazy little orc who whimpered like a wolf pup, and so had gone about his task as he had been told. Later, as an adult, he had asked Drek'Thar if his words were true.

The shaman had chuckled. "It is true that it is foolish to recklessly fell a tree," he said, "and to cut them down too close to our village alerts strangers to our presence. But... yes. I feel that it is disrespectful. Don't you?"

Durotan had to agree, but added, "Do the Spirit's rules always align with what the chieftain wants?"

Drek'Thar's broad mouth had smiled. "Only sometimes," he had said.

Now, as he rode alongside Orgrim, a thought occurred to Durotan. *Felling trees...*

"Gul'dan said that when the southern orcs cut open trees, they smelled... wrong."

"Now listen to who is talking about Gul'dan!" said Orgrim.

"No, truly... what do you think that means? And the blood apple... he showed us the seeds were gone."

Orgrim shrugged his massive shoulders and pointed to a copse up ahead. Durotan saw the dark skeletons of fallen branches resting on piles of dried brown needles. "Who knows? Maybe the southern trees decided they didn't want to be cut open any more. As for the apple, I have bitten into some that had no seeds ere now."

"But how would he have known?" Durotan persisted. "If he had cut open the apple and there had been seeds in it after all, he would have been laughed out of our village. He knew there wouldn't be one."

"Maybe the fruit had already been cut." Orgrim vaulted off Biter and turned to open the empty pack in preparation for filling it with wood. Biter began to turn in circles, trying to lick Orgrim's face, and the orc was forced to follow, chuckling. "Biter, cease! We have to load you up."

Durotan laughed too. "Your dancing leaves much to be..." The words died in his throat. "Orgrim."

The other orc, instantly alert at the change in his friend's voice, followed Durotan's gaze. Several paces away, all but hidden in the gray-green folds of the pines, a white spot on the bark revealed that someone had hacked away a branch.

The two had hunted together since they could walk, stalking make-believe prey and rough toys made of skin. They were attuned to one another in ways that transcended language. Now, Orgrim waited, taut and silent, for instructions from his chieftain's son.

Observe, Durotan's father had taught him. The branch had been chopped, not broken and twisted off. That meant whoever did this had weapons. The cut still bled amber sap, so the harvesting of the limb was recent. Snow was churned up beneath the violated tree.

For a moment, Durotan stood still and simply listened. He heard only the soft sigh of the cold wind and the rustle of pine needles in response. The clean fragrance wafted to his nostrils as he inhaled deeply. He smelled something else: fur, and a not unpleasant, musky scent—the scent not of the strangely floral-smelling draenei, but of other orcs.

And over these two known, familiar smells, a third stood out starkly: the metallic tang of blood.

He turned to Sharptooth and placed a hand over the wolf's muzzle. The beast obediently sank into the snow, still and as silent as his master. He would not move or howl unless he was attacked or Durotan called for him.

Biter, as well trained as his littermate Sharptooth, obeyed as Orgrim did likewise. Both wolves watched their masters with intelligent golden eyes as the two orcs stepped forward carefully, avoiding mounds of snow which might conceal branches that could snap and betray their presence.

They had come armed only with axes, their wolves' teeth, and their own bodies—weapons aplenty to deal with ordinary threats, but Durotan's hand itched to hold a battle axe or spear.

They moved toward the harvested trees. Durotan touched one of the weeping marks, then pointed to the trampled snow, indicating how obvious the interlopers had been. These orcs did not care if anyone knew they were present. Durotan bent to examine the tracks. A few feet away, Orgrim did likewise. After a quick but thorough inspection, Durotan held up four fingers.

Orgrim shook his head and held up a different number, using both hands.

Seven.

Durotan grimaced. He and Orgrim were orcs in their prime, fit and fast and strong. He would have felt comfortable attacking two, even three or four, other orcs, even armed only with hatchets. But seven—

Orgrim was looking at him and gesturing further into the copse. Spoiling for a fight as he had been since his birth, he was eager to take on the trespassers, but Durotan slowly shook his head *no*. Orgrim's brows drew together, wordlessly demanding an exclamation.

It would have made a tremendous lok'vadnod, but while Durotan would have been honored for his exploits to be remembered in song after a brave death, he and Orgrim were too close to the village. Durotan held his arms as if he cradled a child in them, and Orgrim reluctantly nodded.

They returned to their wolves, which still huddled in the snow. Durotan had to struggle not to mount immediately. Instead, he buried a hand in the soft, thick ruff of Sharptooth's throat. The wolf got to his feet, tail wagging slowly, and accompanied Durotan for several paces as the copse and its dangerous tidings fell away behind them. Only when Durotan was certain they had not been heard or followed did he leap atop Sharptooth, urging the wolf to race for the village as fast as his great legs would carry him.

Durotan headed straight to the chieftain's hut. Without announcing his presence, he shoved open the door. "Father, there are strangers who—"

The words died on his lips.

The chieftain's hut was, by clan law, the largest in the village. A banner covered one wall. The chieftain's armor and weapons occupied one corner. Cooking utensils and other day-to-day items were neatly arranged in another. Ordinarily, a third corner was filled with sleeping furs, which were rolled up and stowed out of the way when the family was active.

Not today. Garad lay on a clefthoof skin on the hard earthen floor. A second pelt covered him. Geyah had one hand beneath his neck, tilting his head forward so that the Frostwolf chieftain could sip from the gourd ladle in her other hand. At Durotan's entrance, both she and Drek'Thar, who stood beside her, jerked their heads in his direction.

"Close the door!" Geyah snapped. Shocked into silence, Durotan quickly obeyed. He crossed the space between himself and his father in two long-legged strides and knelt beside Garad.

"Father, what is wrong?"

"Nothing at all," the chieftain grumbled, irritably shoving the steaming liquid away. "I am tired. You would think that Death himself was hovering over me instead of Drek'Thar, though sometimes I wonder if they are one and the same."

Durotan looked from Drek'Thar to Geyah. Both of them wore somber expressions. Geyah looked as if she had not slept more than a few moments during the last three days. Durotan realized, as he had not done earlier, that she had worn the same beads in her hair since Gul'dan's visit; Geyah, who would never wear ritual garb of any sort once the ceremony was over.

But it was to the shaman that he spoke. "Drek'Thar?"

The older orc sighed. "It is no illness I am familiar with, nor injury," he said. "But Garad feels..."

"Weak," Geyah said. Her voice trembled.

So, this was why she had urged Durotan to depart on firewood duty for three days running. She did not want him here, in the village, asking questions.

"Is it serious?"

"No," grunted Garad.

"We do not know," Drek'Thar answered as if Garad had not spoken. "And it is this that concerns me."

"Do you think it has anything to do with what Gul'dan said?" Durotan asked. "About the world growing sicker?"

About the sickness reaching Frostfire Ridge.

Drek'Thar sighed. "It could be," he said, "or it could be nothing at all. An infection I cannot detect that will run its course, perhaps, or—"

"If it were, you would know it," Durotan said flatly. "What do the Spirits say?"

"They are agitated," the shaman replied. "They disliked Gul'dan."

"Who could blame them?" said Garad, and gave his son a wink meant to reassure. But it had the opposite effect. The entire clan had been unsettled by the green orc's dire predictions. It would be unwise for Garad to appear before his people in this condition. Geyah and Drek'Thar had been right to wait until he had recovered to—

Durotan swore. He had been so shocked to see his father in such a state that he had forgotten what had driven him to barge into their dwelling.

"We found traces of intruders in the woods, a league to the southeast," he said. "They smelled of blood. More blood than a simple kill. And it was *old* blood."

Garad's small eyes, watery and bloodshot, narrowed at the words. He threw aside his blanket. "How many?" he said as he struggled to rise.

His legs gave way and Geyah caught him. His mother was strong and had many years of wisdom upon her, but for the first time in Durotan's memory, his parents seemed old to their son.

"I will gather a war party," Durotan decided.

"No!" The protest was a bellow, an order, and despite himself Durotan stopped in his tracks, so deeply rooted was the instinct to obey a command from his father.

But Geyah was having none of it. "Durotan will deal with these intruders," she said. "Let him lead the war party."

Garad shoved his mate aside. The gesture was imperious, angry, but Durotan knew that fear drove his father. Normally, if he had treated her with such disrespect, Geyah would have responded with a blow of her own. Garad might be the chieftain, but she was the chieftain's wife, and tolerated no such treatment.

That she did not chilled Durotan to his soul.

"Listen to me," Garad said, speaking to all of them. "If I do not ride out to face this threat, the clan will know—will *believe*—that I am too weak to do so. They are already agitated, thanks to Gul'dan's nonsense. To be seen by them as unable to lead..." He shook his head. "No. I will command this war party, and I will return victorious. And we will deal with whatever is happening then, from a place of triumph. I will have shown the Frostwolves that I can protect them."

His logic was unassailable, even as Durotan's heart cried out against it. He looked at his mother, and saw the wordless request in her eyes. She would not be fighting alongside Garad, not today. For the first time in their lives, Geyah suspected her husband would not return. The clan could not afford to lose him, her, and Durotan in a single, terrible battle. Pain twisted inside him.

"I will keep him in my sight, Mother. No harm will—"

"We Exile those who are weak, Durotan," Garad interrupted. "It is our way. You will not hover around me, nor interfere. If this is my fate, I accept it, and I will do so unaided, on Ice's back, or on my own two feet." Even as he spoke, he swayed slightly. Geyah caught him, and this time when he pulled away, he was not ungentle with his loving life companion. He reached out for the gourd and looked at it a moment.

"Tell me what you have seen," he said to Durotan, and listened while he drank down the draft.

5

Geyah and Durotan assisted Garad with his battle armor. It differed from hunting armor in that it was specifically designed to block blows from axes, hammers, and maces, as opposed to hooves or horns. Beasts attacked the center of mass: the chest and legs. Orcs went for these as well, but the shoulders and throat were particularly vulnerable on an orc wielding a weapon designed for close combat. Throats were guarded with thick leather collars, and the shoulders sported massive pads studded with metal spikes. But for a race where honor was all, armor was less important than the weapons. And the weapons that orcs bore into battle were massive.

The weapon bequeathed to Orgrim was the Doomhammer, for which his family was named. The huge chunk of granite was wrapped twice around with gold-studded leather and affixed to a thick oaken haft that was almost a weapon in itself.

Thunderstrike was Garad's hereditary weapon of choice for the hunt. But the huge axe he had named Sever was his weapon for battle. With two blades of steel, honed meticulously to a leaf-thin sharpness, Sever did exactly what it was named for. Seldom did Garad strap it to his back, but he wore it with pride today.

Durotan had never been prouder to call himself a son of Garad than when his father emerged a short time later. He strode from his hut as straight as Durotan had ever seen him, his dark eyes flashing with righteous rage. Orgrim had already been speaking to the warriors of the clan, and most of them, too, had donned battle armor.

"Frostwolves!" Garad's voice rang out. "My son brings news of intruders in our forests. Orcs who do not approach our territory openly, as a hunting party would, but who skulk and hide. They hew limbs from our trees, and they reek of old blood."

Durotan fought back an instinctive shiver at the memory. Any orc would deem the scent of fresh blood, spilled in the name of sustenance or honor, a good smell. But old blood, that stale, musty stench of spoilage... no orc would choose to wear it. A warrior reveled in blood, then cleansed afterward, donning fresh clothing for the celebration to follow.

Were these the Red Walkers Gul'dan had spoken of? Was this why they named themselves thus—because they were always covered in the blood of their kill? When Gul'dan had mentioned them, Durotan had been inclined to welcome them, should they arrive in Frostwolf territory. Any orc who refused the warlock was an orc to respect. Or so he had believed, until he had scented them.

Things slain should be allowed to move on—the souls of orcs, and the souls of little brothers and sisters such as the clefthooves, even down to the smallest snow rabbit. They were slain and eaten or burned, returning to the earth, water, air, and fire. Pelts were cleaned and tanned, never worn rotting and bloody.

The thought appalled Durotan—as it did every Frostwolf who listened attentively to their chieftain's words.

"We will ride to confront these intruders," Garad continued. "We will drive them from our forests, or slay them where they stand!"

He lifted Sever and bellowed, "Lok'tar ogar!" *Victory, or death.*

The Frostwolves took up the cry, shouting along with him as they raced to their equally eager wolves. Durotan leaped atop Sharptooth, casting a quick glance over his unarmored shoulder at his father. For just an instant, the weariness that had prostrated Garad a short time ago flitted across the chieftain's features. Then, with what Durotan knew to be an effort of sheer, stubborn determination, Garad banished it.

Durotan's throat suddenly felt tight, as if squeezed by an unseen hand.

* * *

Garad forced his sluggish mind to focus as he rode. The Frostwolves raced toward the cluster of violated trees with no semblance of secrecy. His son and Orgrim had reported seeing the footprints of seven, but doubtless, there were more. It was even possible that the main force outnumbered the Frostwolves, who had never boasted great numbers. One thing was certain: neither orc had seen any sign that the intruders had wolves. In the end, the Red Walkers, if such they were, would be facing more than a score warriors—in truth, twice as many, as the frost wolves themselves had been trained to fight alongside the orcs they regarded more as friends than as masters.

It would be sufficient to wipe them out. At least, Garad had to hope it would be. And he had to hope he would last long enough to do what he had come to do, return home, and continue fighting this crippling, cursed *weakness*.

The symptoms resembled those caused by the bite of a lowly but dangerous insect the orcs called a "digger". The victim was enfeebled for days at a time, with a lack of energy and strength uniquely terrifying to an orc. Agony, racking convulsions, a shattered limb—these things, orcs knew how to embrace. The listlessness and lethargy evoked by this insect truly frightened them.

But neither Geyah nor Drek'Thar had found evidence that he had been bitten by a digger. And Drek'Thar had heard nothing—nothing at all—from the Spirits as to the nature of this mystery illness. When Durotan had come with his talk of blood-steeped enemies, Garad had known it was a sign. He would rise, and fight. He would rally and defeat this malady, just as he had every other enemy.

A victory brought by action would also be good for the clan's morale. Gul'dan's dire foreboding, his unsettling presence, his strange slave, and above all, his green skin—it had cast an unwholesome shadow upon the Frostwolves. Bloodshed of an enemy, would hearten them immensely. And Garad longed to be once again spattered with the hot blood of a justified kill. Perhaps this was a test sent by the Spirits—and triumph would restore his vigor. Illness had stalked the clan—even its chieftain—ere now. As he had done before, he would repel it.

The arrogant interlopers had left a broad trail from the wounded trees, their footprints dark smudges on trampled snow. The Frostwolves followed, overwriting the tracks with the paw prints of their mounts. The trail led to the gray curve of the foothills, the peak of Greatfather Mountain lost to view in the low clouds.

The strange orcs were expecting them, and Garad was glad of it.

They stood in a line, straight and silent, their number a mere seventeen. While the Frostwolves wore armor and bore weapons that reflected their northern heritage, the intruders wore a strange jumble of armor styles—boiled leather, fur, metal plating. Their weapons were similarly mismatched.

But that was not what brought some of his clan members up sharply. Garad knew it was the sight of their armor—their skin, their faces—all covered in handprints of crusted, dark, dried, reeking blood.

One orc, the largest and most physically intimidating of the group, stood in the center, a few paces ahead of the others. Garad assumed he was their leader. His head was shaved, and he wore no helmet.

Garad gazed at him with contempt. These Red Walkers, if such they were, would not long survive in the north. Warriors kept their hair, and covered their skulls, here in the cold lands. Orgrim was the only Frostwolf who rebelled. Hair and helmets helped preserve warmth—and the skull in question atop one's shoulders. Garad would remove that bald head, watch it land in the snow and melt it with hot blood.

Earlier, Geyah had urged him to stay out of the fray; begged, almost. She had never done so before, and her fear alarmed him more than his illness did. She was the most courageous orc he had ever known, but he saw now that he was her one weakness. They had been a mated pair for so long, Garad could not imagine life without her charging into the fight by his side. But here he was, and he knew why she had chosen to stay behind.

This wasting sickness was unbecoming of an orc, and it would not stand. He would not let it.

He would not condemn his Geyah to riding without him.

He growled low in his throat, summoning all his strength and channelling it toward two things—raising Sever, and opening his mouth to shout a battle cry.

His voice was almost immediately joined by the other Frostwolves. He was flanked by his son and Orgrim, and as they and Geyah had done many times before, they rode forward as a unit, tight and terrifying, their wolves so close they touched, before each broke off and headed toward his own target.

Garad focused on the leader. As he watched, the other smiled and nodded. He held an axe that shone with something sticky—tree sap. Doubtless, this disrespectful orc had used it earlier to hack the limbs off the trees. Garad let his anger at the act fuel him, and he felt energy starting to rise within him—real energy, if bought from bloodlust.

The bald orc cried out and raced torward him, thick legs propelling him forward as swiftly as the snow would permit. But an orc on foot was no match for a mounted Frostwolf, and Garad bore down upon his enemy, grinning.

Ice, too, was ready to fight. His jaws were open, red tongue lolling over sharp white teeth. Garad lifted Sever, both hands wrapped around its hilt, timing the moment when he would lean over and slice off the enemy's head.

But then, the orc shouted, "Mak'gora!"

Abruptly Garad shifted his weight and Ice veered off awkwardly. Garad had never heard of an orc issuing the mak'gora in the middle of a battle. The

Red Walkers were facing certain defeat. To ask for the outcome to be decided by single combat was pure cowardice. Had it been the Frostwolves with so few, they would know they claimed honor by fighting to their deaths against overwhelming odds. They would never try to alter the outcome by reducing it to a one-on-one fight!

Garad's disgust with this Red Walker grew, but concern flickered through him as well. Ordinarily, he would likely be more than a match for this southlander. But this was not an ordinary time, and his limbs were already threatening to turn traitor. He could not rely on his strength remaining.

But how could he pretend he didn't hear the challenge? If others heard it and saw he did not honor the mak'gora, the shame would be Garad's, not the interloper's. His enemy saw the conflict on Garad's face, and a cruel grin twisted his mouth around his tusks.

The insolence was too much to be borne. Garad leaped off Ice. He stumbled ever so slightly, but recovered quickly, setting his will to it. *You are strong,* he told himself. *This sickness will pass. It will not claim you. You are a chieftain, and it is nothing. You will defeat this challenger, and your Frostwolves will wipe out the Red Walkers.*

"I accept," he snarled, and charged.

As if the mighty Sever was nothing more than a child's training toy, the bald orc's sap-fouled axe struck it and shoved it aside with shocking ease. Garad recovered, gripping the weapon tightly, striving not to fall. To lose his footing would be death.

The Red Walker went on the offensive now, and Garad grunted with the effort of simply lifting Sever to block the deadly blows. It was all he could do; there was no strength remaining in his arms, his legs, anywhere in his body to mount an attack. Too late, he understood that he had chosen poorly in allowing himself to be goaded into this. Anguish and rage flowed through him, enough for him to rally, heft the great axe, and bring it down in a final strong horizontal strike.

But the other orc was not there. He had leaped aside, and now laughed openly at Garad's efforts. Elsewhere, the Frostwolves were the clear victors in this battle. The Red Walkers fought well, but they were struggling in the snow and faced greater numbers. The bald orc looked around, smirking.

"I had best end this quickly," he said, "as only you and I know this is a mak'gora."

He lifted his axe. Garad grunted angrily, and struggled to lift Sever in return. Helplessly, he watched his arms quiver as he raised the axe only a few inches before it fell from his weak fingers.

Even so. *Let it be thus*, Garad thought. *I will die in a fair—*

And suddenly, he understood. Garad's enemy had known he would be easy to defeat.

The knife—Gul'dan's blade...

His gut went as cold as winter with stark comprehension.

And the Red Walker's axe descended.

6

Ice needed no rider other than the corpse of his master.

The great frost wolf had howled piteously when Garad fell, and had rushed in to swiftly and bloodily dispatch his murderer. Now Ice stood, trembling, as Durotan lashed his father's body to the wolf's strong back. Orc and wolf eyes met, and Durotan saw his own grief reflected in Ice's great amber orbs. Most orc clans regarded the wolves they rode as mere beasts—mounts and nothing more. Less important, in some cases, than a weapon borne into battle, because living things could die and not be bequeathed to one's offspring.

The Frostwolves had never felt so. These animals chose their masters, not the other way around, and they stayed with them until their bond was broken by death. Ice would grieve, not as an orc would, but it would be true grief nonetheless. Durotan wondered if Ice would ever permit himself to be ridden again. Compassion for the great beast, and for his mother, to whom he must bear the wrenching news, threatened to crush Durotan's heart. He allowed himself a single moment to feel the loss: *Father. Friend. Teacher. Chieftain.*

Life was harsh in Frostfire Ridge, and had only grown harsher with the passage of time. It was not unnatural for a father to pass before a child. It was the manner of Garad's passing that was the heaviest burden to bear. Garad had been a wise, strong, successful leader of his people for many years. He did not deserve to have such a cloud over him.

Durotan, and many others, had borne witness as Garad died unable to keep his grip on Sever.

Durotan was now the leader of the Frostwolves—for the moment, at least—and they were all looking to him. Once he felt his father was secured for his final ride back to Frostfire Ridge, he turned away from Ice to survey the party.

"Today, we rode to meet a challenge," he said. "And meet it we did. We were victorious. Our foes lie stiffening in the snow, and we have eliminated a threat to our clan. But this victory was not without cost. We have lost Garad, son of Durkosh, son of Rokuk—our clan leader. He died as he, as any, Frostwolf warrior would wish: In battle, courageously protecting his clan from a clear enemy."

He paused, his nostrils flaring, ready to quash

any wayward comment to the contrary. There was none, though the snow groaned softly as some orcs shifted uneasily, not meeting Durotan's gaze.

"We will bear him home in silence. As his son, I am his heir, unless the Spirits deem me unworthy." *Or unless I am challenged*, he thought. He did not say it aloud. He could not help it if that idea had already occurred to anyone, but he would not plant the seed himself.

But even so, the shadow was there. Garad had fallen when he should not have, and that presaged poorly for Durotan—and for the Frostwolves.

Determination chased away his grief. As Durotan leaped atop Sharptooth, in the midst of all the swirling chaos, he knew one thing: He would do all that was within his power to honor and clear the name of a great orc.

Garad had been a long-lived chieftain, and therefore few present had witnessed the ritual that was about to unfold. Every member of the Frostwolf Clan, from the grayest orc to the smallest suckling child, had gone to the special circle that Drek'Thar had instructed be designed. It was not too far from the village, but a distance away, in an open area that was large enough so that all could bear witness. Durotan realized with a pang that while the area would see grief tonight, it was the same site where the clan would be dancing to celebrate Midsummer.

Garad's body had been placed on a pyre. It had

required most of the wood the clan had stockpiled. Durotan mused bitterly on the irony that it had been a search for firewood that had led to the need for it now.

It all felt so horribly wrong. Four days ago, they had never heard of a green orc named Gul'dan. Only this morning, Garad had yet breathed, and the clan was blissfully ignorant of the true horror of the Red Walkers. Durotan wondered if he would ever be able to get the stench of dried blood out of his nostrils.

Garad's body had been bathed, but the hole in his chest still yawned open. Like scars on living flesh, the wounds of the slain granted them honor. If an orc fell fighting—in battle or in the hunt—the injuries that took his or her life were left to show everyone what had been endured for the clan's well-being. Garad wore the armor in which he had fallen, damaged from the blows that had claimed his life. It sent a pang through the young orc to see his father's limbs so very motionless.

The younger shaman who served Drek'Thar were placing stones in a ring around the pyre, leaving a space for Durotan to enter. The stones were held, chanted to, and laid down with great reverence. Durotan could feel the energy building, increasing as each clan member came to sit around the circle, in silence.

Finally, the circle was almost complete. Drek'Thar had been standing quietly to the side, one hand on Wise-ear. Now, the wolf moved into the ring of sanctified stones, guiding his master inside.

Drek'Thar dismissed the wolf with a soft word and a pat, then straightened.

"Frostwolves!" he cried. "We know that our way of life is worth fighting for, and today our warriors did so. Most returned to us victorious. But one did not live to join us again in this life. For any warrior who died, we would mourn and honor his sacrifice. And this we will do, but we are gathered for another reason as well. The orc who fell today was our chieftain, Garad, son of Durkosh, son of Rokuk. And so we must also seek the blessing of the Spirits of Earth, Air, Water, Fire, and Life, upon his son, Durotan, that he might lead us as well and wisely as his father did."

There were no murmurs, not quite. The rite was too profound for such disrespect. But there was an aversion of eyes, a subtle shift of movement among the crowd that made Durotan's anger rise. He ignored it, keeping his gaze fixed on Drek'Thar and awaiting the signal to move into the circle.

But it was for Durotan's mother that the shaman called first. His voice was gentle as he said, "Geyah, daughter of Zungal, son of Kerzug. You were Garad's mate in life. The hand that loved best is the one that must light the fire."

Geyah's normally braided hair hung long and unbound, falling almost to her waist. Her body was straight as the pines as she strode forward. Only Durotan, who knew her so well, could see the shimmer of unshed tears in her eyes. Later, she would weep; later, they both would, alone with their pain.

But for now, with this bitter pall like a stain upon the memory of a beloved mate and father, they had to embody strength.

If the Spirits feel as some members of the clan do...

No. He would not give such thoughts even a heartbeat's worth of attention. Garad had been a great orc chieftain. Durotan knew he had done nothing himself to disrespect his family, his clan, or the Spirits. All would be well.

It had to be.

His fingers curled into fists.

"Durotan, son of Garad, son of Durkosh. Come forward into the circle. Be judged by the Spirits our people have honored since time began, and which will be, even when we are forgotten and no mouths sing our names."

Out of the corner of his eye, Durotan saw Orgrim staring intently at him. The other orc slowly, deliberately, put his fist to his broad chest and lifted his chin in a show of respect. After a moment, a few others followed, then still more, until, by the time the younger shaman had closed the circle with sacred stones, the entire clan had saluted Garad's son. Durotan threw Orgrim a grateful look, then settled himself for what would come.

Drek'Thar had told him nothing of the experience, saying, logically enough, that as it had never happened to him, he could not properly say. "And I suspect that it is different for everyone," he had added. One thing Durotan did know was that while the Sprits would be evaluating him, they would simultaneously be in communication with Drek'Thar.

Drek'Thar held a bundle of smokeleaf. Dried and tightly braided, the plant gave off a sweet scent when burned. It burned now, slow to be consumed, and the smoke wafted lazily upward. Durotan approached and knelt before the shaman, who held the braid of long grass with one hand and waved the smoke over Durotan with the other.

It smelled good—clean, and fresh. Drek'Thar handed the smokeleaf to Palkar, his attendant shaman. A third shaman, Relkarg, extended a cup to Durotan. He drank it down. The liquid was hot and thick, sweet from the sap that the trees wept. He returned the empty cup to Relkarg, and waited for more instructions.

"Sit, now, young one," Drek'Thar said. There was great affection in his voice. He and Garad had been close, and the shaman, too, was doubtless wrestling with how to manage the sudden void. "The Spirits come when they will."

Durotan obeyed. Now, he felt his eyelids growing heavy. He let them close.

Then they flew open.

In years past, Durotan had seen the night skies in winter shimmer with colors that seemed made of mist. The visions before him, undulating with equal tranquility, resembled that exquisite celestial display, but only as a sapling resembled an ancient tree. Durotan gasped in awe, reaching without thinking, as a child might, toward the phantasms.

Green, red, blue, and yellow, they danced before

him, but he knew they were not physically present. They were in his mind, in his ears and eyes and blood and bone. They darted and hovered, so very real, but he knew that what he experienced was for him alone.

In his vision, the snow beneath him evaporated, and the dancing colors faded, melting along with it. Durotan sat on good, solid earth, held and supported as a babe in his mother's arms. Wonderingly, he placed his hands on the ground and dug in his fingers deeply. His hands came up with rich loam.

Durotan smiled, then gave a surprised, unrestrained laugh as a sprightly breeze came out of nowhere and scattered the handfuls of soil. The zephyr, laden with the scent of fresh, new grass, caressed him. He felt his lungs release their tightness as he breathed in.

The air whirled and began to take on colors. They were not the same soft, fey tones that had danced before his eyes earlier, but bright, strong hues: sharp flickers of red, orange, white, and blue formed, and a fire suddenly crackled around him. His face had been growing numb from the cold, and Durotan welcomed the warmth of the flames. Without fire, no Frostwolf could survive. It was dear to them, and the Spirit of Fire seemed to know that.

Something wet touched his cheek. Fat, white flakes drifted down, and the flames spat and hissed at them. Though he missed the fire's warmth, Durotan was content to let it surrender its place to the Spirit of Water. What was a Frostwolf without frost, anyway? Ice and snow were part of what made them unique—made them strong. Water cleansed and purified. It quenched thirst, and even filled one's eyes, and slipped down one's face, as it did now. Water soothed, and healed, and Durotan accepted its gentleness in this form as he accepted its harshness in others.

The shimmering hues that were real-not-real began to swirl, chasing one another as a pup chased its tail, so fast that they soon began to blur. A white brilliance exploded in front of Durotan, so strong and beautiful that he could not bear to look upon it.

Earth, Air, Fire, Water—they had all come, and now they welcomed the greatest of all: the Spirit of Life.

He had been numb since his father's fall. Since he had watched, unable to reach Garad in time, as the Frostwolf chieftain died weaponless, he had tamped his emotions down to appear strong in front of the clan, but now he could do so no longer. His senses were vibrantly, painfully alive. His heart swelled with love and torment, so much that he thought he could not bear it. How could any single being—

But you are not, came a whisper in his mind. *You are experiencing life with all its joys and fears and horrors and losses and blessings and power. You wish to stand as chieftain for your people—hold all this, just for a moment, and you will be worthy of them. They fear, and lust, and laugh, and weep, and live—know it, Durotan, son of Garad. Know it, and honor it!*

Durotan felt himself being stretched, reshaped,

molded to hold more than he had ever been meant to. He was but one orc. But what else was a chieftain, if not the caretaker of his people? And how could he act for them, if he did not truly feel them? Trembling with fear, Durotan accepted the test of Life. He was filled, more than filled, he had become so vast that he—

And then it was gone.

They were all gone.

He opened his eyes to a world that seemed oddly flat and devoid of color. His heart slammed against his chest, his lungs heaved, but Durotan was himself again, alone. For a moment, the isolation was too much to take; it was as hard to endure as the fullness of his clan had been, but eventually, that sensation, too, dissipated.

His gaze focused. He saw his mother, standing by his father's pyre, a slight smile curving her lips. Her eyes were no longer wet with grief, but fierce with pride. Durotan, dizzy as the Spirits left him, took in the sight of faces that were as familiar as his own reflection in a pool of water, but now also strange to him, new in their sudden precious beauty, their vibrant essence of life.

The Frostwolves had followed his father. Now, they would follow him. He would do what was best for them, as Garad had always striven to do. Durotan tried to speak, but his heart was so full of a tumult of emotions that he couldn't find the words.

"The Spirits have accepted you, Durotan, son of Garad, son of Durkosh," came Drek'Thar's voice. "Do you, Frostwolves?"

The answering cheers were deafening. Durotan got to his feet. He raised his hands, curled into fists, into the air, arching backward as he cried out in joy and hope.

After the cry had subsided, the new Frostwolf chieftain, his ears ringing and his heart overflowing, turned to Drek'Thar. It was only as he gazed at the shaman's solemn visage that Durotan realized that, although they had approved of him, all was not well in the world of the Spirits.

7

After the ceremony, Geyah lit the fire that would take her husband's body. She and her son stood vigil as the flames caught the tinder, then grew higher, creating a wall of light and heat to stand against the cold and the darkness of evening's encroaching shadows. Durotan recalled the leap of the Spirit of Fire and all its myriad hues, seeing them again in his mind's eye as he gazed at the pyre's flames. Members of the clan approached throughout the night to lay wood on the fire, so that it would remain hot enough to burn Garad's body to ashes. When the sun showed its head, it was done. Fire had consumed Garad. Air had scattered his ashes. Water would bring them back to Earth, which would accept them into the welcoming soil. Life had ended, and yet still went on.

When it was over, Durotan moved toward his mother, discovering his body had grown stiff from standing so long beside the pyre. But before he could speak, she said, "I have arranged to have your things moved into the chieftain's hut. I will move into yours, now."

Of course, Durotan realized. He had dwelt in his own hut since his first hunt. Now, as chieftain, he would return to the hut where he had entered the world, under somber circumstances that he wished had not come quite so soon.

"You always see to things before I have even thought of them," he said, sadly.

She struggled to smile. "I am the Lorekeeper. It is my duty to remember what is customary. And you will have more than enough to keep you busy for some time."

"Do not worry, Geyah," came Orgrim's voice. "I will see that he sleeps, if I have to knock him out myself."

Geyah moved silently toward what would be her hut now, where she could grieve privately. Durotan watched her go, then turned to Orgrim. "Mother said I would have many duties in the next few days."

Orgrim chuckled. "If by 'many' she meant 'a few hundred,' then yes," he replied.

"I will need someone to help me with them," Durotan said. "Someone I can trust completely. Someone," he said, "who would lead the clan if anything were to happen to me."

Orgrim was strong, steady, and capable. Little

seemed to disturb him. But now, his eyes widened. "I... Durotan, I am honored. I..."

Durotan laid a hand on his friend's enormous, sloping shoulder. "I am heartsore and weary of words and rituals, and the Lorekeeper has gone to her hut. Please... just say yes."

Orgrim laughed. And then, he said yes.

Next, Durotan met with Drek'Thar, who told the young chieftain what he himself had experienced during the ritual. The Spirits had no quarrels with Durotan. But there was, as Durotan had suspected, something amiss.

"Gul'dan is not to be trusted," Drek'Thar stated bluntly. "The Spirits..." he groped for words, then shook his head. "I would say, 'fear' him, but such terms, such concepts, cannot be applied to them. They would not go near him, although... About some things, this *warlock*—" Drek'Thar spat the word "—does not lie. The world *is* changing, my young chieftain. You follow in your father's footsteps at what is perhaps the darkest time in our clan's history. These hardships will not abate. They will only grow worse."

"But the Spirits *do* approve of me," Durotan pressed. He hoped that Drek'Thar would take the words as he meant them—as evidence of his concern, not a need for reassurance.

"That is clear, yes."

"Then I must be worthy of their confidence. My father led well—well enough for Gul'dan to make a long and difficult journey for the sole purpose of asking us to ally with him. I do not think he did so out of the goodness of his heart, but rather because we have something he wants. Our strength. Our ability to endure. My father refused to join him, because such virtues are not for southlanders, but for us—for Frostwolves—to benefit from. I will lead as he did."

He reached to lay a reassuring hand on Drek'Thar's arm, still strong with muscle beneath his shaman's leather garb. "I will take care of our people."

The gift of the Spirits had been an unexpectedly tender, if fierce, one. After they had both had a little time to rest, Durotan went to his mother, and together they wept for his father. There was no shame in it. He told her of the gift of the Spirits, and his determination to protect the clan.

"They granted you the understanding of the love a parent has for a child, my son," she said, smiling through the tears still wet on her face. "Nothing is stronger. I am still, and always will be, your mother, but you are now my chieftain. I will advise you as best I can, as a shaman and the Lorekeeper. Command, and we will all obey."

That night, he fell asleep on his father's sleeping skins so exhausted that he had no dreams.

The next morning, Durotan summoned the clan's finest hunters—not just those in peak physical condition, but those who in the past had brought down fierce prey with skill and renown. He told them all they were free to speak—even disagree and argue if need be, but were to work together to discover which weapons were truly the finest at hunting which prey. They were to show him, and indeed everyone, where the talbuks were most likely to be found by using the burned ends of sticks to draw maps on dried, scraped hides. They were to indicate which lakes stocked which fish, and what those fish best liked to eat.

"But, my chieftain," Nokrar had said, eyeing a fragile-seeming orc, "all know these things."

"Do we?" Durotan had demanded. "Does everyone here know? Or do we keep secrets, so that we may be deemed valuable when food is scarce?" A few orcs flushed at that, but he continued. "We must think of what is best for *all*, not just one, or one family. *All*. We are Frostwolves—we are skilled, and wise, and brave. Do as I say, and all will eat."

For several days, he repeated this pattern with various groups. He spoke with the warriors about setting up patrols. Hitherto, few outsiders had troubled the Frostwolves. Greatfather Mountain had discouraged all but the occasional trespasser. But no one in the clan, least of all Durotan, wished to see the Red Walkers return. They had killed the orc who had slain Garad, and his party, but Durotan suspected that their clan numbered more than that handful. By that evening, the warriors were taking watches, patrolling by both sun- and moonlight.

Durotan called the shaman, wanting to learn about healing herbs, and asked them to ponder if there might be a way to create a magical light, so that plants might be cultivated even in months when the sun shone little. To the skinners and leatherworkers, to those who harvested and dried the fruits, he spoke as well, and urged them to share their techniques. Durotan even sat with the children and played with them, observing their games and watching to see who the natural leaders were.

There was some resistance at first. But Durotan was stubborn and persevered, and his people did as he bade. Though the spring had been feeble, the Midsummer feast was one of the most bountiful the Frostwolves had seen in some time. The Midsummer bonfire was lit at dawn, and was fed until well into the night. The joke was always that it was tended to until everyone fell asleep—whether that sleep came from exhausted dancing or the cider that flowed as freely as the melting snow.

At one point, during the laughing, drinking, dancing, and drumming, Durotan stepped away from the festivities and looked out across the wide meadow that lay to the west of the village.

"There is still green here," said Orgrim, as he stepped next to his friend. "And not the green of Gul'dan or his slave."

Durotan emitted a bark of surprised laughter. Orgrim joined him. Sobering, Orgrim said, "My old friend, you have made a good chieftain these past several months. Take a look at your people. Their bellies are full. Their children play in safety. They are warm when they sleep."

"That ought to be the very least a chieftain should do," Durotan said, uncomfortable with the praise.

"But these days... it means more than it used to," Orgrim said. "Why do you stand here? Come dance! A chieftain needs a mate, and I tell you, there are many who would be more than willing to be yours."

Durotan laughed, glancing back toward the dancing taking place in the meadow. Sure enough, several females boldly gazed back at him. There was no denying their strength and beauty. "There is time for that yet. I... Orgrim, I keep thinking of those we have Exiled. I wonder if any will ever return."

Orgrim shrugged. "Some do, if they are strong enough. Some don't. Why do you care? It is the way of our people."

Durotan thought about the old orcs who had been fierce warriors, but who had been largely ignored, left to nod by the fires and wait for death. He had invited them to speak, to share their memories, and the clan had benefitted. Why had such knowledge ever been allowed to escape the clan? What had been lost in years past? Would Draka, and others who had been born weak, still have had something to contribute, had they been permitted to stay? Or would they simply have taken precious resources from those who had the ability to contribute?

He sighed. He could not share these thoughts with Orgrim. Not yet; not until he understood them himself. "It has not been easy, Orgrim," he confided. "Being chieftain. Father made it seem so effortless."

"He was a great Frostwolf," Orgrim agreed.

"A great orc. Do not worry, Durotan. He would be proud of you."

Durotan hoped so, but he could not say for certain. He only knew, as he gazed out over the meadow, that he wished he could see an Exiled Frostwolf striding home.

But he did not.

With each day that passed, Gul'dan's grim warnings seemed to recede. The patrols continued, although as the moons came and went, some of the clan began to complain of the duty.

Nokrar, in particular, thought them a waste of time. "Your father's death has been avenged," he said to Durotan. "We have seen no sign that any survived. Warriors like myself and the others would be more useful sent on extra hunts."

Durotan prided himself on listening to all reasonable requests. While Nokrar's comment verged on an insult, Durotan had to admit to himself that there was at least some truth in it. His father's death *did* haunt him. But was a daily patrol truly necessary? Although Gul'dan had spoken of them with contempt, he did not seem to particularly fear them. He believed the Red Walkers would die off soon enough. Besides, if there were any Red Walkers still in the area, it might be that the hunting parties themselves would discover them.

"You are a skilled hunter, Nokrar. Perhaps a daily patrol is not necessary." He reduced the patrols to once every five days, and increased the number of hunts.

The summer was still too short, and the fall harvest meager, but spirits were high. Although looked as though Nokrar's idea had been sound, as more hunts did result in more food, Durotan would not allow himself to slacken. He consulted with Drek'Thar, who heeded the visions of the Spirits, and found himself issuing orders that seemed contrary.

To Durotan, it seemed foolish to ask his people to hoard nuts and seeds through the winter when they could be eaten, but he listened to an old female who advised him to do exactly this. Fish and meat were best fresh caught. Their flesh was sweeter, and a fitter food for warriors. But he instructed his clan to hunt more often, restrain themselves from gorging, and salt fish and meat to preserve it for the lean times. For every bite they ate now, he urged them to lay aside three. He did not need to remind them that there was no way to tell how long the winter would last this year.

"They do not truly understand," Orgrim said to Durotan one evening. "We are orcs. Danger and death come at the end of a spear. That is what we are made for—fighting, not—" he eyed the pile of salt in front of him "—this."

"There are no lok'vadnods sung for those who starve," Durotan agreed, "but it does not mean they are any less missed when they die."

"It annoys me when you speak truth sometimes," Orgrim muttered. "But truth it is."

"This is why I am chieftain, and not you," Durotan grinned. "But I have a task for you, to shut your mouth. Kurg'nal's party has just returned. He says they found tracks, just a few days old. The party had to return before they could follow. Take a fresh group out with you tomorrow, and bring home some juicy meat."

"Ha! If it means no more of this stink for a while, I will make sure we are successful."

8

Orgrim hand-picked those who would ride with him. Kurg'nal told him exactly where his party had found the prints. "I wish I could go with you," the older orc said.

"Let others have some glory, too," Durotan said. It was his custom to rotate rest with activity, for several reasons—not least of which was every orc wanted the honor of bringing home a kill. Privately, he wished he, too, were riding out with his friend. "Orgrim needs something to restore his pride. He is losing his edge."

"He has no *edge*," quipped Nokrar, "he has the Doomhammer!"

Everyone laughed. Durotan could feel the shift in energy among his clan. Fresh meat would lift everyone's spirits—and give everyone strength.

Orgrim's party was cheered when they rode out shortly afterward.

They would not return for at least two days. He hoped they would be successful. Even the supply of dried fish was becoming depleted. He instructed an orc called Delgar to round up a few others to bundle up against the elements and fish in the ice, deflecting the complaints calmly.

Geyah watched them go. "You lead well, my son," she said. "Your father would have had to threaten a mak'gora to make Frostwolf warriors go fishing!"

"Fishing is hunting too," he said. "At least, now it is."

"I will be visiting the outskirts," she told him, speaking of the scattered huts farther away from the communal fire in the heart of the village. "I have been promised some dried roots for a stew tonight. Perhaps it will be fish stew."

The attack came at midday.

Durotan was in the shaman hut, speaking with Drek'Thar, when he heard the wolves howling. It took him an instant to realize that the howls were not in the center of the village, but to the south—the fringes of the Frostwolf encampment Geyah had gone to visit. A heartbeat later, he had seized Thunderstrike and was atop Sharptooth, speeding south toward the savage noises.

There were half a dozen Red Walkers, all covered with those sinister, bloody handprints, and they attacked with a savage vigor. Two Frostwolves lay motionless on the ground. Geyah was screaming battle cries, brandishing a small hand axe as she charged one of the strange orcs, who was laden down with a sack of ground nuts. Other Frostwolves, most of whom were artisans or older children, had snatched up makeshift weapons and were charging their attackers with a courage that made Durotan's heart simultaneously soar and break.

He bore down on the Red Walker stealing the sack and ran him through with Thunderstrike. The orc stared at him blankly, spitted like a talbuk's haunch on the fire.

Another one seemed infuriated by the attack and ran at some of the children. They jumped on him, attacking him with small carving knives, holding him off until Kagra, Nokrar's mate, came after him with a mace and crushed his head.

Geyah hurled her small hatchet at another Red Walker. It caught him between the neck and the shoulder and he stumbled. Snarling, she leaped on him, worked the hatchet free, and dispatched him. Other Frostwolves were riding from the center of the village now, armed with axes and hammers and their righteous fury. Another Red Walker fell before them. The remaining two panicked and turned to flee. One clutched an armload of fur, the other a barrel of salted fish.

Grukag and Durotan ran them down. As he stared down at the still-twitching corpses, panting, Durotan realized two things.

One: None of the Frostwolves living on the fringes of the village were safe. All would need to move in as close to the center as possible.

And two: The attack had come when nearly all the warriors had been gone, either fishing or hunting. Which meant that the Red Walkers had been observing the encampment for some time.

He looked up at Geyah. Their eyes met, and he realized she understood as well. "Everyone," he said, "pack your belongings. You all will dwell close to the main fire from now on."

The fishing and hunting parties were recalled by riders sent after them by Durotan, instructing them all to return to aid their fellow clan members as they moved their lodgings.

At last, the final families arrived with their simple belongings—a few pieces of furniture, hides, and their allotted winter stores. Other orcs would take them in until new huts could be built. Durotan and Orgrim set down the last items, accepted the families' thanks, and went to join Drek'Thar by the communal fire pit.

"The children are older," Durotan observed.

"That happens with children," Orgrim deadpanned. The appetizing scent of roast talbuk wafted into the crisp late autumn air; though interrupted, Orgrim's hunt had been at least somewhat successful.

A flicker of amusement rippled through Durotan. He shoved his friend, who laughed, snorted, and reached to cut another hunk of meat as it turned on the spit. Then the young chieftain grew somber.

"I have seen no newborns," he said, and Orgrim sobered as well.

"Neither have the wolves littered," Orgrim said. "Nor were many calves born to the herds this year."

"There is wisdom in that," Durotan mused. "Fewer mouths to feed when supplies are scarce."

"Yes," said Drek'Thar, who was sitting with them and reaching his hands toward the warmth. "Wisdom. The Spirit of Life understands ebb and flow. But if there are no new calves to grow into adults, what have we to eat? If there are no sturdy young orcs born to the clan, what will become of the Frostwolves?" He turned his blind face in Durotan's direction. "Your attentiveness has saved lives, Durotan."

Durotan scowled and shook his head. "Had I been more attentive, the Red Walkers might not have dared attack."

"Even so. Do not belittle what you have done that has been worthwhile. Children who might have starved to death with lesser care live to play by the fire tonight. But attentiveness cannot create life."

"Has the Spirit of Life come to you, then?"

Drek'Thar shook his head. "The Spirits come less often to me, in these times. But I do not need to have visions or messages to know something this simple. The clan is strong and healthy, for now. But now is not tomorrow."

The words were heavy to Durotan. He thought of Gul'dan and his promises of a new land, fertile and green and bursting with life. He wondered if the warlock and his Horde had already departed, bound for this mysterious place. Durotan recalled the unsettling hue of Gul'dan's skin, the green glow in his eyes, the dead things with which he chose to adorn his body.

He shook himself. Everything in him, and in Geyah, Garad, and Drek'Thar, told him that whatever the warlock promised, it would come at a price. A burst of laughter came from the newly settled family, free, joyful, and content.

The clan was strong and healthy, for now. And for now, Durotan would let that be enough.

The winter was brutal. It came hard on the heels of a dry autumn that yielded wizened fruit and a frost that bit deep. The firewood that had been gathered with muttered complaint in the summer now kept them warm. The dried flesh they had refrained from eating when it dripped sweet juices was now a leathery comfort when snowstorms raged outside, and there was no thought of hunting.

As the clan clustered about the life-giving fire, Durotan told young ones tales about his father and his own first hunt, where he learned what it truly meant to be a Frostwolf. He encouraged Geyah to tell stories of Garad in his prime, and of himself as a child. He invited the elderly orcs who could no longer hunt or fight to sit by the communal fire and share recollections of when they were young.

His only request was that the tales uplift, inspire laughter, or otherwise "make our clan better for the hearing of them."

The Frostwolf clan survived the winter with no loss of life from cold or lack of food. And when spring finally returned, the nuts and seeds so carefully stowed away were planted and tended to.

No one spoke in whispers any more of Garad being "cut down." No one mentioned Gul'dan, unless it was to condemn his fear-mongering. And Geyah told her son that his father would have been proud.

Durotan did not reveal to anyone, not even Orgrim, with whom he shared so much, how he lay awake at night counting barrels of dried grains in his head, or wondering if there were enough kevak leaves to ease the coughing of one of the little ones. Or how he constantly battled a sense of doubt that he was doing the wrong thing.

He knew enough of his parents' interaction to know that Garad turned to his mate for advice and counsel. Doubtless, he had been able to confide his fears to her as well. But although it would likely have been wisdom to have chosen a mate, Durotan did not feel any stirring in his heart.

Perhaps it was simply too weighted down.

9

"I say it will be a dancer, not a drunkard, who is the last orc to throw something on the Midsummer fire tonight," Orgrim said. "The dancing is only beginning. The drinking isn't."

Durotan laughed. Later, he would assume his place on the Stone Seat, but for now, it was too close to the bonfire for his comfort. He and Orgrim stood on the outskirts of the village as the dancers whooped, shouted, and leaped in the flower-starred meadow.

They had made it through a full, and difficult, year with only four clan members to mourn. Two fell in a hunt, one was lost in an accident, and an old orc had died beside a fire, drifting into an endless slumber after telling a story of his youth. Durotan's people were still content. They did not complain about the austere measures their chieftain put on them. They were Frostwolves, accustomed to hardship, and if tonight they reveled, Durotan would be glad.

"I see *you* started early," Durotan replied to Orgrim, gesturing to a waterskin that was, he knew, most definitely not filled with water. Orgrim laughed and passed the bag of cider to his friend. Durotan drank, the tangy but sweet liquid flowing down his throat, and returned the skin to Orgrim.

"Barely a mouthful!" Orgrim said. "Set a good example to your clan, chieftain, and drink up!"

"I will set the example by not having a pounding head on the morrow."

"I won't have a pounding head, either."

"That is because your Doomhammer skull is so thick a clefthoof could dance upon it without causing..." Durotan's voice trailed off.

There was movement on the meadow, a small speck in the distance. None of the dancers had noticed it yet. It did not move like an animal, and no lone Frostwolf would have wandered so far. Durotan realized that it was a figure, and one heading directly toward the village.

Red Walker.

Ever since the attack last autumn , Durotan had had his people on high alert for this hideous "clan" of blood wearers. But today, there had been no patrols. Today, he had let his clan relax and enjoy. Rest. He cursed himself.

Orgrim said quietly, "I will get the wolves."

* * *

Picking up on his master's sense of urgency, Sharptooth flattened his ears against his skull as he ran. The aptly named Biter actually snapped as he bore Orgrim. The two orcs had not raised an alarm, not yet. The Red Walker was out in the open and clearly alone, and Durotan and Orgrim would be more than a match for a single foe. But as they raced across the open meadow, as exposed as the enemy, Durotan turned to see the dancers pause and observe them, their faces tense.

The Doomhammer was strapped across Orgrim's broad back, and Durotan clutched Thunderstrike in one powerful hand. His jaw was set in grim determination. They were downwind of the intruder, and Durotan sniffed, trying to catch the telltale scent of old, dried blood. He frowned when all he smelled was the musk of another orc.

In harmony with him as ever, Orgrim said, "No stink."

The small dot grew larger as they approached. Durotan leaned back and Sharptooth slowed. Biter raced forward for a few paces, then Orgrim circled back to where Sharptooth now stood.

At first, the shape had appeared bulky, and he had assumed it was a male. But there were strange angles on the form, and gradually Durotan realized that he was looking at a female who bore something across her shoulders. Her pace was steady. He now caught a glimmer of something blue and white draped across her torso.

Tension bled out of him so quickly that Durotan

actually trembled. Joy, knife-sharp as torment, sliced through him.

"Orgrim, my old friend, you have an idiot for a chieftain," he said between whoops of giddy laughter.

"I suspected that," Orgrim said, "but why do *you* think so?"

"What day is today?"

"Midsummer, of... course..." Orgrim's eyes went wide.

"That's not a Red Walker out there. That's a *Frostwolf*!"

Orgrim shouted in astonished delight. Both orcs leaned forward and their wolves, happy to be running again, hastened toward the Frostwolf female. She had halted, awaiting their approach, and she bore the body of a talbuk doe on her shoulders. The wind caught a trailing corner of the Frostwolf banner and it fluttered about her. As Durotan and Orgrim came to a halt in front of her, her dark eyes met Durotan's. She grunted as she shrugged off the talbuk and let it fall to the earth. Her belly was flat and bare, her strong, muscular legs encased in roughly made leggings. Her arms were sleek and knotted with muscle, her skin a warm, rich brown. A purple crystal hung about her neck on a cord made of sinew. It caught the sunlight as she threw back her head and laughed, lifting a single small axe in salute.

"Hail, Durotan, son of Garad, son of Durkosh!" she shouted in a bright, clear voice. "I am—"

"Draka, daughter of Kelkar, son of Rhakish," Durotan said, and grinned.

Durotan walked beside Draka almost in a daze as they made their way back to the celebration, her offering of meat slung across Sharptooth's back. His heart was so full. Surely, this was a sign from the Spirits that things would improve soon. He had never seen an Exile return, and it seemed more like fate than coincidence that it was Draka, who exemplified weakness becoming strength, coming home when the clan most needed to be strong.

She was welcomed like a returning hero, and Durotan supposed she was. Skin and bone she had been, weak and frail and slight, almost as slight as the female slave who had accompanied Gul'dan. Now, she was muscular, strong, fierce. He recalled she had bowed her head to no one, departing for what everyone—including herself, perhaps—believed to be certain death. She had returned every bit as proud.

The two years since her departure had seen the death of Draka's parents, but Geyah welcomed her with a warm embrace. Draka was stiff at first, but gradually her arms crept up to hug the older female tightly. Drek'Thar's smile was broad and his voice trembled as he gave her the formal blessing of the clan. Durotan surrendered the Stone Seat to her, which she accepted after a brief hesitation. He himself cut her a dripping slice of roasted flesh, and she ate hungrily. She was muscular, but lean, so very lean. Not an ounce of superfluous flesh softened her frame. He made sure she ate her fill and refused to let her be besieged with questions while she did so.

At last, Draka sighed and sat back, placing a

hand on her full belly. She let her gaze travel over the scene before her. "Durotan. I grieve for your father."

"He died in battle," Durotan said. "Do not grieve."

They looked at one another for a moment before she said, "Do you know, I almost did not return."

"Why not?"

She chuckled without humor, staring at the leaping flames of the bonfire. The sun had set, and the warmth was now welcome. "I was an Exile. My clan had turned against me."

Durotan felt his stomach clench. "It is our way, Draka."

"Which is why I did not return. It has been..." She shook her head. "The Frostwolves have done well. Others have not. The world out there is harsh, Durotan, son of Garad."

"So is the world here."

She turned to him, her brown eyes intense. "The world out there is bigger than here."

"What happened to you? How did you survive? What did you see? I want to hear everything."

Draka scrutinized him. "Why?"

There were many reasons, all of them entirely proper coming from the chieftain of a clan. And yet, he hesitated. "Things have... happened here. I will tell you of them. But I want to know what *you* have seen."

"For what reason?" she pressed.

"I am chieftain now. I need to protect the Frostwolves as best I can. You are a Frostwolf again—if you wish to be. You can help them. Help... us."

Draka smiled. "And?"

He didn't answer immediately. He owed Draka nothing more than what a chieftain owed a returned Exile—an offer to return to her place in the clan. But there was something remarkable about her. Something that made him want to not be a chieftain, always mindful of his words, always trying to lead and do the right thing.

"I watched you leave," he said at length. "You stood straight and proud, though you were so scrawny the weight of the pack alone should have crushed you. You didn't look back. I thought that was the bravest thing I would ever see. Last year, I stood and looked out to the west, and wondered if you would come back. But you didn't."

"But I did," she said quietly.

"You did."

Draka chuckled, low and soft. Her eyes searched his boldly, as if she had earned the right to regard him as an equal because of what she had endured. Perhaps she had. Finally, she seemed to make up her mind about something. She rose from the Stone Seat, stretched her long, strong body, then lay on the earth, watching the smoke as it rose in a gray, twining trail as if trying to meet the stars.

"For as long as time," she said at last, "the south was lush, and our north, our Frostfire Ridge, was starkly simple. This, we know. We were proud that we did not grow lazy, that the challenges honed us. Made us Frostwolves, and not some other clan. And they did, and I was glad of it. Even though I was an Exile, in some ways, I was prepared for what I saw, and the southern orcs were not. I knew what was expected of a Frostwolf, and even if my body was weak, my heart..." She clenched a fist and brought it between her breasts, thumping it firmly. "My heart was strong. My heart and my head kept me alive. Alert. Clever. Alert and clever enough to *stay* alive until my body caught up with them."

He watched her intently, then realized he was staring. Instead, he lay down as well, not touching her, but beside her, and they both looked up at the stars overhead. He envied them their impassivity.

Draka continued. "I could have returned last Midsummer. I chose not to. I wondered if there had been a reason for my weakness, my being sent into Exile. I wanted to learn what was out there. So I went on a journey."

"Where did you go?" Could he have done such a thing? The clan was so important. So tightly knit. Would his heart have been strong, as Draka's was, or would it have broken at leaving his family and their way of life behind? And if he had managed to last a year alone, would he have been able to choose to walk away, simply to see what else was out there?

"Many places. South, west, east, north. I have seen the sun rise from a mountain peak in the east. I got lost in a forest so ancient it makes Greatfather Mountain seem young. I learned how to hunt, and to eat, many things. What plants were wholesome, and what were not."

She turned her head to look at him. Her eyes glittered orange in the firelight.

"There is a blight there that is not here, not yet. Sickness. Ugliness. Things not just dying, but..." she groped for words. "Being twisted first. It is difficult to explain."

"Did you encounter other orcs?"

She nodded. "Yes. From many different clans. Some were hunting parties, as we had encountered here. They carried tales of their lands. They told me how hungry they were, and how frightened."

"They *said* that?"

She laughed. "Not in so many words. But I could smell it on them. They were afraid, Durotan." She fell silent, then said, "I saw others, too. I traveled with the draenei for a time."

"What?" Durotan was shocked. He knew the draenei were more common in the south, but there were some near Frostfire Ridge, as well. He had glimpsed them only once, fascinated by their blue skin, their curving horns, their long tails, their hooved legs that made them look closer kin to talbuks than to orcs. They had been in retreat. Garad had said they were always in retreat; the draenei were notoriously shy, immediately melting away if the Frostwolves ever came across them. The two races avoided one another, which resulted in peace. The draenei never offered offense or violation of the Frostwolf territory, and Garad said only a coward looking to feel better about himself would pick a fight with one who never challenged him.

"Only for a little while. I came across them while they were hunting. They were kind, and wise.

They gifted me with this," she said. She held up the necklace Durotan had observed earlier. Even in the dim light, it glittered. "They had created a small refuge they called Haven, to the north, a safe place where they could rest while traveling. They let me share it, one time when I was injured and needed to recover. They are not what we thought."

"They seem so..." He struggled for words. "Passive. They will not fight. Even the talbuks fight back."

She shook her head. "No. They have honor, and they are strong, just not the way we are. We worked together."

"How?" Draenei spoke gibberish. Draka's laugh was robust and hearty.

"They are not so unlike us that I could not be understood. I learned a few words and phrases as well. They are not orcs, but they *are* people. In the end, I do not regret my Exile, son of Garad. Your father might have thought he was giving me an honorable death. He gave me something else, instead. But when all is done, when the sun of my life sets, I would see it do so here, in Frostfire Ridge."

They lay beside one another for some time, neither feeling the need to speak more. The revels went on around them—drums pounding, laughter filling the air. Orgrim was nowhere to be seen. Durotan wondered how his friend's head would be feeling on the morrow, and he found himself smiling. He was content, for the first time in so very long. He was sure that Draka had many exciting stories to tell, of her two years away from the clan, and he wanted to hear them all.

His smile faded. There was a question that needed to be asked, but he was loath to do so. He postponed it for as long as he could, enjoying the simple comfort of lying beside her, not touching, not speaking. But he had to know.

"Draka," he said, "during your travels, did you ever hear of… a warlock?"

As he had feared, Draka's sneer of distaste soured the soft moment. "Pagh!" She turned her head away from him and spat angrily. "Gul'dan, the green-skinned slaver. Indeed, yes, I heard of him. He is gathering the orcs to him with a tale of some faraway, perfect magical land, where the beasts fight amongst themselves to decide which will be your dinner, fruit falls so often it bruises your head, and birds piss cider."

Durotan bellowed with laughter. She joined in, and they lay grinning at one another for a while. Then, Durotan told Draka of Gul'dan's visit. She listened intently as he described both the warlock and his slave. When he spoke of Garad's death at the hands of the Red Walkers, she propped herself up on one elbow, her gaze never leaving his face.

He spoke for a long time, telling Draka everything that had happened since her Exile, the words flowing out of him. It seemed so easy to talk to her, and he wondered why. Some of these things he had not even said to Orgrim. Maybe it was because she was a returned Exile, someone who had not been present when the incidents occurred. Or because she had learned things during her travels, and could offer a fresh perspective. Or perhaps it was the peaceful intensity emanating from her, as if she listened with her whole being, not just her ears.

When he finally fell silent, she spoke.

"Red Walkers," she said. Her voice was as cold as a glacier. "I have seen them."

Now Durotan, too, rose up on one elbow to peer at her. "Tell me."

"They call themselves so, because they cover themselves with the blood of their prey. But the name is wrong." She shook her dark, braided head slowly. "They are not *red* walkers, not any more."

"I don't..." And then he did understand.

"The blood... Draenei?"

She nodded. "And... orc."

10

The first snow followed Draka by a mere twenty-nine suns.

It was not much, a few crystalline flakes that melted before settling on the ground. But snow had never come this early, and Durotan felt both furious and sick.

In the summer there had been some protest at his miserliness with their supplies, but now that vanished almost as quickly as the snowflakes. Resignation settled in, but the clan knew they would greet the swiftly approaching winter prepared. Durotan was proud of them.

Draka's unexpected arrival heartened the Frostwolves. She would tell stories to rapt young orcs—and some rapt not-so-young ones, too. At Durotan's request, she drew maps on dried, tanned hides, showing where she had traveled, and what lay there. She offered techniques the Frostwolves had never seen before: ways to hold the bow that granted a steadier aim, methods to rewrap sword hilts to make them easier to grip. But most of all, Durotan realized she offered hope. If an Exile could return to the Frostwolves after two full years, alive and even stronger, surely they could all survive.

Shortly after the snowfall, Durotan asked Geyah, Orgrim, Drek'Thar, and Draka to join him in the chieftain's hut. The first three had become trusted advisors, and he sensed Draka had much to contribute as well. At first, the others were stiff and uncomfortable around the newcomer, but gradually everyone started to relax.

"I have missed frostweed tea," Draka admitted, accepting a hot cup from Durotan. "Other herbs are nourishing, but none is as tasty."

Drek'Thar, holding his own cup between his hands, turned his head in her direction. "Other herbs?" he inquired. "Only the frostweed and the kevak leaf are safe for us to eat."

"I thought so, too," Draka said. "But I have since learned that I was wrong. Fireweed and arrowroot can both be eaten. Arrowroot saved my leg when I chewed it and made a poultice to treat a red maka sting. And starflower..." Her eyes sparkled. "Well, if you need a long sleep and interesting dreams, simply drink a cup."

Geyah looked stunned and sat down awkwardly. "Starflower gives death, not sleep. So we—and you—were taught, Draka. Why would you drink it?"

"I did not know what it was when I was offered it," Draka said. "The Thunderlord clan says it is good to quiet the mind."

Geyah shook her head slowly. "That you are here to tell us this is proof it is not poison, but..."

"No doubt our ancestors had reason for teaching us this," Durotan said. "It could be that someone drank too strong a potion and never awoke."

"This could be of great help," Drek'Thar said. "Anything that can heal or feed this clan is a gift, Draka, daughter of Kelkar, son of Rhakish. Later, come to the shaman hut and tell all of us what else you have learned."

Draka's cheeks turned dark. Durotan almost laughed. Draka, who had survived what most orcs considered a death sentence, who had traveled far and wide, who had a gleefully coarse sense of humor and who had seen orcs who wore the blood of their own kind like an obscene decoration... Draka was blushing. And abruptly he understood.

Gently, he placed a hand on her arm. "You are no longer an Exile, Draka. You are one of us. You always have been."

She shook off his hand with a grunt and muttered something he couldn't catch. But the look she gave him was grateful.

Later, taking advantage of the good weather, Durotan assembled a hunting party. Anxious to see Draka demonstrate her various techniques against living prey, he invited her to join the group, and was taken aback when she refused.

"Why will you not come?" he demanded.

"Because I do not wish to."

"We require your skills, Draka. We must know what you know."

"I have taught you enough here, in the village," she said. "Your archers and warriors learn quickly."

She strode off. He followed. "The Frostwolves need you to hunt with us."

"You have not needed me for two years," she shot back, and kept walking.

Clan members did not simply walk away from their chieftain when he was speaking to them! Irritated now, Durotan grabbed her arm to halt her. She tried to jerk away, her black brows drawing together, her strong jaw jutting fiercely.

Like the hands of all orc males, Durotan's were huge on her smaller form. "I am your chieftain," he growled. "You will do as I command."

Her eyes, brown as the earth, deep as its secrets, bored into his. "Is this how you lead, then? Perhaps I should have stayed away."

He released her and stepped back. "No," he said. "It is not how I lead. And I am gladder than I can say that you came home."

He waited for her to stalk away again, but she stood where she was. Encouraged, he said, calmly this time, "You do not have to accompany us if you do not wish to. But I don't understand. You have so much to teach us, Draka. Why won't you come?"

Her frown deepened and she turned away. "You know I was sickly as a child. No one taught me the ways of weapons; no one thought I would survive long enough to use them. I had to learn them myself, or die." She shrugged. "I learned."

"You did. You amaze me, Draka." She turned to look at him, surprised at the honesty and humbleness in the admission. "Show us what you have learned. I, for one, long to see it."

"But there were things I did *not* learn in my Exile," she said. "Things I didn't have the chance to learn. I can hunt, Durotan. But... I cannot *ride* to that hunt."

If she had struck him, he could not have been more astonished. He had not paid much attention to her when he was young; he was the son of a chieftain, and, like most children, had focused mainly on his own wants, desires, and perceived hardships. He had assumed all Frostwolves learned how to ride, even those who were Exiled. But Draka had been delicate, and clearly even her parents had assumed she would be Exiled and die. What did a corpse need with riding skills?

"Yes," he said gently, "you can. Today, you will ride with me, in a place of honor, atop Sharptooth. You will sit behind me, and speak in my ear, telling me what to do, how to hold the weapon, and I will obey your instructions. All will see you teaching me. And then, when there are no other eyes to see or voices to carry tales, I will take you away from the village and teach you how to ride Sharptooth, or whichever wolf chooses you, without any guidance from anyone."

Draka's face, her beautiful, sharp-toothed, square face, had gone from closed and wary to open and amazed. She stared at him, then bowed her head and dropped to one knee.

"You honor me, chieftain," she said. Her voice was thick.

Durotan leaned down and lifted her up. "No, Draka. I—all of us—are the ones honored. Come." He extended a hand and grinned. "Show us how it is done."

Tentatively, she extended her own hand. It was callused and strong, the nails chipped from hard use. Yet his own massive palm swallowed it as his thick fingers closed gently around it, as if holding a great treasure.

They returned with six talbuks, and the clan feasted that night.

Despite the early snowfall that chilled in more ways than one, the fall was kind. The trees gave forth plenty of nuts, and the fruits were dried and stored with great diligence. The clan had learned the wisdom of so doing last autumn. There was even a brief false summer, which invited Durotan to feel enough at ease to ride alone with Draka.

She had now been chosen by a wolf of her own. When only a few days old, a Frostwolf child was permitted to play with the pack and bond with the pups. This first great friend could live to see fifteen turns of the seasons. The death of one's first wolf was a respected occasion of tremendous grief—often the first great loss of an orc's life. Another wolf would choose the bereaved clan member. This pattern was repeated until the death of a Frostwolf left the wolf behind, alone, just as Ice had been when Garad was killed. The bereft wolf grieved until it chose another clan member. Sometimes, that never happened, and the wolf was unrideable for the rest of its life.

No one had been more shocked than Draka when, one evening, Ice had separated from the pack and lain down beside her as she sat by the fire. Bold and strong as she was, she had gazed at the huge wolf with the innocent wonderment of a child, hardly daring to believe what she was seeing.

"Am... has he chosen... *me*?" Draka had asked. Her voice had cracked on the last word. When Durotan assured her that Ice had indeed done so, she had thrown her arms around his father's wolf, and he had seen the glint of tears of joy in her eyes. Durotan had worried at first, as Ice was powerful and stubborn. But he seemed to sense Draka's uncertainty and treated the former Exile like a pup.

Orgrim teased him relentlessly. "She would be a worthy mate. Even your father's wolf thinks so! You would sire fine children. She is strong and beautiful—and," he added, "smarter than you."

"All that you say is true, old friend," said Durotan, "even the last."

"Do you not find her pleasing?"

"More than I can say. But I do not feel that the time is right to ask her. Not with things as they are." *Not with winter coming.*

Annoyed, Orgrim growled. "If you weren't my

chieftain, I would box your ears. I certainly couldn't harm your brain further, if you lack the wits to gratefully accept what is right in front of you."

"You could try," Durotan challenged. And for the first time since the world had turned harsh, he and his childhood friend engaged in a scuffle with much bruising, and more laughter.

Winter, as reliable as death, did come. And it was cruel. Game was even scarcer this year, though such a thing would have seemed hard to believe the year before. Hunting parties had to range further to find their quarry, sometimes staying away for several days in a row. Kurg'nal, who had led one such hunt, took his chieftain aside upon the group's empty-handed return.

"We saw talbuks," he said bluntly, "but we did not pursue them."

"What?" Durotan had to modulate his voice. Something in Kurg'nal's grim, lined face told him that this was not news to share with the clan. More quietly, Durotan asked, "Why not?"

"They were sick," Kurg'nal said. "Sick in a way we have never seen before. They looked like they were not alive, yet they moved. Patches of fur were worn away and the skin… looked green."

Durotan felt a chill that had nothing to do with the coldness of the air. "It could be that they have been reduced to eating poison," Durotan said. "Sometimes that can change the color of the skin before death."

"Even to green?" Kurg'nal asked doubtfully.

"My father once told me he met an orc almost as blue as draenei. He said it happened when the other clan's water supply became tainted. If blue, then why not green?"

Kurg'nal looked relieved. "That is likely what it is. I had never seen anything like it before. I am glad to know your father spoke of such things."

"Me too," Durotan admitted. "Still, say nothing of this. We have enough troubles for our waking hours. We do not need our dreams to be filled with worries, too."

One evening, the clan gathered by the fire to listen to Gurlak, whose voice was the strongest, sing a lok'vadnod. The laughter and cheering of approaching orcs mingled with his words; since there was a group on patrol, as usual, Durotan knew these must be the calls of the returning hunting party. Everyone's face brightened at the sound—it meant food, and it had been over twelve days since they had eaten anything but dried fruits and salted fish.

"Chieftain!" cried Nokrar as he approached, still on his wolf. The firelight caught the glitter of the rings in his nose and pointed ears, as well as revealing his enormous grin. "We bring good news!"

"Your safe return is good news all on its own, but I suspect you do not come empty-handed."

"We bring three talbuks... and a sign from the Spirits!" Nokrar said as he swung down from atop his wolf. Drek'Thar turned his head in Nokrar's direction at the words.

"I will be the judge of that, Nokrar, but I would be as pleased to hear it as any Frostwolf," he said. "What is this supposed sign?"

"We followed the trail of the talbuk herd to the base of Greatfather Mountain," Nokrar said. "There is a lake there that wasn't there before."

"There is *grass* around it," Shaksa, Nokrar's daughter, put in, so excited that she interrupted. This was only her third hunt. She was shaping up to be one of their best trackers, with a sharp eye matched only by the sharp tongue she had inherited from her father. "Chieftain, the water is *hot*!"

Excited murmurs arose. "Surely this is a blessing from the Spirit of Fire, isn't it, Drek'Thar?" Nokrar persisted. "In the midst of the worst winter we have ever seen, to find an oasis like this?"

"I have heard of springs that produce heated water, but never one suddenly appearing," Durotan said.

"Nor have I, and I have lived long and listened well to the old stories," Drek'Thar said. He looked cautiously optimistic. "It is strange that the Spirit of Fire did not come to me, but it certainly is not beholden to do so. Nor are any of the Spirits. I do believe this is a good sign. We now know of a place where our prey will gather, if they are to eat. And this means that we, too, will eat."

"And bathe!" said Nokrar. "It is nothing like the cold lake water in summer. You must come, Chieftain, and see this gift for yourself!"

The very next morning, Durotan and a few others, including Orgrim, Geyah, and Draka, rode to the base of Greatfather Mountain. Durotan's eyes widened at the sight. It was exactly as Nokrar and Shaksa had described it: a small spring, which by all logic ought to have been frozen solid, bubbling and emitting steam. It was surrounded by a patch of green, startlingly verdant against the thick white blanket of snow. And when Durotan sank into the welcoming waters, the near-scalding liquid first shocked, then soothed, and he, too, believed that the Spirit of Fire was smiling upon them.

11

In his dream, Drek'Thar could see.

And in his dream, he had come to the hot spring at the foot of Greatfather Mountain. All manner of creatures grazed peacefully on the green grass, from snow hares to clefthooves. As always when he regarded the mighty summit, Drek'Thar could see Greatfather Mountain's face, ancient beyond reckoning. Hitherto, his expression was stoic but benevolent; distant but kind.

Now, Greatfather Mountain's stone face was contorted in a soundless cry. As Drek'Thar stared in horror, his feet sprouting ugly black roots that lashed him to the earth, he saw a tear gather at the corner of Greatfather Mountain's eye. It was not clear like water, but a colossal drop of red that coursed down his stone face. It grew in size as it ran, becoming a stream, a torrent, a river of blood.

Thick and scarlet, the bloody tear cascaded into the pool, turning it into a churning crimson cauldron. The creatures which had been grazing calmly now bellowed in pain. Their bodies turned to sickly gray ash, which drifted to briefly cover the spring with a grisly blanket before the red reservoir devoured it.

Drek'Thar heard a horrible noise and realized it was his own scream of agony. He looked down at his brown skin, then deeper, seeing past the muscles and bones to the veins coursing through every part of him. They ferried not blood but fire, white and yellow and orange.

His screams continued, raw and violent, lacerating his throat, until he opened his eyes onto darkness.

"Wake up, Drek'Thar!" The voice was calm, familiar—Palkar's. For a moment, the shaman didn't understand why he couldn't see and thought that somehow his eyes had been burned away by Greatfather Mountain's bloody tears, but then he remembered the wolf.

He sat up, thrashing about wildly for Palkar's hand, and clutched it hard.

"Bring Durotan," he rasped. "*Now!*"

Always, Drek'Thar had been a wise and calming presence, though even the shaman would have admitted he had been reckless in his younger years—

which had cost him his sight. But to see him now, trembling and groping for Durotan, spitting out words as fast as he could think them, shook the young chieftain to his core.

He grasped the flailing hands, stilling them, and strove to speak calmly. "Drek'Thar, it's me, Durotan," he said. "Take a breath, old friend, and tell me what you have seen."

Durotan had brought Geyah with him, and they listened with growing concern as the words poured out of the shaman, like the strange, bloody river Drek'Thar described pouring down Greatfather Mountain's craggy face. Nothing about the images made sense to Durotan, though they chilled him to the bone.

"What do you think it means?" Geyah asked.

Drek'Thar shook his head. He was still trembling, Durotan observed. "It is a warning. This much is clear. A warning about the spring!"

"But we all thought that it was a good sign," Durotan said. His heavy brow knit in worried confusion.

"If it was, it is blood and ash now, and death is all around," Drek'Thar said. He lifted his blind face to Durotan's. "The clan must leave, while there is still time!"

"Leave?" Geyah stared at him. "We cannot *leave*! Frostfire Ridge has been our home for as long as we have been Frostwolves! The Spirits themselves gave us the Stone Seat. Greatfather Mountain has guarded us. Our roots are here!"

"It was roots that kept me from fleeing in the vision," Drek'Thar reminded her. "It was roots that doomed me."

The hair on the back of Durotan's neck and arms lifted at the words. He had never given much thought to what it must be like to be a shaman, and when he did, he had envied them their deep connection with the Spirits. Now, listening to Drek'Thar with increasing horror, for the first time he was grateful beyond words that such had not been his fate.

Geyah turned to him. "This is our home, Durotan," she said. "It is possible Drek'Thar might be misinterpreting this vision. The spring has brought us nothing but good things. Would you abandon all that we have known for generations simply because of a single dream?"

"You wound me, Geyah," Drek'Thar said. "Though if I am wrong in this, I would be joyful."

Durotan sank back on his haunches, torn. Both orcs before him were wise and had earned his respect and that of the clan. Both had ancient traditions to support them. Never before had the weight of the chieftaincy sat heavier upon him. He loved his mother and trusted her. But Drek'Thar could speak with the Spirits, and in the end, the urgency, the raw, gut-twisting certainty of the shaman's words, was what decided Durotan.

"Mother," he said quietly, "get Orgrim. Remind him of the map Draka drew, of the Haven the draenei showed her. We will leave our home. If Drek'Thar is wrong, then we will return, with no loss other than our time. If he is right, and we stay..." He couldn't even speak the words.

Geyah gave her son an anguished, angry look. Her lips twisted around her tusks, but she nodded curtly. "You are my chieftain," she said, stiffly, and went to obey.

He sat a little longer with Drek'Thar, making sure the shaman had told him every chilling detail, then told Palkar to prepare Drek'Thar and the other shaman for evacuation. Durotan stepped outside the shaman hut to find Geyah and Orgrim arguing with a cluster of Frostwolves.

"We respect Drek'Thar, but perhaps this is a simple dream?" Grukag asked.

"We'll need time to move all the barrels of grain and salt fish," Gurlak said firmly. "Everyone should be working to do that first."

"No," came Nokrar's voice, "we will need our weapons first. If we are to move we must defend ourselves."

Fury descended upon Durotan, as red and hot as the river Drek'Thar had described. He strode forward, but before he could speak, Draka's voice came to him from the crowd.

"Your chieftain has given you orders!" she cried. "Since when did Frostwolves mutter and disobey, like milk-toothed wolf pups nipping at one another? It is not your place to argue. Even I, who have been away for two years, remember *that*!"

Even at this moment, when tempers were high, Durotan felt something warm and strong surge inside him at Draka's fierceness. Orgrim was right. He had never met a worthier female. Indeed, he wondered if he were the one who might be unworthy of *her*.

"Here I am," he said loudly, stepping forward so that he could better be seen in the firelight. "I am Durotan, son of Garad, son of Durkosh. The Spirits have accepted me, and you did as well. Now they have sent a warning to our wisest, most experienced shaman that might save our lives. Did I hear my orders being questioned?"

No one replied. He met Orgrim's eyes and nodded. Orgrim raised a fist. "Warriors and hunters, to me. We will prepare our weapons."

"I will speak with those who have harvested the seeds and dried foodstuffs," Draka said.

"I have birthed a child," Geyah said. "Those who wish to assist in tending them, come to me. We will bring them to my hut and watch them while the others—"

A long, haunting cry filled the cold night air, starting low, then rising, and then falling again. Durotan tensed, listening, trying to understand what was happening. Was this Greatfather Mountain's cry of pain, of which Drek'Thar had spoken? He realized almost at once that it was something much more familiar, if no less alarming.

Every frost wolf in the village was raising its voice in an eerie harmony of dread.

A heartbeat later, Durotan felt a sudden blast of heat on his face, although his back was to the fire. He flung up his hands to shield himself and turned away, utterly at a loss to comprehend what was happening. The nearly unbearable heat came from the south. He turned his head and opened his eyes the barest slit, trying to find the source of—

Fluid fire, glowing the bright red-orange of the blacksmith's forge, spurted from the highest peak of Greatfather Mountain. The liquid climbed high into the sky, illuminating the angles and crags of the mountain's edifice before pattering down to trickle a meandering path that outlined the mountain's shape in stripes of molten stone.

A river of blood.

A moment later, the night exploded.

The keening cry of the frost wolves was drowned by a deafening *boom*. The orcs cried out, clutching at their ears. Many of them fell to their knees. Durotan's face contorted in pain and he, too, covered his violated ears.

Glowing globules of molten stone rained down around them. Durotan heard terrified, agonizing cries and smelled burned flesh. He inhaled a breath of the heated air and was about to shout orders when another voice rose up, strong and calm.

"Spirit of Air! Hear our cry for aid!"

The voice was Drek'Thar's, and Durotan turned from the hypnotic, horrifying sight of Greatfather Mountain's agony to see the shaman, standing in a row, arms spread and backs arched as they pointed their staffs toward the sky.

The night had been still, but now a wind came from the north. Cold as death and icy with moisture, it buffeted Durotan and the other Frostwolves and they shivered violently. He turned to look at the exploding mountain bleeding orange fire-blood, and saw thick gray smoke spreading upward from the still-spurting peak. He watched as the invisible wave of cold, wet air forced the smoke to retreat. Misshapen lumps of stone continued to slam down around them, but they were cool, though still smoking.

"Spirit of Water! Lend us your tears!"

Now the air was laden with fat, white flakes, borne by the Spirit of Air toward the fire-mountain. Durotan's heart surged with gratitude toward the other Spirits as they worked together to shield the Frostwolves from their now-dangerous brother Fire. Even so, he knew this was but a temporary respite. Fire was fighting back, and fire-blood flowed implacably toward the Frostwolf village.

There would be no time for an orderly, calm evacuation. Durotan moved forward, his feet liberated from the roots of the fear that had anchored him. Fiercely hot air scalded his lungs.

"Orgrim!" he shouted, looking around at the frightened chaos. "Geyah! Draka!"

"Here, Durotan!" Orgrim's voice trembled ever so slightly, but the big warrior pushed his way toward his chieftain. "Give me your orders!"

"Find the warriors and hunters. Each of you take a wolf, a weapon, and someone to ride with you. Then head north. Find the Haven Draka told us about. You have seen the map. Do you think you can you find it?"

"But—"

Durotan grabbed his second-in-command's arm, shoving him around so Orgrim faced Greatfather Mountain. "The fire-river is coming fast. The shaman can only hold it back for so long. I ask again, do you remember where she said it was?"

"Yes. I do."

"Good. One weapon each! *Go!*"

Orgrim nodded curtly and pushed his way through the crowd, bellowing for the warriors. Coughing, Durotan turned to Geyah and Draka. The shaman's wind wall held back the worst of the smoke and gases, and the snow calmed the heat of what the orcs did inhale, but Durotan's words to Orgrim were true. Already, the shaman's defense was starting to weaken.

"Mother—find Singer, then go to the shaman. Your task is to recover the scrolls and healing herbs while they hold back the fire. You're our Lorekeeper, you know which are the most precious. But," and he squeezed her shoulder, "do so swiftly. Gather only what you can easily carry. Listen to Drek'Thar. When he orders the retreat, go. And if he refuses to go—make him!"

She winced at his words, but nodded. He understood that the thought of losing the clan's histories broke her heart. But she was a Frostwolf, and knew well that the clan's survival came before everything else.

Another loud *crack*. Durotan whirled to see a huge chunk of Greatfather Mountain's face simply slide down as cleanly as if chopped off by Sever. A fresh wave of fire spewed forth, like blood pouring from a wound.

A hand closed on his arm. He turned to Draka, and their gazes connected. A heat that was not of the fire-blood passed between them, but every moment counted. "Round up the wolves," Durotan told her. "Search every hut and give every two people a wolf. More if they have children. Make sure no one is left behind. Then—"

"Due north, to the Haven," she interrupted, speaking quickly and urgently. He realized she still gripped his arm. For a heartbeat, he covered her hand with his own, then jerked his head toward the huts. Without another word, Draka sprang like an arrow loosed from the bow.

Once, the north had been the Edge of the World, even for the Frostwolves. It was there that the Spirits dwelt; it was there that life was harshest, sometimes impossible. The southlands had always been the lush, fertile parts of Draenor, overflowing with luxuries and ease granted to its denizens that Frostwolves would never taste. But now it was the south that was sick, the southern mountains that were being tortured by Fire, and it was the north which offered a chance of survival.

Durotan took another breath of scorching air. The pain in his damaged lungs was agonizing, but necessary. "Frostwolves!" he shouted. "Do not despair! Drek'Thar's vision warned us! Our brave shaman now hold back the fire-blood of Greatfather

Mountain so that we might find our families and head north. Orgrim and Draka will come among you with wolves to bear you to safety! They speak with my voice. Obey them, and we will live through this night!"

As if Fire itself were mocking him, there came another barrage of head-sized stones. Some were turned by the shaman's spells, but others struck the ground and huts. Fresh cries of terror rent the already tattered night.

"Listen to me!" Durotan shouted, though his throat felt as though he had drunk the fire-blood. "You are not talbuks! You are not prey, to scatter and panic in the face of danger! Listen to Draka, Orgrim, and the shaman. Stay calm. Go north! You are Frostwolves! Now, more than ever, *remember what that means*!"

"Frostwolves!" came a lone voice in the back of the crowd. "Frostwolves!" another one echoed, and then the cry was picked up by others. It rose and swelled, defying the steady, awful roar of a mountain being consumed by fire. The word was no ritual chant uttered by shaman, but it had a magic and a power all its own. The crowd no longer clustered together in a tight knot like a clefthoof herd, but began to move—not with the rush of panic, but the swift step of purpose.

Durotan stood for a few heartbeats, watching Draka calm a small, frightened group and see to it that they had the steadiest mounts. Elsewhere, he heard battle cries uttered by the warriors he had ordered

Orgrim to seek out. Durotan darted into his own hut for a moment, to collect Sever, Thunderstrike, and the map Draka had made of her travels. Before he called for Sharptooth, he did the same thing that he had told Draka to do: he visited every hut.

His heart felt raw at the sight of spilled drinks, rumpled sleeping furs, abandoned wooden toys. So many things would not be coming with the Frostwolves. The Stone Seat, the meadow where for time immemorial his people had danced on Midsummer; soon all this would be buried beneath the river of fire-blood. But the Frostwolves would endure.

They always had. They always would.

12

Durotan had left the doomed village first, leading the largest wave of the clan. He had instructed Orgrim and his warriors to depart soon after to defend the rear. Draka and Geyah, who would bring any stragglers and the shaman, would follow as soon as they could. Durotan's group rode north on wolves that needed no urging to go at their top speed. But even so, the smoke gave chase, stinging their eyes and utterly obliterating the night sky, even the tops of the trees. There was no way to navigate by the stars, whose faces were hidden from them by the choking gray blanket.

But Durotan had the map, and did not need the stars and moon. He was able to locate the place Draka had called the Haven. It was several hours' hard riding due north. According to Draka, there was a large, freshwater lake at the Haven. Where there was water, there were animals, and soil that could be cultivated. There would be shelter from the elements, too, she had assured him: huge stones, some squat boulders, others longer and thinner, had tumbled down over the eons to form natural chambers. The fact that the stones were in the center of a wide, clear area meant that they would have an excellent view both of prey and of encroaching enemies. Finally, there were trees, and trees meant fuel.

She had marked landmarks on the map as well: here a tree struck by lightning, there an old river bed. As he passed them on the journey, Durotan's heart lifted for the first time since the wolves had started howling.

At last, they found Haven. There were indeed dozens of clustered boulders whose positions provided the promised shelter. He sent a small group to gather firewood, instructing them to cut limbs if need be. He would ask Drek'Thar to beg forgiveness from the Spirit of Earth later for the transgression. Durotan's lips twisted at the irony; a river of fire had destroyed their village and forced their evacuation, but a small, contained fire would mean life.

Many members of the clan were exhausted from fear and the grueling ride. Durotan urged those who could do so to sleep. Those, like him, who could not would tend the fire and keep watch.

Shortly after Durotan had lit the fire, Orgrim arrived with his warriors. All had survived, and despite their chieftain's firm orders, they had burdened their wolves with more, sometimes much more, than one weapon each. He chastised them for their disobedience, but was secretly glad of it. Everything had happened so quickly there had been time to bring little more than their own bodies, but now that the threat—the immediate threat of the fire river, at least—was over, every weapon would count.

The hours ticked by. At last, Geyah and Draka arrived. His heart lifted to see them, and the group they led. Geyah slipped off Singer and her legs quivered for a moment before she strode to her son. He embraced her fiercely.

"I am glad you are here, Mother," he said. He looked around at the shaman, so weary they could barely dismount. "But… where are Drokul and Relkarg?"

"They would not come," she said, quietly. "They chose to stay, and hold back the fire river to the last moment. All the others wanted to stay as well. Palkar and I had to struggle to convince Drek'Thar to leave."

It had been foolish to hope that the clan could escape without loss, Durotan knew, but he had done so anyway. "Their sacrifices will be remembered in a lok'vadnod. As for Drek'Thar and the other shaman who are still with us, we will need them now more than ever. What of the medications? The scrolls?"

The lines of sorrow that creased his mother's features deepened. "Most are lost," she replied. "I could bring only a few." The scrolls were ancient and irreplaceable. The shaman had sacrificed their lives to save their fellow Frostwolves; Geyah would have died to preserve the scrolls, but nothing she or anyone could have done would have saved them.

Someone called for her, and she turned. Durotan let her go, his gaze searching the crowd of newly arrived orcs for Draka. Their eyes met. Only now did Durotan realize how concerned he had been for her.

She had her arm around a weeping Shaksa, but when she saw Durotan, Draka said something to the girl and embraced her before making her way toward her chieftain. Her face was grim, and she wasted no words.

"We lost clan members," she said.

"Geyah told me of the shaman," Durotan began, but fell silent when Draka shook her head.

"We lost Kelgrim, Pagar, and all their children."

Durotan felt like he had been kicked in the gut by a clefthoof. "What? The whole family? How..."

"I led the group," she said, and there was self-loathing in her voice. "The fault is mine. Shaksa just now told me. The family was in the rear. Shaksa said that the youngest, Zagu, had forgotten a toy." Draka's voice trembled slightly. "He slipped off the wolf and ran back for it. The family followed. They promised Shaksa they would catch up." Pain flitted across her face. "I did not even know they had gone."

Durotan placed his hand on her shoulders. "You only have two eyes, Draka. If no one came to the front to tell you, how could you have known? As for Pagar and Kelgrim... I cannot imagine such a choice as they faced. I do not believe that you could have stopped them from turning back, Draka, even if you had been aware that Zagu had fled."

He empathized with her. Logically, the right thing for the parents to have done would have been to press on, abandoning one child to save the others. But as he looked at Draka, he found himself imagining how he would feel, had he fathered a child with this remarkable female. Would he have been able to make that choice? Or would he, too, have gambled everything to save his son? A small, unique life, born from love and a true bond?

His emotions were both compelling and uncomfortable. He forced his voice to convey a calmness he was far from feeling. "We are Frostwolves. Other orcs might have found this an easy choice, but not us. And now more than ever, children are precious to us. Could you have ridden on, Draka?"

The answer was strangely important to him. She looked away for a moment, her throat working, then turned her warm brown eyes up to his.

"No," she said, quietly. "Had it been my child, I would have done everything I could to save him. No matter the consequences. You do not know this, Durotan, but that is something Frostwolves share with the draenei. They love their children, and would die for them."

For a fleeting instant Durotan thought the reference odd, but then he remembered—the draenei had brought Draka to this place. Not for the first time, he found himself full of wonder for what this fierce female had undergone.

He let his hands fall from her shoulders and stepped back. "Rest, Draka. You have earned it."

She smiled sadly. "I will not be able to rest for a long time, Durotan. Nor, I think, will you."

The morning after the exodus from Frostwolf Ridge dawned gray and cold. Lingering smoke still drifted in from the south. The air was not clean, but at least it did not scorch the lungs when one took a breath. What water and food the Frostwolves had been able to bring with them—a bag of nuts here, a waterskin there—had been consumed the night before. Durotan decided to seek out the lake, and Draka had asked to accompany him.

Draka had told him this place was a haven. But as the two Frostwolves stood beside the lake, Durotan saw that it could be called one no longer. While the trees and stones were still there, providing shelter from the elements and a defense against attack from beast or other enemies, the lake they now regarded was coated in fine gray ash. Rotting corpses of animals foolish enough to drink water that had grown poisonous had been frozen, paritially in ice, bloated and obscene. It was winter, but it was clear to Durotan that the grass and trees in the area had died months before. There were no fresh droppings to alert them to the presence of any game in the immediate area.

The cold gray morning did nothing but illuminate

a scene of despair as they solemnly regarded the dead lake, which should have promised life.

"Forgive me, my chieftain," Draka said at last. "I have led you on a fool's errand."

"We would have ridden blindly otherwise," Durotan reassured her. "Here, at least, there is shelter and a chance for us to regroup."

Draka snorted, clearly irritated with herself. "I keep failing the clan."

"Do you not think I feel that *I* keep doing so?" he asked her.

She looked at him with surprise. Clearly, the thought had never occurred to her. His clan had lost nearly everything—their home, their history, and even the lives of children. Durotan had led them to a place that was nearly as barren as a village covered in hardened liquid stone.

"We must deliver the news about the lake," he said.

Draka took a deep breath. "We will find clean water. And land that supports life. You must believe it, my chieftain. And more importantly, you must make *them* believe it."

She was right. Without faith in their leader, the clan would be destroyed. Durotan grunted his agreement, then turned and headed back to the stone shelters.

13

The very young and the very old were the first to die.

As the grim gray light crept over the land, a wail went up when a mother discovered her sleeping child would never awaken. Others developed racking coughs and followed over the first few days, their tiny lungs unable to recover from the heat and the smoke. The oldest, too, were not strong enough to fight off the brutal effects of those first devastating minutes of Greatfather Mountain's destruction. Fights broke out over the heartbreaking task of burying the dead. Some wanted to cut trees to burn the bodies. Others insisted they be offered to the earth. But firewood was needed more by the living than the dead, and the earth was frozen solid. In the end, the orcs gathered stones and covered their dead so that, at the very least, scavengers would not feast on the corpses of brave Frostwolves.

Groups of Frostwolves departed daily, some to hunt for game, others to forage for food and search for sources of fresh water. There was not enough of either, and some who set forth never returned to the Haven. Those who went in search of them came across bodies that had been food for predators, or who had simply wandered too far and lost their way. Some of the missing were never found at all, even though parties were sent out after them. Durotan's first thought was that Red Walkers had attacked them, but no sign of those disgusting creatures was ever found. He dared to hope they had perished with Frostfire Ridge—perhaps the only good thing to come of the disaster.

Some water was found—caught in tree hollows that had escaped most of the direct ash fall. The first snows were filthy, gray instead of white, but after a time, they became cleaner. Boiling and flavoring the water seemed to help. Soups made with pine-needle broth, herbs and ground nuts became a staple. In the early days of her Exile, Draka had not been strong enough to hunt larger game. She had subsisted on insects and small animals for a time, and had mastered the art of snares. She taught the children how to make them while the adults were out hunting. Every few days, the snares would yield some small creature, which was cut up and added to the broth so that all might have at least some nourishment.

In an effort to both keep up the clan's spirits and

to replace the items they had to leave behind, Durotan encouraged the tanning of what few hides they were able to obtain. Once, the proud Frostwolves would have scorned the idea of sewing together rabbit hides for bedding, but no longer. Branches and twigs were gathered to make rough baskets and other containers. Wood was hollowed out to hold water that became increasingly hard to find.

Drek'Thar and the other shaman sought answers from the Spirits, but they were speaking less and less frequently. One memorable night, though, Drek'Thar was told by the Spirit of Water to watch for a redjay flying overland in a straight line, in either the morning or the evening. The children made a game out of keeping watch for the bird, and Durotan promised that a special song would be made for one if they found it.

It was the only sign they had, and after many days passed with empty skies, Durotan began to doubt it would ever appear.

Until it did.

Draka, Durotan, and Geyah had been out on two different hunts since before dawn. Orgrim had been left with the task of defending the encampment, and by the time Durotan returned Orgrim had been stalking up and down the camp. "I am so glad you are back," Orgrim said. "I have no idea how to deal with the realm of the Spirits, and Drek'Thar knows it."

Drek'Thar was sitting on one of the stones, still and calm. Beside him, decidedly not still and calm, was Nokrar's youngest, Nizka, who fidgeted and played constantly with her one single, long braid. Currently, she was chewing on it with her tiny teeth. Durotan's brow furrowed and he turned to the elderly shaman.

"What is going on?" he asked.

Drek'Thar said, "The Spirit of Water has sent us the redjay, as promised."

"What?"

"Young Nizka saw it first, right after dawn. She and the other children followed it. She tells me that it landed upon a boulder not far from here. We have been awaiting your return before investigating."

"You promised me a song, great chieftain!" Nizka piped up. Standing behind her, but not taking any attention away from their daughter, stood Nokrar and Kagra. For a moment, Durotan couldn't place a finger on what was different, and then, when he understood, he almost stumbled.

Everyone was *smiling.*

Without thinking, he found himself turning to look for Draka. She, too, looked astonished, but happy. Her smile widened when her eyes met his. It was with difficulty that Durotan returned his attention to Nizka.

"You deserve a song," he said, "and what is more, I think you deserve to come with me and Drek'Thar as we go to this stone the redjay guided you to." He swung Nizka atop his unarmored shoulder and she shrieked with laughter. How long had it been since he had heard the sound?

Spirit of Water, he thought, *please do not toy with us. Not now.* "So, tell me, little Sharp-Eyes, where did this redjay fly?"

"That way," Nizka said, pointing before sticking her braid back in her mouth. Palkar assisted Drek'Thar in rising, and the four set off in the direction the child had indicated. They were not alone. Draka fell into step beside Durotan, smiling at him and the obviously delighted child. Geyah, too, accompanied them, and before Durotan knew what was happening, he had a small crowd in tow.

Nizka led them to a pile of stones in the midst of the flat area between the poisoned lake and the tree. "That one. No, no, not that one, the other one, over there. The one that looks like a sleeping duck."

It did not look like a sleeping duck to Durotan, and his steps slowed as they approached. What was this? It was just a rock in the middle of nowhere, one they had noticed but had never paid attention to. There seemed to be nothing special about it; he knew there was no water here.

Draka stepped beside him, offering silent support. Orgrim strode up to the rock, puzzled. Palkar leaned over and described the scene in Drek'Thar's ear.

Drek'Thar looked annoyed. "The Spirit of Water has sent us a sign," the shaman insisted. "It is up to *us* to interpret it. Nizka, child, where did the bird land?"

"Just on top," Nizka said. Durotan handed the girl to her father and strode up to the boulder.

Carefully, he examined it, searching for some fissure through which the precious fluid might trickle. He found nothing. He knelt beside it and pressed his hand to the bare earth. No moisture. The rock was not merely sitting atop the earth, it was partially buried in it.

Straightening, he turned to Orgrim. Their gazes locked. His old friend knew him so well, Durotan needed to say nothing. Standing beside one another, brothers in spirit if not in blood, they placed their shoulders to the boulder, and shoved.

Nothing happened. Again, they tried, and again.

All at once, Draka was there, positioning her own body against the massive rock. She was strong for a female, but she lacked the bulk, the sheer physical power, of a male orc. Nothing she could do would help shift the boulder. He started to say something to her, to ask her to step back, and her head whipped around. The determination in her eyes was absolute. He nodded. The three tried again.

"We have been deemed worthy!" came Drek'Thar's voice. "The Spirit of Water tells me that you have shown faith in its word. I had been forbidden to help, until now."

Drek'Thar was on his feet, and as Durotan watched, he walked toward the boulder, moving his staff from side to side in front of him. Sliding the staff gently against the curve of the great rock, he inserted the end about a hand's breadth into the sandy soil beneath the boulder. The earth was too hard for him to do more than that. Even if he had managed to dig deeper, the staff was a small, slender thing, barely the width of a sapling. The only thing Drek'Thar would get for his effort was a broken staff. And even though Durotan knew this, he *knew* it, he found himself hoping he was wrong.

As he watched, hardly daring to breathe, Drek'Thar leaned on the staff. The wood bowed beneath the pressure. Durotan braced himself for the inevitable heartbreaking snap. But then... the boulder shifted. Drek'Thar continued to push, and, impossibly, the great stone was torn from the earth in which it had been nestled for years beyond counting.

It teetered. Durotan, Orgrim, and Draka sprang forward, pushing with renewed strength, and abruptly the huge rock rolled a few feet to the side. Panting from the exertion, Durotan turned to the crater it had left.

He was startled to see not dry, frozen soil, but mud. He fell to his knees and began shoveling out great chunks of sodden earth. Puddles started to form. A gift indeed from the Spirit of Water—and the Spirit of Earth as well, which had kept this source hidden and, thus, protected it from the ravages of the falling ash.

As carefully as he could, Durotan caught as much clean water in his huge hands as possible. Rising, he saw Nizka, her eyes wide with excitement. He got to his feet and went to her.

"This little one saw the sign from the Spirit of Water," he said to all those gathered. "She followed it here. She will be the first to drink from it, then

Drek'Thar, who had the vision."

Nizka licked parched lips, looked longingly at the water, then said, "No. It should be Drek'Thar. He is our elder. I'd never have known to look for the redjay if he hadn't told us to."

Durotan's eyes burned. When he spoke, he had to struggle to keep his voice from breaking. "Nizka, daughter of Nokrar, son of Gozek… you are a true Frostwolf."

Nizka stood very straight, her eyes shining with pride, as Durotan turned to Drek'Thar and offered the slightly muddy water to him. Palkar guided the shaman's hands to Durotan's. Drek'Thar drank eagerly, then lifted his wet face.

"Pure and clean," he said, his voice shaking with emotion. "Save for a trace of our beloved Earth," he added, laughing. The last bit of tension dissolved, and everyone broke into relieved laughter and cheers. Little Nizka was swept up and passed from one pair of loving arms to the next, the hero of the day…

"Everyone, drink your fill!" Durotan said. "Then we will return to the encampment and bring the bowls we have carved. We will drink till we can drink no more. Although we were driven from our home by the death of Greatfather Mountain, the Spirits of Water and Earth have shown us that we are not forgotten."

He stepped back and watched them, his heart fuller than it had been at any time during these long, dark weeks. Clean water would mean fewer illnesses. It would mean endurance for longer journeys in search of food. When they widened this source, the beasts would come here to drink as well, which meant food for bellies that had long been far too empty.

"Today is a good day," said Draka, who had come to stand beside him.

"It is," he said. "One we will remember on days that are not." He turned to her. "You put your shoulder to the stone, when you had no hope of moving it," he said.

She shrugged, looking uncomfortable. "I felt called to do so. And Drek'Thar had no hope of moving it, either."

"Drek'Thar walks a different path than the rest of us. He has the companionship and advice of the Spirits. You had nothing."

Draka regarded him evenly, shaking her head so that her long braids danced. "You are wrong. I had you, my chieftain."

Her words touched him profoundly. Suddenly, he wanted her to know something that he had shared with no one, not even Geyah or Orgrim. If she understood this, Durotan knew, she would understand him. He was unused to being vulnerable, to giving someone the power to hurt him. But he sensed that Draka would never abuse the trust he was about to place in her.

Durotan took a deep breath. "It has been difficult since my father's death," he said. "You may have heard the whisperings."

Draka cocked her head, uncertain as to where

the conversation was going. "I have heard, yes," she said, honestly. "That he did not even lift his weapon at the end."

"It is not that he was afraid to fight," Durotan said, and, quietly, while others celebrated around him and went to follow his orders, he told Draka about the strange malady with which his father wrestled prior to his death. Geyah and Drek'Thar knew, of course, as they had been present during Garad's sickness. But Durotan had told no one, not even Orgrim. Draka listened intently, not interrupting, as he told her what had happened, and how it had driven him to do all he could to remove the stain from his father's memory.

"So," she said at last, when he had fallen silent, "not only have you had to deal with the loss of a father, and challenges and hardships we have never before encountered... but you do so with the extra burden of trying to honor Garad's legacy. The true strength of a clan lies in its ability to support one another. I am glad you have had your mother and Orgrim to help you, Durotan, but even so, you have been tested beyond what anyone could expect to endure."

Durotan had always been treated with respect. And, he now realized, he had lived, until Garad's death, an easier life than the rest of the clan. He was not used to being refused. But now, he felt nervous as he reached for Draka's hand, so very small in his.

"I have been blessed, yes," he said, "with the wisdom of the elders and with a friend who could not be dearer to me if we had shared the same womb.

But you are right. There is much that lies heavy on my shoulders."

Durotan looked over at his clan. Someone had already brought back tools and several orcs were hard at work widening the precious reservoir.

He turned back to Draka, his eyes on her small hand in his palm. He didn't want to see her expression until he had finished saying all that was in his heart. "Draka... your wits are sharp when good counsel is needed. Your heart is kind when the clan is hurting. I have been reluctant to speak. I felt that I have so little to give. There was a time when being the wife of a chieftain meant honor and ease. In these times, I can offer neither. You will know burdens, and be forced to watch as I make difficult decisions. But... I think my decisions would be better if you helped me reach them. I think my heart would be stronger if it held your love. And..."

Now he risked taking a look at her. Her eyes had widened as he spoke and her breath came quickly, and she had not pulled away her hand. "I would do everything in my power to be a good husband to you. Even with all the burdens I bring. Draka, daughter of Kelkar, son of Rhakish... will you have me?"

Her expression softened. Her warm, dark eyes shimmered with unshed tears. "Durotan, son of Garad, son of Durkosh," she said, "You are right. This is a dark and frightening time for us. You are laden with many burdens. No one knows what new challenge awaits us on the morrow. And that is why—"

Durotan braced himself for her rejection.

"—You are an *idiot* for not speaking sooner. And I will have you for as long as you let me speak truth to you."

His people were still on the verge of starvation. Their shelter was insufficient, and no one ever grew fully warm. Until just a few moments ago, they had no reliable source of water. But none of that mattered as Durotan gazed into Draka's sweetly sly, loving face.

"It is because you speak truth that I love you," he said simply. "And I will unto my last dying breath. Whatever happens."

"Whatever happens," she agreed.

The Frostwolves, already rejoicing over the fresh water, received the news with thundering approval. Though initially Draka had been looked upon as a curiosity, she had swiftly proved her value to the clan with her knowledge and skills. They were bonded that very night in a small, private shelter of stone and wood that had been quickly constructed for the new couple. The setting was, Durotan lamented aloud as she lay in his arms, far from what Draka deserved. She shoved him, just hard enough, and said that all she needed was him.

They had one another, and the clan had them—a united, devoted, and determined pair. They would both serve the Frostwolves as best they could for as long as breath was granted to them.

Whatever happened.

14

Through the winter, the Spirits were venerated with a fresh urgency. Although Fire had caused the destruction of their Frostfire Ridge home, it was welcomed every moment of every day through the long, dark, lean months. The underground spring the clan had discovered thanks to the redjay sent by Water was tended so that it did not freeze. As Durotan had predicted, fresh, readily available water attracted game, so there was more to eat as well as more to drink. At least, there was at first. But as time passed, fewer animals came, and those who did seemed smaller and frailer than any Durotan had seen before. He was reminded of Kurg'nal's tale of "green" talbuks, and while no such were seen, thank the Spirits, it was clear that sickness was rampaging through the herd animals. Determinedly, the Frostwolves began to recreate what had been lost in the frantic flight—clothing, tools, weapons, all crafted with cold fingers in the weak winter light.

One terrible night, a snowstorm swept in. There was no warning: moments before, the sky was clear, and there was no wind. It was actually even warmer than many days they had seen. But when the storm struck, it was merciless.

Two hunting parties found themselves stranded and survived only by huddling with one another and their wolves. Two orcs, a mother and son, who had been en route to the spring became lost mere steps from the safety of the encampment, blinded by the snow, disoriented by the wind that pulled them this way and that and snatched away the voices of those calling out to them. Those still in the encampment were snowed in. It took days to recover from the abrupt, seemingly random onslaught.

Durotan was forced to forbid any attempt to respectfully attend to the dead until spring. To recover and clean the bodies and gather stones to cover them would take more energy than anyone could spare.

"This is my wife!" cried Grukag. "My only child!" Grukag was known for his level emotions as well as his physical prowess. Even when he had challenged the Thunderlord to the mak'gora so many years ago, he had done so because it was an affront to clan honor, not because he was hot-blooded and angry. But now, his heart was open and raw for all to see. He had just lost all the family he had.

"I do not belittle your pain," Durotan said. "I know your bond was strong. We are becoming so few that each loss hurts the clan—each loss hurts us, as individuals. But would Margah and Purzul want you to die just so you could cover their bodies with stones? Would they want *any* Frostwolf to die doing this?"

Grukag clearly wanted to protest, but there was no arguing. While there was some food and water to be had, there was precious little of it, and even through his pain, he understood. He simply stared at Durotan for a long moment, nodded bleakly, and turned away.

That night, Durotan could not sleep. Draka lay beside him, her hand tenderly stroking his chest, letting him think. At last, he spoke, and his words were blunt.

"I am lost," he said. "The black wolf of despair is only ever a heartbeat away. How can I lead my people well when I can predict nothing? When all I have learned, all my father taught me, could be destroyed by a single snowstorm? If more of the clan had been away from the shelter—"

"But they were not." Draka propped herself up on an elbow and regarded her husband. "It is easy to have dark thoughts in dark times, when the sun does not show its face." Then, she smiled, which struck him as incongruous. "But even when the world seems dead, there is life."

Durotan snorted. "Lives were lost today. Even the Spirits are barely speaking to us. The Spirit of Life is—"

Draka took his large hand and placed it on the flat plane of her belly.

"Is here," she finished for him, softly, her voice trembling.

Durotan stared at her, hardly daring to believe what she was telling him, then he took her in his arms and embraced her tightly.

Spring arrived, sullen and cold. The children climbed trees in search of birds' eggs, but more often than not returned to the ground empty-handed. Creatures that had once gravitated to the area for what little grazing there was seemed to have disappeared, traveling on to other feeding grounds.

During the winter, a grim resignation had settled upon the clan. Now, with the thaw, there was a restlessness, a need to move, to *do*.

But when the feeble spring returned, so did Gul'dan.

A runner sent word ahead that the "Gul'dan, Leader of the Horde, would parley with Durotan, son of Garad, son of Durkosh, Chieftain of the Frostwolves."

Durotan regarded the orc atop the lean gray wolf for a long moment before replying. "How does it happen that Gul'dan knows that my father is no longer chieftain?"

The runner shrugged. "Gul'dan is a warlock," he replied, "and he has ways of discovering what he wishes to know."

The words sent a shiver down Durotan's spine. Gul'dan had not bothered to display his power to Garad when he had last visited, and Durotan expected he would not do so this time, either. He recalled Geyah's dislike of the warlock, and Drek'Thar's insistence that the Spirits disliked Gul'dan. Durotan debated refusing the warlock a second audience under the parley banner, but he had to admit to some curiosity. The Frostwolf clan could not have been easy to locate. Why had Gul'dan gone to so much effort to meet with him? What was he offering this time?

And more importantly, what did he want from Durotan and the Frostwolves?

More than ever, Durotan was interested in the idea of orcs working together. Draka had spent time away from the clan, and had hunted side by side not only with other orcs, but even with the strange draenei. The experience had done nothing but enrich her—it had taught her skills and in some cases kept her alive. He thought about the horrors of the night when Greatfather Mountain had bled a river of fire, spouting smoke and ash into a sky that still suffered. Of herds of weak, sickly creatures, bitter fruit that would not ripen, and grass that refused to grow green and lush. Of those who had not had enough food to make it through the winter, or who had perished in the blizzard mere steps from safety.

"I will parley with Gul'dan," he told the runner. "But I make no promises."

Geyah, Drek'Thar, and Orgrim were not pleased with their chieftain's decision. They sat with

Durotan and Draka in his new shelter, which had been improved since the night of the pair's joining. It was still a cramped space for so many, but they had crowded in together so that they could converse unheard. Geyah spoke up almost before they had all arranged their cloaks and extended their cold hands to the comforting flames. "He has already been refused by a Frostwolf once," she said.

"Durotan is not his father," Orgrim pointed out reasonably, "and much has happened since Gul'dan first approached the Frostwolves. Perhaps he thinks Durotan will have a different response for him."

"Durotan is his father's child, and a true Frostwolf," Geyah said. "Our clan has suffered so much." She turned imploringly to her son. "Surely you will not abandon our ways now?"

"I am not my father. Orgrim is right about that. But I do believe in the ways of our clan, and my father led us well. There is no harm in listening. Perhaps this time, he brings us solid proof of this fertile land he spoke of."

"Where the animals fight to be your dinner," added Draka. They shared a smile. "I confess, I am glad you have decided to meet with him. I have never seen this warlock, but I have heard much about him." She sobered as she touched his arm lightly. "Be careful, my heart. I joke about him, but from what I know, he is dangerous."

"I think," Durotan said, staring into the crackling flames and remembering a river of fire, "that I have learned to be respectful of danger."

The Frostwolves did their best to display at least some semblance of tradition and formality when Gul'dan rode into the encampment. Drummers started striking their instruments' taut hides as soon as Gul'dan's party came into view, pounding out a steady, heartbeat rhythm. Durotan stood to meet their guest wearing an outfit that had bone and bright-colored feathers painstakingly gathered by the children on the calmer days sewn into it. A long cloak fell from his shoulders. In one hand, he grasped Thunderstrike. Sever was strapped to his back. If the cloak was of rabbit fur, and the bones those of small animals, it was of no matter. Whether he wore the skin of a clefthoof or a rabbit, if it was new or stained and worn, he was Durotan, and he was chieftain of the Frostwolf clan.

Draka stood beside him, a necklace of bone and feathers about her dark brown throat. She wore ritual beads braided into her thick black hair, the same beads that had adorned Geyah's hair two years past, when the Lorekeeper had been the wife of the Frostwolf chieftain. Orgrim stood, massive and silent, on Durotan's left. Geyah stood next to Draka, and Drek'Thar, leaning on the staff that had, with the aid of the Spirits, unearthed a boulder, was beside Orgrim.

Gul'dan, "Leader of the Horde" came, this time, with more retinue in tow than he had when Garad was chieftain; a half-dozen surprisingly healthy-looking orcs, who had doubtless helped him to travel safely through the ravaged land. They wore cloaks with heavy cowls, so their faces could not be glimpsed, but their bodies seemed to be fit and strong.

But these newcomers were in addition to, not in place of, the peculiar, reed-slender female slave Garona. Why did he persist in bringing her? Surely it was risky, unappealingly delicate as she was. Durotan felt as if he could snap her arm between his thumb and forefinger. Yet twice, the warlock had felt compelled to bring her. She must have some value to him.

Gul'dan slid off his wolf, and came forward. Durotan's gaze flitted over him, observing everything. He was more stooped, but bulkier than Durotan remembered. The green skin was darker, too; or perhaps that was just a trick of the weak, late-afternoon light. But Gul'dan's smile—that confident, sly, slightly sinister smile—had not changed.

Nor had his clothing. He still wore the cloak of spines and tiny skulls, and still strode with the aid of a carved staff. And those eyes burned with the same green fire that made Durotan's skin crawl.

He heard Draka growl softly, so low that only he could hear it, and saw that his mate was staring not at the imposing but repugnant Gul'dan, but at Garona. Durotan could now see the huge collar about the peculiar half-breed's too-thin neck had rubbed so often that it had left scars. Even so, she still had that upright, defiant expression, as if the abrasive collar were a beautiful necklace. Durotan felt a jolt of surprise as he recognized it. It was the same expression Draka had borne for so long, when she was still newly returned. He recalled that, even then, thoughts of Draka had been in his mind when he had first seen Garona. He wondered if his wife, too, could see herself in this fierce-eyed slave. Had it been only two short years ago when all his questions, it seemed, had been about Garona? Why was she green? Why was she so important to Gul'dan? He had not voiced these questions. It had been his father's meeting, not Durotan's, but now that the meeting was indeed his own, he realized—as, doubtless, his father had—that there were more pressing matters.

The drumming ceased when Gul'dan came to a halt in front of Durotan. Gul'dan leaned on his staff and shook his head, chuckling slightly.

Durotan returned the warlock's gaze confidently. He had seen and learned—and lost—so much since his last encounter with Gul'dan that the older orc did not intimidate him as he once had. Geyah had briefed him on what to say to properly enact the ritual, and he spoke clearly and with the authority that he had earned over the last two years.

"The ancient banner of parley has come to the Frostwolves, borne by Gul'dan, son of No Orc and of No Clan."

Gul'dan wagged a chiding finger at him. "Chieftain of the Horde," he corrected.

A muscle tightened in Durotan's jaw, but he continued in the same voice. "Gul'dan, son of No Orc, Chieftain of the Horde. You have come with respect for the puissance of the Frostwolves, demonstrating veneration for the praxis of our people. For your bearing of the banner, you have safety. For your deference, we will feed and shelter you and yours like our own. Our ears we will turn to you, for as shedding blood shows our prowess in battle, listening shows our prowess in reason."

The sneer never left Gul'dan's face. When it was his turn to speak, he said, "Custom and the ancient rites that stay your hand compel me to tell you three things: Who I am. What I offer. And what I ask." He lifted his hunched shoulders in a shrug. "I think you already know these things."

"The ritual demands it," Geyah said, her voice icier than the winter.

Gul'dan sighed. "You have my name. I offer to you, Durotan, what your father spurned: Life. And I ask that you accept this offer."

Durotan did not reply, but he nodded to the two rough-hewn wooden chairs by the fire. Gul'dan eased his twisted frame into one, mindful of the spines that had been attached to his cloak. Even in daylight, Durotan couldn't see how they had been sewn on. Gul'dan jerked Garona's chain, and she knelt beside him in the snow. Her back was as straight as one of the great trees.

"As you said, my father spurned your offer of some mystical new land," Durotan said as he took his own seat. "But I am not my father, and I will listen to you and judge for myself what is best for the Frostwolf clan."

"So I saw in you, then, Durotan. I am pleased by these words."

"Wait until you hear my decision before you speak so," Durotan cautioned.

Gul'dan chuckled, his voice low and deep. Draka's hand, resting on her husband's shoulder as she stood behind him, tightened, her sharp fingers digging in.

"When last I visited your people," said Gul'dan, "your father told me that the hardships we suffered were merely part of a cycle. He spoke eloquently of legends that told us this, of ebb and flow, life and death. He told me that he believed things would change. Then, your troubles were lesser, were they not? All you feared was longer winters, thinner herds, decreased harvests."

He lifted his arms, covered with bracelets of braided hide and hair, and indicated their surroundings. "Garad was right. Things have changed. Now, the noble, confident Frostwolves no longer dwell on Frostfire Ridge. Your ancestral home is covered by once-molten stone, gone beyond recovering even in a thousand years. Your people were forced to flee north. Your water is poisoned, your shelter crude. The grass does not turn green, even though spring has come. The trees bear no buds."

He turned his glowing green gaze to the clan members clustered about to watch. "I see fewer Frostwolves before me," he said, his voice sad. "And children… I see fewer still. Tell me, Durotan. If you love your people, why do you stay here?"

"Silence, you twisted monster!" came a cry from the back. "You know nothing of what it means to be a Frostwolf!"

Durotan shot to his feet, his gaze raking the

gathered clan. "Frostwolves, for shame! This is a guest who has come under the banner of parley! You will not speak so to him," he said, adding, "No matter what you think."

Gul'dan nodded his appreciation. "I am not a Frostwolf," he agreed, "and I imagine I must seem a monster to those who do not understand. I appear as I do because of the power I have been given. The power to take every single one of you to safety. Tell me," he continued, "even if this is a cycle, as your father believed… can your clan survive until it changes? What good would longer summers be, if all the grass does is grow over Frostwolf graves?"

Draka's nails dug deeper into Durotan's cloaked shoulder as the Frostwolves murmured angrily. Durotan held up a hand, and the muttering subsided.

"You said it was worse in the south. Is this still so?"

"It is," Gul'dan replied.

"Then why should we leave here at all? How do we know this is not a lie of some sort?"

It was an extraordinarily disrespectful comment, but it needed to be said. To Durotan's surprise, Gul'dan smiled. "When I came to your clan before, I brought a blood apple with no seeds. This time, I bring something even better: the word of someone you know."

He gestured, and one of the orcs who had accompanied him stepped forward. Flipping back the cowl from his face, he regarded Durotan with a smile.

Durotan's eyes widened in recognition. "Kovogor!"

15

The other orc made as if to bow to Durotan, but the Frostwolf chieftain had risen and gone to him, gripping his forearms tightly. "Kovogor! By the Spirits, it is good to see you!"

"And you, Durotan. Chieftain, now," Kovogor said. His grin was wide and his eyes were bright. He looked older, though Durotan supposed they all did; the years since the Frostwolves and Thunderlords had joined together to hunt had not been kind to anyone. But there was the calm patience in his mien that Durotan remembered. "Although it pains me to see the hardships the Frostwolves endure. With respect, Lorekeeper," and he turned to Geyah, "I would speak of what I know of how the south fares, and how Gul'dan leads the Horde."

Geyah nodded that he might proceed. As

Durotan resumed his seat, Kovogor stepped forward and knelt in front of him.

"I once thought as you did. I sided with my chieftain when he was skeptical of Gul'dan's magic, and when he talked of orcs forming a single, mighty Horde. It made no sense to us. Surely, we would overhunt an area. We would have quarrels. It could never work even in times of plenty, and in a time when every scrap of food was precious, it would be disaster."

He looked over at Gul'dan. "Except… it *did* work. Not at first, certainly. There was many a mak'gora. But we found that we each knew different things. One clan knew how to make a call to summon boar. Another knew how to make white leather. We could teach throwing techniques," and here he smiled knowingly at Durotan, "and share the knowledge that starflower—"

"—was good for sleep," Draka interrupted.

Kovogor's head turned to her, his face surprised and delighted. Geyah scowled. Draka had not been given leave to speak, but Durotan reached to cover his mate's hand with his own. "My wife, Draka, understands what you say better than most," he said.

Garona's eyes widened as they flickered to Draka. The slave's tiny fingers crept to her throat, touching the collar that encircled it, then she lowered her hand. Always before, Garona had seemed aloof, as if she were trying to distance herself from her situation. Now, she gazed with open curiosity at Draka, and, to Durotan's surprise, a slight smile curved her thin lips.

What is so interesting to her about Draka? Durotan wondered briefly before turning his attention back to Kovogor.

"Then Draka has likely told you of things that have been useful in this bleak time," Kovogor said. "So it was with the Horde. We learned that the enemy was not another clan. The true enemy was starvation. Thirst. Violence directed at each other, not at solving problems. This understanding, this sense of unity, is what Gul'dan has given to us." His eyes searched Durotan's. "Do you remember, when we met, when our clans hunted together? I recall that time fondly."

"As do I," Durotan was forced to admit.

"I had never thought to enjoy the friendship of anyone who was not of my clan, but I did. That connection, that sense of working together for a common goal—this is what drives the Horde. We are working, together, to prepare to enter this new land, which will have enough for all of us to prosper."

Durotan looked searchingly at the orc he had once, for a brief time, considered a friend. Draka had already opened his eyes to possibilities. Now Kovogor was confirming that this Horde was doing the same thing she had done, except on a scale he could barely grasp. He returned his gaze to Gul'dan. Could it be that this warlock, who seemed so dark, whom the Spirits shunned—could it possibly be that he was putting the sense of cooperation, of unity, into play not just for a few orcs, but for them *all*?

Was this what it meant to be part of the Horde?

Gul'dan said he had returned because he had seen Durotan's interest in this precise thing. And the Frostwolf chieftain realized Gul'dan had also been right about Draenor's troubles only growing worse.

"So, you have come to the Frostwolves because we are the only clan that has not yet joined the Horde?"

Gul'dan frowned. "No. There are others like you, who refuse to join us," he confessed. "Some have become Red Walkers, like the ones who slew your noble father. Others simply keep to themselves. And they are dying because of it. I said before, and I will say it again: the Frostwolves are known throughout Draenor as proud, individualistic, and strong. If you joined my Horde, you would show by example that there is no shame in doing so. You would be able to feed your people. Your children would eat good meat, and grow strong and healthy. The Frostwolves will be given a place of honor in my Horde. You will help me lead them, for where you lead, Durotan, these stragglers, these who hold out—they will follow. I am asking you to be to these other clans what Kovogor has been to you today—a voice of reason, one they will respect."

"And you need them."

"I need you to convince them to lay their pride aside—for the good not only of the Horde, but of themselves. They need *us*," Gul'dan insisted. "They will soon find themselves facing a choice: join my Horde, join the Red Walkers, or die. This world is dying, Durotan. You are not a fool, you *must* see it!"

A moment before, he had looked benevolent,

almost avuncular, while Kovogor spoke. Now, irritation slitted those strange green eyes. Durotan looked from the warlock to his slave: small and bird-boned compared to true orc females like Draka and Geyah. But so very proud.

No. Durotan, son of Garad, son of Durkosh, was not a fool. He had almost been one, though. He had almost been taken in by Kovogor's words about the unity of the Horde, the things they could accomplish. He had almost turned his back on traditions that were nearly as old as Greatfather Mountain. He had come too close to debilitating a clan that was, and had always been, free, proud, and passionate.

He had almost become a slave, and worse, he had almost enslaved his own people.

Gul'dan's words had betrayed him. It was not "the Horde," or even "our Horde." It was "*my* Horde." For all his talk of caretaking, of saving orcs from hardship and perhaps extinction, Gul'dan was no kindly uncle, selflessly gathering devastated clans to his breast to nurture them. He wanted something from them. He *needed* something from them. And if the Spirits did not wish his company, then the Frostwolves did not, either.

Durotan believed that the rewards of which Kovogor had spoken were true. But what had been the cost? Yes, the orcs were working together toward finding this new land. But what if this promise was a lie? Or what if the rewards were only for a select few? Even if it were true, the Spirits had taken care of the Frostwolves. They had guided them to pure water. And the clan had survived the winter.

Garad might have refused Gul'dan out of a desire to preserve Frostwolf tradition. Durotan would make the same decision out of a desire to preserve the Frostwolves.

Gul'dan's sickly coloring and strange eyes, his lack of clan ties, his penchant for keeping slaves—none of that would nourish Frostwolves. Durotan would not gamble his people's spirits and, in the end, their lives on the promises of this… *creature*.

"My father said to you, that we do not suffer," Durotan said. The memory of the words was as clear, as strong, as if he had heard them but a moment past. "We *endure*. And we will continue to do so."

Garona understood him before her master did, and her delicate nostrils flared with surprise. Her eyes had been fixed on Durotan, but now they darted to Draka.

"Draka! *Jeskaa daletya vas kulduru*!"

All eyes now turned to Garona in utter shock and disbelief. Until now, Durotan hadn't even been certain that the slave had a tongue in her head, so silent she had been. But now, she was speaking—directly to his wife. Durotan turned to look at Draka. She stood, her hand clutching her necklace.

The purple crystal given to her by the Draenei.

"*Kulshuri kazshar*," Draka said. And then he understood. Both his wife and Gul'dan's hitherto silent slave were conversing in the draenei tongue! Durotan regarded the slave with new respect.

Gul'dan, however, was angry. His eyes narrowed.

The green flame in them grew in intensity, and his lip curled as his gnarled green hands tightened on the staff.

"What did you say to her?" he hissed at Garona.

"Your—Garona said, that my mate was a fool to refuse you." Draka's voice was calm, measured. "My apologies, husband, but those were her words."

Durotan kept his face impassive. He did not know the Draenei language.

But he knew that Draka was lying.

"My slave is right," Gul'dan said, his voice soft and sinister. "You *are* a fool, as your father was. No doubt if you conceive children, they too will be fools. Honor and duty are noble concepts, Durotan. You would have seen them embodied in my Horde, had you chosen to join it. Honor cannot feed your people when there is no food to be found, when the growing things wither and the beasts drop in their tracks. Duty cannot shelter them when snowstorms freeze them where they stand, or when mountains crack open and bleed fire. Only my magics can do that—magics that will make the orcs mighty once more!"

His eyes gleamed fiercely, and Durotan wanted to draw back from them. He forced himself to stay seated, unmoving. Behind him, he heard Geyah and Draka both take quick, swift breaths.

"Do you truly not comprehend how powerful I am? Do the Frostwolves, and the Red Walkers, and a handful of others wish to be the only orcs left behind to die in a barren wasteland? I could have *saved* you, stubborn son of Garad!"

And then he sighed. The flames in his eyes subsided to green embers. "And I may yet save you. I have never turned away an orc who asked to join me, and I will not make you the first, much as I wish to at this moment. When you are ready to see wisdom, head south, to what was known as the Tanaan Jungle." He smiled bitterly, the gesture twisting his mouth. "It is now a desert, utterly devoid of life. It is there that we prepare. It is there you may find us. But do not tarry overlong. This world is sick. And its death throes may take you with it sooner than you bargained for."

He turned to leave. Geyah cried out, "The test of the blade! You cannot leave without our promise of safety!"

Gul'dan turned around slowly and impaled Geyah with a contemptuous look. "I need no promise of *safety*," he snarled. "Neither your son nor your mate could have laid a finger on me and lived to boast of it."

He jerked sharply on the chain in his ire. Even though Garona was clearly expecting it, the action forced a sharp hiss of pain from her and was so strong that she fell forward.

Draka was there so swiftly Durotan marveled at it. The chieftain's mate knelt in the snow beside the slave, helping her up. Garona jerked back at first, then hesitated and allowed herself to be raised. Draka smiled at her, kindly, then regarded Gul'dan with a scornful look. The warlock merely tugged on the chain a second time and Garona followed, turning at one point to regard Durotan searchingly before falling into step behind her master.

Kovogor was the last to leave. Unlike Gul'dan, he did not look offended. His eyes were sad and his brow furrowed in concern. Durotan longed to speak to him, but the time for words had passed, and they both knew it. Kovogor flipped the hood of his cloak over his head, and turned away to follow his chieftain.

The sun had almost set. Under other circumstances, Durotan would have invited Gul'dan and his retinue to stay, to share a meal and shelter with the Frostwolves, after he had traveled so long to reach them. But Gul'dan's scathing comments had rendered that impossible.

Most of his clan glared angrily at the departing warlock. Most, but not all. Some regarded their chieftain and Draka instead, and Durotan wondered if perhaps Gul'dan had managed to plant seeds of discontent on fertile ground after all.

As soon as he could he walked with Draka away from the others and whispered, "What did Garona really say?"

Draka answered equally softly. "She said, 'My master is dark and dangerous.'"

Garona was not only proud, she was smart. She had seen the crystal, realized that Draka had been in contact with the draenei at some point, and guessed she might know some of their language. She had given Durotan's clan a warning—at great risk to herself.

"And what did you reply?"

"I told her, 'We know.'"

16

No one, it turned out, was happy with how the meeting with Gul'dan had gone. After the clan had eaten—another meager meal of birds and rodents boiled in an earthenware pot that satisfied neither taste nor hunger—Durotan spoke with his advisors.

Geyah was livid at Gul'dan's disregard for the ritual. "It is *ancient*," she said. "Sacred to all orcs. Who are we if we forget everything? He comes to our encampment with this talk of unity, and then leaves unhindered after insulting us!"

It was more than the warlock's rudeness that was upsetting his mother, Durotan realized. The terrible strain had affected all of them. Geyah in particular had lost so much since the last meeting with Gul'dan: her mate, her home, the Frostwolf scrolls that were so old and fragile they had to be handled with exquisite care. No doubt, they had gone up like kindling from the simple heat of the fire-river as it consumed their village. Her identity and ability to contribute, as both mate of the chieftain and Lorekeeper of the clan, had been dealt devastating blows. It made Durotan's chest ache to see her so frustrated and uncertain.

Gently, he placed a large hand on her arm, pained to discover how fleshless it was. "You once said the dishonor is his," he reminded her. "We honored the rituals, Mother. The shame is Gul'dan's alone to bear."

"Shame it is, indeed," Drek'Thar said, "and you showed wisdom, Durotan." He shook his head. "The darkness around him has only grown. I would have had grave misgivings had you decided to follow him."

Durotan and Draka exchanged glances.

"When I see him and hear him speak, I have an urge to throttle him," Orgrim muttered. "My fingers itch just thinking about doing so. But I wonder if perhaps..." He trailed off.

"Speak, old friend," Durotan said, "your bluntness is at the heart of you. I would hear all views."

Orgrim looked at his chieftain. "We have struggled day to day, heartbeat to heartbeat," he said. "Your father met the challenge with faith that it would change. You have met it with cunning and innovation—and you have outsmarted it. So far."

Durotan felt a prickle of unease. Beside him, Draka scowled. "Go on."

"Before the river of fire, we could plan; dry flesh and fish; store nuts and seeds. But now, we have no nuts and seeds, and if we tried to dry fish for a later time, we would not eat at all. There is..." he groped for the word.

Draka found it. "Immediacy," she said quietly.

"Yes. An immediacy now that we did not have then. How much longer can we outsmart disaster? We hang on by the most slender thread of spiders' silk to existence. You and I both knew Kovogor. He would not lie. And he has faith in Gul'dan."

Durotan did not answer at once. He turned to his wife. Garona had reached out to her, not to him; he would let her decide what she wished to share. "Draka," he said, "your knowledge of things beyond our experience has helped us. You have been a major reason why we have survived this long. There is much that Gul'dan said that was familiar to me because of you."

Draka shook her head firmly. "He and I may both understand that orcs can work together," she said, "but it is the *how* of it that is as different as night and day." She paused, looking at them, measuring her words before speaking. "I feel kinship with the slave, Garona. We have never seen her like before; she must be a stranger to this place. I, too, have been alone among strangers."

She lifted a hand to forestall their protests. "You will tell me there is a difference. I was never forced to walk about on a chain, never 'owned': I have always been a Frostwolf. And yes, this distinction is true. But I do know what it is like to be *other*. Garona has spirit. Intelligence. And courage—she told me, in the draenei tongue, that her master is dark and dangerous. Gul'dan dominates Garona. I feel he would dominate us *all*."

Durotan looked from face to face in turn: at his mother's, drawn and tight; at Orgrim's, concerned and open; at Drek'Thar's, his sightless eyes focused on something Durotan couldn't see; and finally, at his wife's.

He would dominate us all.

"No beings who can think, who can feel, who can understand what is happening around and to them, should be enslaved. We see how Gul'dan treats her. I believe you are right, wife. And I promise you all: Frostwolves will never be dominated. Our own spirits, and the elemental ones as well, reject this green orc and his promises."

But even as he said those words and later lay with his mate in his arms, Durotan wondered if his decision was the right one.

Six days after Gul'dan's arrival, and two days after a late spring snow, Durotan and his hunting party were returning to the encampment, empty-handed and frustrated. When he saw a small group of orcs assembled awaiting their return, he assumed the worst and urged the exhausted Sharptooth to hasten toward them.

"What has happened?" he said.

The orcs exchanged glances. "Nothing... yet," Nokrar said. Durotan looked at their faces. The orcs seemed determined but oddly furtive. No one but

Nokrar would meet their leader's questioning gaze.

Weariness draped Durotan like a cloak. "If nothing has happened," he said, "both we and our wolves require food, water, and rest." He made to ride past them, but Nokrar stepped into Sharptooth's path. It was a bold move—but contentious.

"We *all* require these things, Chieftain," Nokrar said. "And… some of us think we know how to get them."

Durotan was bone-weary. The fact that they had found no prey to bring back—not even a few birds to toss into a pot with old, worm-chewed grain—sharpened his ire. He should have dismounted and asked Nokrar to walk with him, listened to his concerns, but Durotan suspected he knew well enough what they were.

"Unless the Spirits have called you to their service, Nokrar, or you have a new method of finding game or harvesting food, you know all the ways that I know. Those who have spent the last six days tracking meat for you to eat should be allowed their rest, and Sharptooth is short-tempered."

"We want to join the Horde."

So, it had finally come.

Durotan had been expecting this, but not quite so soon. Until now, aside from Nokrar's group, nobody in the bustling encampment had paid much attention to the returning hunting party, but he could see a few heads turn at the word "Horde." "I know you want to be a good mate and father," he said, as kindly as he could manage. "I know you fear for them. I have a little one on the way myself. After a fashion, the clanspeople are also my children, and I have the same concerns for all of you. You know I will listen to all reasonable suggestions. Come to me later today, when I am not so weary, and we will talk."

Nokrar shifted his weight. Durotan also knew that Nokrar's family had been close to Grukag's. He had taken the deaths of Purzul and Margah hard, and Durotan suspected he still had not recovered fully.

Have any of us recovered fully from what we have been through? he wondered. *Will we ever? And* should *we ever?*

"We think... you chose wrongly," Nokrar said at last. He stuck his chin out and drew himself up to his not inconsiderable height. More Frostwolves were wandering over, listening to the conversation.

Durotan stared at Nokrar, unblinking, and straightened as well. "I am your chieftain, Nokrar," he said, his voice low and dangerous. "Tread carefully."

Nokrar was impulsive and passionate. He had raised his voice before on behalf of his mate and younglings. Durotan wanted him to back down, now, not simply for his own reasons, but for Nokrar's safety. Durotan was a patient orc. But even he would have to do something he had no desire to do if Nokrar persisted.

But Nokrar could not see that. He tossed his hair out of his eyes and met Durotan stare for stare. "Let those of us who want to go depart."

At least two dozen Frostwolves had gathered now. They watched both Durotan and Nokrar intently. More clan members emerged from their shelters and joined the crowd.

"And take precious food and supplies with you, only to be lost when you die within seven suns? I am not so foolish as that." Durotan tried one last time, keeping his voice calm. "Stay, Nokrar. I understand why you feel thus, and we can—"

"Let us go, or…" Nokrar stopped abruptly, as if only now, when it was too late, he realized what he had done. His eyes widened slightly.

Quietly, Durotan asked, "Or what?"

Nokrar swallowed. "Or I will challenge you to the mak'gora."

Durotan closed his eyes. "You just did."

17

The argument had drawn attention as it escalated, and now nearly the half the clan had assembled. Gasps rose, and Nokrar turned pale for a moment, before the hot blood of anger rushed into his face.

"Durotan, son of Garad, son of Durkosh—I challenge you to the duel of honor. Do you accept—or refuse?"

"I accept," Durotan said. There was no other option. "We will meet by the spring pool. Prepare, Nokrar. Gather your family. Tell them you love them. And apologize for depriving them of a mate and father because of your own arrogance!"

Durotan stormed off toward the chieftain's small hut. He was shaking, but with anger, not fear. Anger at Nokrar, for being so stupid. Anger at what he now must do if he were to continue to command respect.

Anger at Gul'dan for inciting this. And even anger at the Spirits, for the difficulties and tragedies that had driven a Frostwolf to the worst possible error.

Durotan began to divest himself of his armor, flinging it down in frustration. The crude door opened and Orgrim, who had overseen the camp in his absence, entered, followed by Geyah and Draka.

"You are angry," he said.

"Do you think so?" Durotan was not fond of sarcasm, but he could not bite back the retort.

"You could do nothing other than what you have done." Geyah's voice was cold and unemotional, but her cheeks were dark with outrage. "No Frostwolf has challenged a chieftain for generations. The insult could not be allowed to pass unaddressed."

"Geyah is right," Draka said, though there was a trace of sorrow in her voice. Of course she knew what he was thinking, she knew him better than anyone. She could see through the rage to the grief that fueled it. He reached for her and drew her close, then pressed his forehead to hers.

For her ears alone, he whispered, "I do not wish to kill a Frostwolf."

She closed her eyes, then opened them. Tears stood in them. One hand crept to her swelling belly, caressing the child within.

"I do not wish to search for stones to cover my husband's body," she murmured.

He winced. She pulled back slightly, one small hand on his cheek. "The challenge was made in full view of the clan," she said. "No one thinks you come to this duel with hate in your heart. Do what you must."

Durotan grasped her hand tightly and pressed it to his chest for a moment. Everyone here knew that, unless thc Spirits willed otherwise, he would win the battle. Although weary from the fruitless hunt, he was larger and a more experienced fighter than Nokrar. He was not concerned for his own life. He was concerned for Nokrar's.

He emerged a few moments later. Word had spread, and now he saw that the entire clan was present. The gathering was subdued. Durotan recalled the one mak'gora he had witnessed, when Grukag had been challenged by a foolish Thunderlord orc over something as trivial as a slain talbuk. Then, there had been anger, as offense had truly been given, and cheering as Grukag fought to an easy victory.

But Grukag's family was dead now. And there was no one to cheer for when Frostwolf fought Frostwolf.

Nokrar stood with Kagra and Shaksa beside him. In his arms he cradled his youngest daughter, little Nizka, who had followed the redjay to fresh water. When he caught sight of Durotan, Nokrar gave the little girl to Kagra. Nizka began to cry and reached out for him, but Nokrar gently pushed both her and her mother to the side and strode forward. Shaksa was openly weeping.

They stood facing one another as Drek'Thar was led forward. The elderly shaman halted and released Palkar's arm. "I am glad my eyes cannot see today," he said, "if they would witness a battle to the death between two Frostwolves. It pains me, and it pains the Spirits, who have watched our struggles. I have known you both since you drew your first breaths. My heart aches to think one of you draws your last today. I will bless both of you, for only the Spirits will decide the outcome of this imprudent battle."

He reached into his pouch and withdrew a vial of oil. "Nokrar, give me your hands," he said. Nokrar did so. Gently, Drek'Thar placed a drop in each huge palm. "Spirits of Earth, Air, Fire, Water, and Life guide you to your destiny. Greet it well, as a Frostwolf should. While life is to be valued, death is not to be feared."

He repeated the ritual with Durotan. When Drek'Thar had finished the blessing, Durotan rubbed his hands together, then placed them on his heart, letting the sweet scent waft up to his nostrils.

Drek'Thar bowed his head and let Palkar lead him away. The younger shaman threw a backward glance over his shoulder. Once the two were safely away, Durotan and Nokrar looked at each other. Durotan wanted to urge Nokrar to withdraw the challenge, but that was impossible. He would appear weak for doing so, and Durotan would appear weak for allowing it.

Oh, Spirits, has it truly come to this?

Durotan had barely had time to form the thought when, head lowered, howling a wordless cry, Nokrar charged him like a raging clefthoof bull. Durotan leaped to the side, striking the still-hard earth and rolling. Nokrar's forward momentum carried him several paces before he was able to turn. Durotan was on his feet in a fighter's stance, ready to leap in whichever direction served him best.

He let his focus narrow to himself and Nokrar. It was almost, but not quite, a trance, this hypersensitivity to his opponent. He had learned it from his father when he began to hunt, and had honed it in battle since then. Durotan could still not believe he was using those skills now against a fellow clan member.

Nokrar grunted, taking a breath to size up his opponent. Durotan took advantage of the pause and leaped forward, angling himself so that his right shoulder slammed into Nokrar's upper chest while his left arm snaked upward. He tangled his fingers in Nokrar's long hair and yanked hard. Nokrar howled as his head was hauled down. Durotan continued his forward motion, letting his body roll over Nokrar's back and relentlessly driving the other orc forward down into the dirt.

But Nokrar rolled too, jerking his head free as he hit the ground on his side, rather than his front. Durotan was left holding nothing but a bloody chunk of hair and scalp. The sudden release of tension threw him off balance, and Nokrar was able to slam his fist into Durotan's face. Durotan felt teeth break and tasted blood as he stumbled backward. He stayed on his feet, but Nokrar slammed into him and they both went down.

Nokrar shouted wordlessly as he punched his chieftain's face, once, twice—

Durotan shoved both hands up and between

Nokrar's swinging fists. He cupped Nokrar's jaw in the heels of his palms and snapped his arms upward so violently that Nokrar's head jerked and he was flung backward.

A heartbeat later, Durotan was on his feet. But so was Nokrar. The two orcs snarled and slammed into one another. Their bodies, slick with sweat and blood, collided, and Durotan felt a rib crack. Judging by Nokrar's yelp, he too had been injured. Growling deep within his throat, Durotan let the bloodlust take him. He had been challenged. He had to win, or die.

Lok'tar ogar.

Instead of pulling away or attempting to attack, Durotan forced himself to go limp, bent his knees, and wrapped his arms around his opponent's waist.

"Gyaaaahhhhhh!" he bellowed, lifting up the other orc and hurling him a distance away. Nokrar struck the ground hard and struggled to rise.

Durotan was there. He curled his fingers into a fist and put all his force behind the blow as his hand crashed into Nokrar's square, bony jaw. He felt bone snap beneath the force. One tusk had been knocked loose and now dangled from a bit of skin. Durotan drew back his arm for another blow. Nokrar was wounded, nearly unconscious. Blood now covered his face. One solid strike would end him. End the mak'gora.

Durotan stayed his hand.

Through the mask of gore, Nokrar's eyes stared up at Durotan.

Durotan had been challenged. He had been offered no choice. The law, ancient and always obeyed, was clear. The honor duel was to the death.

Slowly, he uncurled his fist and leaned back. He stumbled to his feet, his enormous chest heaving as he sucked in air, calming himself. He heard the murmuring, but did not look at the crowd. He kept looking at Nokrar.

Nokrar's chest continued to rise and fall, but he was beaten. He struggled to rise and failed, finally collapsing back and waiting for the death blow.

It did not come. Durotan turned to the silent, watchful crowd and spoke.

"We have suffered greatly," he said. "First, the longer winters and shorter summers. The decrease of the herds, and their sickness. We survived. Then Greatfather Mountain wept a river of fiery blood, destroying our ancestral home. We survived. We have endured poisoned lakes, withered trees and grasses, and lack of shelter and food. We have buried those whose struggles were not successful, and we mourn them. This world offers us challenges aplenty to show our courage, to prove that we are worthy to dwell in it. Challenges that should make us stronger—not set us at each other's throats.

"Our numbers are small, and they dwindle. I fight to lead you. To protect you. To keep you alive. I will not, by my own hand, add another Frostwolf's name to the list of the dead. My wife is with child—the only one of our clan at this time. Nokrar is a father himself. Nizka, Shaksa, and our other children are the future of this clan, and we must do all we can to be there for them. We will fight, yes—fight to protect them and the rest of the clan. Fight prey, for food, and fight against the ravages of the elements. But to fight one another is folly of the highest order, and I refuse to do it.

"I am Durotan, son of Garad, son of Durkosh. I lead this clan. And I will *never* turn down a challenge. But I will not see one of us die for daring to make one. Does anyone else wish to fight?"

His eyes roamed the faces he had known all his life. Some looked angry. Some relieved. Draka's eyes shone with pride, and she gave him a subtle nod. His mother, the Lorekeeper, looked distressed, but said nothing.

No one accepted his challenge.

Durotan wanted to reach down and help Nokrar rise, but he knew the gesture would not be welcomed. Nokrar needed to keep what Durotan had left him of his pride, and Durotan could not afford to be seen as weak—or, perhaps, weaker than he already seemed to some.

So instead, Durotan strode back to his shelter without a backward glance. Once the door had closed and he was inside, he let himself wince at the pain and sink into a chair. Draka and Geyah entered, followed soon by Orgrim, and, leaning on Orgrim's arm, Drek'Thar.

"You fought well, my heart," Draka said as she reached for a small earthenware pot and filled it from a container of water. "And you chose well, to spare Nokrar. He will nurse injuries and a sore ego, but he will live to strengthen the clan." She lit the fire and set the pot to boil.

Geyah glanced at Draka, then at her son. "You should have told me what you intended to do," Geyah snapped. "Our traditions have already been eroded—nay, attacked and almost destroyed—by what has happened over the last few years. Now *you* attack what shreds remain!"

"Mother," Durotan said tiredly, "I did not know myself what I would do. Take a look around you. Nokrar is a strong warrior and will be again, when he heals. I have seen him bring down a clefthoof by himself. With him, we have one more hunter to bring home food. Should I deprive the clan of that simply for tradition?"

"Simply for—"

"Geyah," interrupted Drek'Thar. "Your son's choice was in line with all I have been able to learn from the Spirits—when they choose to visit me." He sighed. "There is enough destruction and death all around us. The Spirit of Life urges us not to feed that fire. There is… an interconnection I cannot yet grasp. But rest assured that Durotan did the right thing."

"I am more than happy to be your *second*-in-command in these times," Orgrim said.

Durotan chuckled, even though it made him wince. "In these times? In other times, you'd prefer to be chieftain?"

Orgrim reached to shove his friend playfully, then, mindful of Durotan's injuries, stopped just short of doing so. "It would keep you from getting fat and lazy if you knew I was always ready to challenge you." He grinned. Then, more seriously, he added, "What you did... it would not have occurred to me. And yet, I, too, think the choice was sound."

Draka had tossed a handful of herbs in the boiling water. Now, she strained them and set them aside to cool. As they did, she dipped cloths into the herb-scented water and cleaned her mate's wounds. What was left would be mixed with starflower and given to Durotan so that he might sleep deeply. The strained herbs would be mixed with animal fat and made into a poultice for his injuries, and later, Drek'Thar would ask the Spirits for aid in healing the clan's chieftain. Elsewhere, Durotan knew, another shaman was tending to Nokrar in the same manner.

Durotan smiled at her gratefully as she tended to him. "Let us hope you are all correct. Rather than letting the clan fall into chaos, I will take a life, if I must. But I ask the Spirits that it will not come to that."

The hot poultice felt good and smelled better. Orgrim and Draka eased Durotan to his sleeping furs. Within moments of drinking the starflower concoction, Durotan drifted into sleep as Drek'Thar chanted over him.

He awoke in the morning to his wife's voice.

"Durotan," Draka was saying, her voice low and urgent, "wake up. We need you!"

The starflower had left him groggy, and Durotan

struggled to clear his head. He sat up with only a little pain, pausing to offer gratitude to the Spirits and to Drek'Thar, their vessel. Draka's expression made his heart sink.

"What is it? What has happened?"

"Nokrar is gone. And he took his entire family with him."

18

Drek'Thar had been the last to visit the missing family, checking in on Nokrar after tending to Durotan. Nokrar, Drek'Thar said, had been sullen and embarrassed, as was only to be expected.

"I am sorry, Chieftain," the shaman said. "I had no suspicion they would try to leave."

Draka snorted as she helped a still-aching Durotan into his armor. "Of course you didn't. You, like the rest of us, assumed that Nokrar and Kagra had some sense in their thick skulls. It would seem we gave them greater credit than they deserved."

"Them, Grukag, Delgar, and Kulzak as well," said Orgrim as he entered. "Five adults and three children, in all. I say let them go," he growled, though he, too, was clad in armor and ready to depart with his friend. "They will not catch up with Gul'dan, nor will they likely be able to even follow him. That last snow saw to that. Let them starve to death. Or mayhap they will run across some stray Red Walkers who will do the job more swiftly than hunger."

"You forget, Orgrim," snapped Durotan, fastening Sever to his back, "they have taken children. I will not allow them to die because their parents are foolish. These are Frostwolf children, the future of our clan, and they are in danger. Our duty to them is clear."

"What of their parents?"

Durotan hesitated. He was furious at Nokrar's stubbornness. His decision, and that of the others who had had accompanied him, had not only put the children at risk, it had necessitated that a whole party be sent to hunt them, instead of food. For a brief moment, he regretted his decision to spare Nokrar, but he pushed that thought aside as quickly as it had come.

"I will decide what to do with them when we find them. I will do nothing to jeopardize the clan." Perhaps a night spent alone at the mercy of the elements might have changed Nokrar's demeanor. A clanking sound drew his attention from his dark thoughts and he looked up to see Draka reaching for her own armor.

"Wife," Durotan stated, "you will stay behind."

She paused and arched an eyebrow. "Husband," she replied, "I will ride with you, as I have always done."

"You are with child, my heart," he said, rising and laying a gentle hand on her belly. It was only slightly softer, as the child was still new. "And one of the reasons we ride is to recover these precious little ones. If we do not find them, our child will be one of a mere handful; no one else is carrying one."

Her expression could have withered the strongest tree. "In years past," she said, "I was deemed too frail to be a true Frostwolf. That time is over. I go where you go. Whatever happens."

There was no arguing with her, and Durotan found he did not want to. Their place was at one another's side. That was part of the legacy he would bequeath to his child—be it male or female.

"Whatever happens," he agreed. He turned to Orgrim. "I will need you to stay behind," he said. "In case we do not return, there will be tension here. The clan will need a strong leader."

Orgrim grunted unhappily. "I will serve my chieftain better by smacking the upstart soundly," he said, "but I will obey."

"Keep your armor on," Durotan said, "Just in case." He did not need to spell it out. The Frostwolf clan had been rocked by this event as never before. Durotan had never expected a challenge from one of his own, but it had come. Orgrim should be prepared in case things grew ugly.

Orgrim nodded, all humor gone. "Lok'tar," he said.

"Lok'tar," Durotan said, and went to the waiting Sharptooth.

Durotan and Draka rode side by side, surrounded by their hunting party. Sharptooth and Ice loped at a mile-eating but steady pace that allowed the couple breath enough to speak.

"I should have been better prepared for such a challenge," Durotan said. "Gul'dan's words would be intoxicating to the fearful, and Nokrar has a family to care for. And he has ever been impulsive. A few words from his wife or friend might have led him to believe that, somehow, this," and he indicated the harsh terrain before them, "was the best option."

"You have a kinder heart than me," Draka said. "I have faced this terrain alone. I know how unforgiving it is." She looked up at him. "I know how hard it is on the young. My anger at Nokrar is less that he left, than that he took his children with them."

"He and the..." Durotan frowned. What should he call them? Frostwolves? They had scorned the title. Rebels? After the mak'gora, they had not offered violence. Traitors? He shook his head. There was no precise word in the orcish tongue for what Nokrar and his group were. "The deserters," he said, unhappy with the word but knowing no better one, "will not elude us for long. If Gul'dan's trail is hard to find, I think only the trail of a wounded clefthoof bull would be easier to follow than theirs."

Draka threw back her head and laughed. Durotan grinned, warmed by the sound.

He had not exaggerated. The group had taken five wolves with them. It was clear that Nokrar was trying to catch up with Gul'dan: the tracks led almost directly south.

The hunting party was five strong: alongside Durotan and Draka were Gurlak the singer, and

Kruglar and Melakk, both experienced trackers. Ice, Sharptooth, and the other wolves ran amiably, ears forward, tongues lolling. Durotan envied them their innocence. They ran not in pursuit of those who had betrayed them, but to join with their fellow pack members—both lupine and orcish.

What would he do with them? Durotan wondered. The children would have to come back, of course. Their chances of survival were higher with the protection of the full clan—and the children *must* survive. But Nokrar and the other adults? Nokrar had now challenged Durotan's authority twice, first with the mak'gora, and now by absconding like a thief in the night with the most precious things the Frostwolves had. Even now, Durotan did not wish to kill the foolish orc, but he saw no way out of it.

Sharptooth halted abruptly, and Durotan found himself having to grab his wolf friend's thick scruff to stay atop him. Sharptooth's body tensed and he crouched, his ears flattening against his skull. A low, dangerous growl emanated from him. All the wolves were behaving in a similar manner. Durotan signaled to the rest of the hunting party to emulate him as he drew Sever.

He sniffed the air. He scented nothing that signaled danger. While an orc's sense of smell was keen, it was feeble compared to that of a wolf. Durotan trusted his friend. He could not smell what the wolves did, but he realized he scented enough—the beasts' musky tension and his party's own sweat. Something very bad lay ahead.

Initially, the trail appeared no different here from what they had seen before. The carelessly paw-trampled snow led on for a while before being swallowed up by a thick cluster of pines. The rest of the party awaited their chieftain's orders. Durotan silently dismounted, and the others followed suit. He pointed at the trail ahead of them, and held up two fingers. He then pointed to the wolves and, keeping his hand palm down, swept it in front of him. The orcs would proceed two by two, and the wolves were to be released. Unlike the orcs Durotan was tracking, frost wolves would never desert their pack, and in the closeness of the forest, if it came to a fight, they would fare best unhindered by riders.

The group moved forward, taking care not to disturb the snow-laden boughs, a lifetime of practice rendering them able to maneuver almost soundlessly through the snow. The forest was still as they entered. There was no sound of birdcalls or the rustling of small creatures going about their business.

The tracks revealed that the deserters, too, had dismounted, walking alongside their wolves. There were no prints of small children's boots, so Durotan assumed the parents had permitted the children to ride. He looked ahead along the path, noting that it bent to the right.

The wind shifted. Durotan gasped. He could smell it now, the reek of blood from both orc and wolf. It was not fresh. Whatever had happened had occurred hours ago.

He looked back at his companions and pointed

left and right, indicating that they were to separate and close in on the site of the battle from different directions. They nodded and obeyed.

Durotan did not know what to expcct. Bodies, almost certainly, of both wolf and orc. But what—or who—had killed them?

He could glimpse the site now, through the tall dark shapes of the pine trees: a clearing spattered with blood, both red and brown. But…

"Where are the bodies?" asked Draka, who was a slight distance away from him.

The wolves had come forward, sniffing at the partially frozen puddles of snow. Ice lifted his muzzle to the sky and began to mourn its fallen pack mate. The others joined in. Convinced now that there was no immediate threat, Durotan lowered his axe.

The rest of the party drew closer, also lowering their weapons. The entire area had been churned up, snow and pine needles alike drenched in a veritable lake of red blood. As Durotan approached, he saw a wide, bloody trail continue through the woods.

Something must have slain all five wolves and dragged them off. There was too much blood, and besides, the wolves would never flee if their riders were in peril. Durotan could think of only one predator that could—or would—do that.

They had not left the Red Walkers behind with Frostfire Ridge after all.

Durotan stepped closer to the wide red trail. He could now see that boot prints led away from it. He followed the prints with his eyes as they disappeared into the shadowy darkness of the forest. The wolves were already bounding in that direction, whimpering and growling. Draka sprinted off with them, taking care not to disturb the tracks.

"There is too much orc blood," Gurlak pointed out. "Someone died here."

Durotan looked at the brown-stained snow and realized that the lok'vadnod singer was right. He had assumed, naively, that a member of Nokrar's group had been injured, but—

Another mournful howl rent the air, this one sharper, more heartfelt with the rawness of grief.

"Durotan!" called Draka. Her voice, barely audible over the frost wolves' own lok'vadnod, was sharp and laced with something he had never heard in it before: fear.

The rest of the group raced to her. They found her and their mounts in a small clearing. The wolves had their muzzles raised to the sky. Draka stared, transfixed, at the carnage before her.

The five wolves had been skinned and butchered, only carcasses remained. That, Durotan had half-expected. Their pelts would provide clothing for an orc, and their flesh would feed them. Even the Frostwolves worked the skins of their wolf brothers, so that the wolves would be remembered and still serve the clan even in death. While he would have ached at the sight of their slaughter, that was not what had him, and the others, rooted with shock.

Orc life was often brutal. Death was no stranger. Durotan had witnessed fellow clan members, some close friends, trampled beneath raging clefthooves. He had watched them bleed out after being gored by the horns of talbuks. He had even witnessed death in battle and shocking and violent accidents.

But this—

Before them lay a body—*no,* he thought wildly, *that wasn't even right, what was* left *of a body.* It was naked; the murderers had taken all of this orc's clothing and supplies—and more. His flesh had been carved from his bones, as the flesh of the wolves had been. His entrails had been scooped out and laid to one side. With a peculiar clarity in the midst of his shock, Durotan noticed that a few organs were missing.

The orc lay face down in the snow and pine needles. Swallowing his gorge, Durotan extended Sever. He could not bear to touch the blood-slicked bones. Prodding gently, he rolled the corpse over.

Nokrar's face stared up sightlessly at him.

"I knew they adorned themselves with orc and draenei blood," Draka said softly. "But this..."

"They... they cut him up like..." Gurlak couldn't finish the sentence. He swallowed hard and said, "Was this a trophy?"

Durotan looked from the wolf to the orc and shook his head.

"No," he said grimly. "Food."

19

"The children," Draka said at once. "The Red Walkers took them!"

Durotan shook his head to clear it, fighting back the daze of revulsion. "The Red Walkers needed to kill the wolves outright, and swiftly," he said, working it out as he spoke. "That was the greatest threat, and the most… the most meat. Orcs could be overcome, subdued, and made to walk under their own power. They took the wolves' meat and hides and they took…"

For some strange reason, Durotan's mind seized on a careless comment he had made years ago, when they had first seen Gul'dan. He had said that Geyah looked like she wanted to make a feast out of the warlock. And Ogrim's words before they left: *Or mayhap they will run across Red Walkers who will do the job more swiftly than hunger.*

He thought of the times when some hunting parties had simply never returned, and his stomach clenched.

If you can't say it, you give them power, Durotan told himself. His fists clenched hard, bruising the palm that clutched Sever. *Name the thing you fear, and you become its master.*

"They took Nokrar's flesh as well," he said. His voice was steady. "The others, including the children, I believe they have taken prisoner. Food for later."

"Then," said Draka, speaking as bluntly as he had, "they are perhaps all still alive."

Durotan and the others had been single-minded in their purpose when they set forth that morning. They had come to hunt down deserting clan members. Now, that quest had turned into a rescue mission.

"The Red Walkers are not mounted, and we are," Durotan said. "We will find them. And when we do… they will die. Lok'tar!" he shouted, and the others joined in. Their voices rang in the unnatural stillness. Doubtless, the Red Walkers heard them.

Durotan did not care. Let them know what awaited them.

Let them know the Frostwolves were coming.

The scent of their pack mates' lifeblood filled the nostrils of the frost wolves, and they ran with all that was in them. Their riders hung on tightly, giving the magnificent, huge white beasts their heads. They ran swiftly but steadily, as they did when in pursuit of a herd, but Durotan could feel Sharptooth's tension. This was a very different sort of hunt, and both wolf and orc knew it.

It was Gurlak who spotted the stream of smoke curling upward, so thin that Durotan had to look carefully to see it. His stomach lurched as the wind shifted. It carried the smell of cooking flesh. It might have been appetizing, if Durotan had not known what it was.

Like his father before him, Durotan prided himself on being an orc of reason, not just battle prowess. Seldom had he felt the red haze of bloodlust, but it descended upon him now full force. He had not realized that he had shouted a battle cry until his throat was raw, or that the sound in his ears was his own voice. The others picked up the cry. Their mounts, sensing their riders' desire, lowered their heads and ran as swiftly as they could.

The hunting party was made of five orcs. The tracks of the Red Walkers indicated that there were twelve. The Frostwolves didn't even slow down. They burst out of the trees and into an open area, the encampment before them nothing more than a stopping point in the snow. The haze of bloodlust lifted long enough for Durotan to note the camp's layout: a central fire pit, with several spits of meat part-roasted, a pile of still-bloody wolf pelts, a bulging sack leaking pools of red and reddish black, and—bound together like so many pieces of kindling—the missing, living, Frostwolves.

The Red Walkers who had slain Garad had been horrifying enough. They had dipped their hands in animal blood and marked their bodies and faces with it. But the ones who turned to face the Frostwolves now looked like animals themselves. *No, not animals,* Durotan amended. Animals were natural creatures. What stood before him looked like the embodiment of nightmares.

They did not have merely a few handprints of dried blood on their bodies. They wore the blood like *clothing*. Layer upon layer had crusted on their chests, arms, and legs. It was impossible to guess what color the blood had been when it had first been spilled, or how long it had been on their bodies. The new flies of spring clustered on the things that had once been recognizable as orcs as they charged the mounted Frostwolves with a crazed recklessness.

One, a female with long, matted hair and wild eyes, raced toward Durotan with her spear. The blade was still coated with red wolf blood. Durotan leaped off Sharptooth. The wolf knew this maneuver and veered left when Durotan turned his attention to his attacker. Sharptooth bounded forward, springing on a second Red Walker who was swinging a mace at Melakk. The wolf's jaws yawned wide, his teeth as white as his coat, and then clamped down on the orc's neck. The Red Walker went down at once in a flurry of snow, ash, embers, and a fountain of his own brown blood.

Draka stayed mounted as her wolf ran in a tight circle. Her hand was a blur as she nocked and released arrow after arrow. One of the Red Walkers, snatching up a piece of flaming wood from the fire, dived for Draka's mount. Durotan could smell burning fur and Ice howled in pain, but the Red Walker went down with two arrows through his throat.

Durotan was glad he had selected Sever and not Thunderstrike. He would not have wanted to dispatch these creatures from Sharptooth's back. He wanted to thrust his snarling face within inches of theirs, smell the caked, rotting blood, and watch the light of life in their eyes wink out as he split their chests open or sliced off their heads. He had never hated before, but he hated these orcs.

He fell into his trance-like focus, losing track of time as his blade found flesh or blocked a strike, ceasing to count the number of times he ended a Red Walker's life so that he or she would never, *ever,* do to another orc what they had done to a Frostwolf. Finally, his body wet with sweat and blood—some of which was his own—Durotan slowed, blinking, to behold the area littered with corpses. Most of them were the hideous, fly-covered ones of the Red Walkers, but he saw Draka kneeling over the still body of Gurlak.

"He fell under three," she said simply. "He took them all with him."

Durotan realized he was panting and simply nodded. Gurlak, who loved to sing the lok'vadnods, would have been pleased to think he had earned a glorious one of his own. Melakk and Kruglar were in the process of sawing at the ropes that bound the remaining Frostwolves. It took Durotan another moment to come back to himself, and he realized with an icy jolt that the prisoners were all adults.

"The children!" he shouted. He strode over to the rescued prisoners, treading without caring upon the corpses of the Red Walkers. They were not orcs. They were insane, twisted monsters, and they earned even less respect in death than they had commanded in life. "What happened? *Where are they*?" He grabbed Grukag by the front of his tunic.

"They fled!" Grukag said, his voice was close to a sob. He and all of the former prisoners wore desperate, stunned expressions, but Durotan had no time for sympathy. "When we were attacked—they bolted and fled into the trees."

"Some of the Red Walkers went after them," Kagra said, "but they returned empty-handed. The children must have escaped."

"When was this?" Durotan demanded. He remained furious with them. Gurlak and Nokrar were dead because of the ill-advised decision to slink away in the night, and the thought of the children—

"Half a day ago," Grukag said. His voice was somber. He knew what that meant. There were dangers in the woods for three children, two of whom were quite young. Wild wolves seldom attacked adult orcs, but would view such small ones as prey. Insects, whose bites were lethal, had emerged with the spring. Venomous snakes would still be too sluggish to slither away at a child's approach, choosing to strike instead.

And night was coming.

"Hurry," Durotan ordered. "We will search as best we can." He hoped that the Spirits would guide them to the no doubt terrified youngsters.

But the Spirits were not kind. Six fruitless hours later, in the middle of a dark and bitter night, the party was forced to abandon the hunt. It would be foolish to continue. The Red Walkers had taken most of the clothing from the Frostwolves they had captured, and had not bothered to feed them or give them water. They were in bad shape. The darkness was so deep that the children could be lying unconscious a few feet away, and the adults would walk right past them.

Quietly, Kagra began to weep. Draka put an arm around her. Durotan had to force himself not to rage at Kagra and the others. He knew they were suffering enough.

"Frostwolf children are strong and smart," Draka said confidently. "They have Shaksa with them. She is the same age I was when I was Exiled, and I survived. We will return on the morrow with the whole clan to search for them." She looked at Durotan. "Won't we, my heart?"

"We will," Durotan promised. He didn't trust himself to say anything further.

The ride back was cold, long, and silent. Durotan could not recall his heart ever being so heavy, not even when Garad had been slain before his eyes. Draka rode by his side while Durotan brooded, trying to make sense of what he had just seen.

Except… he *couldn't*. This was not an orc clan.

This was a hive of madness. He was fiercely glad for a moment that his father was dead and could not bear witness to a depravity Durotan had never even conceived of. What in the name of the Sprits *were* these Red Walkers? Could they even truly be called orcs any longer? For an orc to kill another was not unusual. Disrespect for the body was rarer, but it happened on occasion.

But to *feed* upon it…

"Durotan!" The voice belonged to Orgrim and snapped Durotan out of his dark reverie. His second-in-command had ridden out to meet them. "You found them!"

"Not all," Durotan said heavily. "We lost Nokrar and Gurlak. And… and the children had already fled before we arrived."

Orgrim's face fell at the mention of Nokrar and Gurlak, but brightened, inexplicably, at the mention of the children. "Yes," Orgrim said, "they did."

"Mama!" came a shriek of delight.

"Nizka! Shaksa, Kelgur—"

Durotan stared in astonishment as wolves bearing the three missing children raced from the encampment. The two littlest ones launched themselves at their mother, leaping with the fearless trust of the young straight from the backs of their wolves to be caught in a loving embrace. Shaksa vaulted from her wolf and ran to Kagra. Durotan felt a stab of sorrow as the girl asked, "But… where is Papa?" and saw Kagra's face crumple.

Geyah stood at the edge of the firelight, awaiting

them. "I am so pleased you have returned, my son," she said. "I have not been sure how to handle our visitors."

Durotan was utterly confused. "Visitors?" Why would she call returned children "visitors?"

"There is nothing in the lore about this situation," Geyah continued. "Drek'Thar says they were sent by the Spirits, and considering they have returned our children to us, I have made them welcome."

Durotan had thought he had received more than enough shocks today, but it seemed there was a final one in store for him as he looked past his mother to the three shapes she indicated.

They rose on legs that curved backward like those of a talbuk, standing taller than even the tallest orc. The firelight caught the gleam of horns and illuminated their blue faces and their glowing, sky-colored eyes.

Those faces wore shy, happy smiles.

"Draenei," Durotan breathed.

20

Durotan had only ever caught fleeting glimpses of the draenei. He knew they were tall, and blue, with tails, horns, and hooves. But he had not appreciated how physically intimidating they were, even as they stood, outnumbered in an orcish camp, smiling down at him. The males seemed to be as massively powerful as any orc, and even the female was muscular and toned—and half a head taller than he.

"They saved us!" Nizka said. "When the... the bad orcs attacked us, Papa told us to run. And we did. The draenei found us almost right away!" She looked at Durotan hesitantly. "I thought about running away from them, too, but Papa always said they wouldn't hurt us. And what was chasing us..."

Her voice trailed off and her face crumpled as she recalled the horror. Durotan was relieved that she had been spared the worst of it. She had not had to witness the sight of her beloved father lying butchered like a talbuk in the snow.

He called over Grukag and murmured to him, "Take the children. Give them a draft of starflower, so they may sleep deeply tonight. Tell them only that Nokrar and Gurlak fell. Do not tell them how." Shaksa, at least, would soon need to know, as she was of an age to fight in battle, and deserved to know the truth about her enemy. But the youngest two needed no further horrors to haunt their dreams.

"Say good night and thank your rescuers again, then go with Grukag," Durotan said. Kelgur, the youngest, carried in his mother's arms, reached out to hug one of the draenei females around her long, slender neck. The draenei's face lit up with tenderness, and Durotan shook his head wonderingly. This world, surely, was not as it once had been. For ill... and, at least in this case, for good.

The male draenei had recognized Draka, calling out her name in a rolling, musical tone. She went to him, taking his outstretched hand warmly, and said a few halting words in his language. He made some exaggerated gestures, pointing up at the sky, pretending to run. Now, she listened carefully to his reply and, once the children had left the tight circle around the fire, she spoke.

"Deskaal says that they saw the—" She had been about to say "deserters," but after what had happened, clearly she, like Durotan, could not find it in her to speak ill of them. "They saw Nokrar and the others last night. They knew Red Walkers were in the area, and were worried when they saw *detishi*... children. So they followed, and when the children ran, they were there."

"*Detishi*," Deskaal repeated, and placed his hands over his heart. Durotan recalled Draka's words from a few months past, when they fled Frostfire Ridge: *That is something Frostwolves share with the draenei. They love their children, and would die for them.*

Or risk their lives for any child, he thought. Would we have done the same for them? He knew the answer, and felt a flush of shame.

"*Detishi*," he repeated, imitating the draenei's gesture. "Children."

"*Ch-cheeldrrren*," Deskaal repeated, and nodded. He looked sad and said something else, pointing at the rescued orcs, then shaking his head.

"They regret they could not save the others, but there were only three of them, and they could not risk the lives of the little ones."

"Tell them we understand, and are grateful."

Draka made a wry face. "I'll try." She seemed to succeed, for the draenei looked pleased and smiled warmly at her and Durotan. The draenei had never been the orcs' enemy. Nor were they friends now, not precisely. But right now, that did not matter to him.

"Sit," he told them, suiting action to word, and they did so hesitantly. "Share our food and our fire as thanks for our *detishi*."

Out of the corner of his eye, he saw Geyah

perched on a stone at the very edge of the firelight, her arms crossed in front of her, and a look as hard as stone on her face.

No one was allowed to leave the encampment alone, and the patrols were doubled. The extra tension manifested itself in the clan with arguments, fights, and—due to the need for more patrols to stand guard—fewer hunts, which meant fewer opportunities for food. Still, after the horror of what had happened that night, no one objected.

The spring went from cold and gray to bright and scorching almost overnight. The flat area surrounding the encampment did not have enough green to be properly called a meadow, only here and there erratic patches of shoots stretching forth that were soon scorched by the sun. The lake continued to be unwholesome, and the baking heat—strange this far north—seemed to want to suck it dry. As the water level grew lower, more decayed bodies—mercifully only those of animals—came to light and began to stink.

Thankfully, the spring that had lain hidden beneath the boulder continued to provide water, though it was muddier than it had been in the past. While there was no longer any sign of larger prey, smaller creatures provided enough meat to feed the clan. For now, anyway. Durotan said to Draka once that she was the only orc in the clan getting bigger instead of smaller. Unruffled, she had shot back that if the child she carried did not box Durotan's ears for the comment one day, she'd do so for him—or her. They had laughed and Durotan had pulled her close, and for a time they escaped the world and its troubles in each other's arms.

While there was no longer any talk of leaving the clan or formal challenges to Durotan's leadership, he did not need to hear unhappy words to know his people were suffering. He sought out Drek'Thar, begging him to contact the Spirits and ask what to do. "There is one source of water, and one source of food," Durotan said. "If we lose these, the clan will die. We have no fruit, no grains or seeds. We need aid, Drek'Thar!"

The old orc, who so seldom lost his patience, lost it then. "The Spirits are not wolves to come when we call for them, son of Garad!" Drek'Thar snapped. "They are the essence of the elements, and we are fortunate that they come at all! I am a shaman. My task is to listen to them when they appear, and to tell you, my chieftain, what they tell me. What to do with that information—or what to do when it is not forthcoming—is *your* duty, not mine."

It was true, and Durotan's face grew hot to hear the words spoken so bluntly. But he had exhausted all his options. He called his counselors to him, and held nothing back as he outlined the full gravity of the situation. Orgrim scowled and drew shapes in the dirt with a stick. Geyah sat quietly, her hands folded in her lap, letting her son speak, as was his right. Drek'Thar appeared to be exhausted, and leaned heavily on his staff even though he was seated. Draka sat beside her mate, one hand on her swelling belly, listening and offering silent support.

"The Spirits once sent us a sign in the form of a redjay," Durotan said. He could hear how disheartened he sounded, how he was grasping at the faintest of hopes. "Drek'Thar, have any of your shaman seen anything to guide us? I speak not of visions or messages, but more earthly signs. Ants or birds heading a certain direction, perhaps, or patterns of plant growth?"

Drek'Thar sighed, rubbing his temples as if his head hurt. Palkar spoke in his stead. "We have been paying close attention to what has been growing, as we use the herbs for medicine. We've... well, it's almost as if it's still winter. Or perhaps autumn—I have noticed some mushrooms, and they usually only grow in the fall."

Durotan wondered for a moment how it was that mushrooms, which liked water, were growing when there had been no rain, but he shrugged it off. The shaman seemed unconcerned, and they knew much more about such things than he did.

"I do not care when or where or what mushrooms grow on if I can eat them," Orgrim said. "Can I eat them?"

Palkar shook his head. "I have never seen ones like these before. I would not risk it."

Disappointment knifed through Durotan. Only one thing seemed to be growing, and that might be poisonous. He sighed deeply. "Well," he said, "if something can grow, even if it is of no use to us, perhaps something else will grow, too."

Nothing did. So it was that when word came of a flock of birds passing over to the northeast, Durotan announced that there would be another hunting party assembled to follow them. The birds might be heading to water, and water could mean chances for larger game. If not, at least the archers might be able to shoot a few birds for roasting. It was the most hopeful sign they had seen in some time.

"I will go with you," Draka said when he spoke of the idea.

"Not this time," Durotan said firmly.

"I am as fine a warrior as any you have," she said, and it was true. She might not have the physical strength of an orc male, but she was stronger than any female he knew, and quicker than a snake.

They lay on their sleeping furs, and Durotan rolled onto his side to look at her. "Draka," he said quietly, "I know you can defend yourself. And ordinarily I would say, 'Wife, hunt till the baby drops, and then hand him a spear.'"

She chuckled. "I like that. *She* would take that spear and promptly kill a talbuk."

"I've no doubt *she* would," Durotan said, smiling down at her. The smile faded. "But there seems to be no talbuk for her—or him—to kill. Draka, these are no ordinary times. There are no other females with child but you. I worry enough that you will lose this child to things like poor water and lack of food. To think of a Red Walker attacking you—"

"I understand your fear. I share it. These are troubling times. You are correct—I should not engage in fighting until our child arrives."

Relief washed through him. "So you will not come."

"I will come as an archer, and promise to attack from a distance."

He paused. For a moment he was furious, and then he started to laugh.

The idea of a hunt was well-received. Durotan assembled a group of ten, half of them archers, as they might discover only birds, and there was much laughing and talking as they milled about before departing.

"It almost looks like the old days," Orgrim said. His eyes were on the hunters, saying farewell to their loved ones with smiles instead of grim, determined expressions.

"Nothing looks like the old days anymore," Durotan said. "Still, it is good to see."

Orgrim squinted up at the sun. "We have more sun here than we had in Frostfire Ridge," he said. Durotan had noticed it, too, but had said nothing. What was there to say?

For a moment, he despaired, despite the happy sounds surrounding him. Was this all there was to life? Simply hanging on from one day to the next?

He remembered a childhood full of stories, of play, of sound sleep and full bellies and four full, true seasons. Winter was a lean time, but spring always came. It had been a good childhood. What would his son's—or daughter's—be like? Would he or she even live to see it? He did not tell Draka, but he worried constantly for her, that she was not getting enough of the right food, enough clean water… enough of anything.

He had scorned Gul'dan's offer, understanding that the promise of betterment came with a price and with no certainty. Even Garona had warned him against her master. But what was their life now? There was no certainty here, and he had already paid a grim price.

His people were excited about the opportunity for flesh in their meals, even bird flesh. They needed it. Lack of food was no longer just a hardship—it had become life or death. Durotan suspected that many of the older Frostwolves were sneaking food to the younger clan members, becoming themselves little more than skin and bones, kept alive seemingly only by water and will.

And it was not enough, not even for Frostwolves. Stones to cover bodies were more plentiful than anything growing in the ground, and that bitter harvest grew with each passing day. Since they had arrived, the hitherto flat area now had seventeen cairns. Durotan shook off the gloom. It would not serve him. Who knew what possible bounty awaited them if they followed the flock of birds? The spring was a symbol that there was always hope.

The thought of the spring reminded him. "Send them to fill up their waterskins before we depart," Durotan told Orgrim. "We cannot count on finding fresh water elsewhere."

Orgrim nodded, turning Biter back toward the milling group of wolves and hunters. Most of them went off right away toward the spring. Orgrim lingered behind, waiting for Durotan, who in turn was waiting on Draka.

She was having trouble with Ice. The great wolf sat on his haunches, refusing to allow Draka to mount him. She glanced up at Durotan as he approached her, exasperation plain on her face.

"If it were you," Draka said, "I would cuff him on the ear."

"If it were me, that would be fine." Frostwolves were rough on each other; even displays of affection could leave bruises. But they never laid a hand on the great wolves who bonded with them.

"Maybe you can talk some sense into him," Draka muttered. Durotan went to the wolf that had served his father since puppyhood. He scratched Ice behind his ears and the wolf whimpered, jerking his head away and sniffing the air intently.

Durotan reached to pet him again, and then his hand froze mid-motion. He recalled the awful howling of the wolves on the night when Greatfather Mountain had spewed forth a river of fiery blood, and their home had been destroyed.

He whirled, looking at the other wolves in the pack. Now he saw that all of them seemed to be in some form of distress. Some sat stubbornly, like Ice, forcing their riders to dismount. Others who had ranged further toward the edge of the field were now racing back, ears flat against their skulls, ignoring their riders' protests to halt or turn around.

"*The earth is hungry!*"

The eerie, awful cry barely sounded like Drek'Thar. He had retired to his hut a few hours ago, saying that he felt unwell and needed to rest. Now, he stumbling out unescorted and screaming the single phrase. "*The earth is hungry! The earth is hungry!*"

Durotan spun back toward the hunters. Beside him, Ice yowled and crouched down low. The great wolf was trembling. Durotan cupped his hands about his mouth and shouted, "Come back! *Come back now!*"

Some of the watering party did, turning their wolves back toward the encampment. Some of them tried to, and others found that their wolves, like Ice, were so terrified they wouldn't move.

"*The earth is hungry!*"

And so it was. As Durotan and the rest of the clan watched in sick, helpless horror, there came a low, grinding noise that sounded almost like... *chewing.*

The ground simply vanished beneath four of the clan's hunters and their wolf mounts. They were there, then they were not, and all that remained was a perfect circle, and the desperate shrieks of the dying.

The earth had been hungry, and it had devoured them.

21

Those who were closest to the disaster rushed to lend aid, but the hole continued to widen. More soil, grass, orcs, and wolves toppled in. Durotan saw Grukag scrabbling at the edge for just a moment, his eyes wide and frantic, before the lip crumbled. The hole opened like the massive mouth of some hidden creature.

Those who could scattered in all directions, fleeing the growing sinkhole. Still it widened, and more victims vanished into the depths. Durotan realized that although the hole had opened some distance away, it was expanding so swiftly that the encampment itself was in danger. Others saw it too. Jolted from their frozen horror, they turned and began to run as far away from the monstrous gaping void as possible.

Sharptooth quivered beneath Durotan, suppressing his natural desire to flee. Ice still huddled, refusing to move. Durotan reached out a hand and hauled his pregnant wife onto Sharptooth's back, forced to abandon his father's frost wolf to find his own courage, or die.

As he rode away, Durotan glanced around and saw that others, like Ice, were paralyzed with fear. His clan was a brave one. They faced their foes with courage. But who would have ever thought the earth directly below their feet, the earth that grew food and nurtured them, would become an enemy?

Draka held on tightly. When Durotan thought she would be safe, he lifted her off Sharptooth's back. She uttered no word of protest, sliding down and landing lithely. The life of the child within her was more important to Draka than her pride. But as Durotan wheeled Sharptooth back to try to save others of the clan, she called after him, "Strength and honor!"

She had been an Exile, yet Draka was more of a Frostwolf than any Durotan had ever known. He would return to her, and their child. Grimly he pushed Sharptooth to disobey the clamor of his own instincts, and his friend obeyed. Durotan scooped up Kagra, who clutched Nizka, and raced back to solid ground with them both. Others followed their chieftain's example, conquering their fears and rushing to aid their clan members.

Still the mouth gaped wider, hungry for more. Durotan was reminded of an orc from another clan describing the motion of the sea; the tides that rushed forward, then retreated. Except this "tide" moved only in one implacable direction—outward.

Hungry.

Durotan snatched up more Frostwolves, his wolf never slowing. As he urged Sharptooth back for another run, the chanting of the shaman reached a fevered pitch. Drek'Thar had stretched himself out on the earth and was now silent. Durotan didn't know if that was for good or ill.

He came upon a running little boy—Kelgur. Durotan bent and caught him up with one huge brown arm and the child sprawled in front of him. He wasn't crying; Durotan could see by the blank expression in the boy's enormous eyes he was too frightened for that.

And then—the awful, rhythmic chewing noise stopped. The only sounds were the chanting of the shaman and the howling of the wolves. The wolf song, too, died down, until all that remained were the prayers of the shaman to the Spirit of Earth, begging it to be still, to leave the Frostwolves their lives and their home.

Durotan thrust Kelgur into Kagra's arms and turned to look back, his skin slick with sweat, his lungs heaving for air with exertion and, yes, fear.

Nothing else fell into the gargantuan maw. The earth's hunger, it would seem, was sated.

Quiet sobs of relief went up, marked by keening wails of loss. Durotan's breathing slowed. He saw with a fresh burst of nervous sweat that there was but a few feet of still-solid ground between the hole's mouth and the outlying stones that comprised the encampment.

"Ropes!" Durotan shouted. "We must rescue our fallen brothers!"

"No!" Drek'Thar cried as Palkar helped him up. "Durotan! Where is he? He must not let anyone go near it!"

Durotan and Sharptooth raced over to the shaman. "But they may still be alive!"

Drek'Thar shook his head. "No," he said, brokenly. "Even if they are alive, they are dead. Earth has told me its hunger was too great. It is starving... like we ourselves are starving. The Frostwolves have fallen too deep, and if any survived, Water has borne them away to the dark places in the center of our world. They have become one with the Spirits of Earth and Fire, far beyond our reach. So the Spirit of Earth tells me, and so I believe."

Durotan slipped off Sharptooth's back. For the shaman's ears alone, he asked quietly, "Has the Spirit of Earth become as the Spirit of Fire, then? Turned to destruction?"

His mind went back to something Draka had said, that Midsummer night when she had returned from her Exile. *There is a blight there that is not here, not yet. Sickness. Ugliness. Things not just dying, but being twisted first.*

Drek'Thar reached out blindly for Durotan, who caught his hands in his own. "Fire called out to me, that night," he said. "I heard its cry in time for us to flee with our lives, if not our way of life. But recently, the Spirits' voices have become faint. I do not feel them when I seek them out. Earth tried hard, so hard, to warn us, but I... I could not *hear*..."

The wolves had heard. As wild things themselves, closer to the Spirits even than the orcs who venerated them, they had known. Both times. From this moment on, Durotan vowed, he would look to the wolves for warning as he did to the shaman.

"What has happened to them, Drek'Thar?" Durotan demanded. "To Fire, and to Earth? Are they... are they dead?"

Drek'Thar shook his head. "No, not dead. But silent. And in torment. Even Water's voice is faint, now, and Air... Air is in pain."

A chill brushed Durotan. Water. What could live without water? "What was it you said about Water? That it had borne away the Frostwolves who fell? Taken them to the dark places deep inside Earth?"

"Water," murmured Drek'Thar. "Water. It was Water that made Earth hungry. It was Water that ate away at Earth, beneath the surface, and then Earth needed to feed..."

"The spring," Durotan said. Now, too late, he recalled the sudden increase in mushrooms, which thrived in damp areas. Water had tried to warn them of what it was doing to Earth. Had tried, and failed, and now more Frostwolves and their beloved mounts were gone. Swallowed up as unwitting offerings to Earth's twisted appetite. "We cannot go near the spring, can we?"

"Hole," was all Drek'Thar could say, but the single word told Durotan everything he needed to know.

Orgrim had come to stand beside his chieftain

and friend. Draka was with him. "There is water further north," Orgrim said. "Snow."

"Nothing lives in the snow," said Draka.

Durotan thought hard about what he knew of the north. "Some creatures live," he said. "They must have something to feed on."

"Other creatures," said Orgrim.

Durotan was nodding. "The fox must eat, so there must be rabbits. Mice. And they must eat roots and... and moss. There will be water, and fish in those waters. We will survive."

Palkar had been speaking quietly with Drek'Thar while Durotan spoke with Orgrim. The older shaman seemed calmer, more himself. Now, he spoke up.

"Yes," he said. "We will go north. As north as north can be. We will go to the Seat of the Spirits, as the long-ago Frostwolf chieftain did. We mustn't go south." Drek'Thar shook his head firmly. "The Spirits will not be found there. They are in the north, they have retreated as far as they can. We must retreat there as well." He turned his blind face in Durotan's direction. "My chieftain... perhaps we can help them. Heal them."

Hope surged in Durotan's heart at the words. "Heal the Spirits? It had never occurred to him that perhaps the Spirits themselves needed help. And yet, Drek'Thar had insisted they were in pain.

"How could we possibly help them?"

"I do not know. But if we can..."

"Then," Durotan finished, his voice hushed with awe, "perhaps *they* can heal the world."

22

The shaman's work in soothing the Spirit of Earth had saved the vast majority of the clan. The total loss of life was seven, and thankfully, there were no children among the dead. Mercifully too, there were no sounds from the sinkhole. Durotan was not sure that he would have been able to stop himself or others from attempting a rescue if anyone had been calling for help from the depths.

The hole still loomed, an enormous grave beside the place that had once been a haven for Draka and the draenei. It had been the Frostwolves' home for many months. Now, they would need to press on. Again.

There had been moments when Durotan had revisited his decision to refuse Gul'dan. He knew the whispers were racing around the encampment now, but this time, there was an answer. After the initial wave of grief over the tragedy had passed, and the orcs were calmer, he called them all together and shared what Drek'Thar had said.

"Our wise shaman believes that if we go south, if we join the Horde and ally with the warlock Gul'dan, the Spirits may never be able to speak with us again," he told the listening crowd. "But if we travel north, to the Seat of the Spirits, it may be that we can help them."

"Us? Help the Spirits?" Kagra asked. "Why would they need us?"

"These disasters—the hard winters, Greatfather Mountain, the sinkhole—we thought they came because the Spirits had turned against us. But we were wrong. They've been crying out for us to *help* them. They've been falling ill, somehow. Spinning out of control." He took a deep breath. "Drek'Thar thinks it's possible that they could be dying, the way the grasses and trees are dying"

"What?" cried Shaksa. "How can this be? They are the Spirits of the elements! They cannot die!"

Drek'Thar pounded his staff on the ground. "Listen, please listen to me!" When the clan quieted, he continued. "I am but a humble shaman. I have always listened with open heart, and the Spirits have spoken to me for most of my life. They warned me of the fire-river, and they warned me today, but not in time. Like Fire was, Earth and Water now are sick. And just as Fire did, they are manifesting as tainted and violent. They are asking for our help."

"But... the north," someone muttered.

Durotan stepped forward again. "If beasts can live in the far north, so can Frostwolves," he said. "We will find a way. It will be difficult, but we have no choice. We cannot stay here, and we should not go south."

He looked from face to face. Quietly, he said, "I know you are heartsore," he said. "I know it seems that for the last several years, all we have known is loss. We are forced to keep moving, to keep starting over, each time with fewer friends, or mates, or children. I would surrender my life to give you a place to call home that can truly nourish us. But I do not trust one whom the Spirits do not trust. And I would not see Frostwolves turn away from the Spirits when they cry out for our aid."

They looked up at Durotan with bleak, sad eyes, but he saw heads nodding in agreement. "Good. Then we will gather up all that we may, and on the morrow, we will head north. As north as north can be, to the Seat of the Spirits, just as a Frostwolf chieftain did long ago. And we will go, as always, with honor."

That night, the Frostwolves prepared to leave their homes for the second time. How many lok'vadnods, he brooded, had been written since he had taken over as chieftain? How many since the winters had first starting growing too long?

Action was needed lest he fall too far into a foul mood, and there was plenty to do. First, Durotan held a strategy meeting with his counsel. Geyah, surprisingly, was more than firm on the idea of heading north.

"Your father would do whatever was necessary to take care of the clan," she said, "and we Frostwolves have always been associated with the north. The Seat of the Spirits is mentioned frequently in the scrolls, and while the Spirits are honored by all orcs, we have always had a unique relationship with them. I think we will be glad of this journey."

Drek'Thar nodded in agreement. "We will be able to help one another. The Spirits are in need, and so are we."

Orgrim sighed. "This place was never meant to be a home. I don't know how we will survive in the north, but I do know that with a poisoned lake and a hungry earth, anywhere is better than here."

"Most clans have an ancestral homeland," Draka said, "but not all. Some clans are nomadic, as the scrolls say we once were, following the herd animals they hunt across Draenor during their migrations. I have met a few of them, and I will be happy to show you how they traveled."

Geyah looked at Draka. "You have given me an idea," she said. "I will search through the scrolls, to see if they can tell us anything about our nomadic heritage."

Between Draka's experience and Geyah's research, the clan soon had many ideas for how to make the journey. Geyah found a scroll that contained sketches depicting how the trunks of smaller trees could be fashioned into poles and placed together, touching at the top, wide at the bottom. Other scrolls had different designs for larger buildings to shelter several orcs at once.

"Then, they draped hides about this structure,"

Geyah said. Durotan peered at the illustrations.

"Yes!" Draka confirmed excitedly. "I have seen these! And some of the poles—or, sometimes, the tusks of great beasts—have a second use when they are following the herds," she said. She reached for two small pieces of kindling to show them as she spoke. "They take two of the poles and lay them alongside one another, narrow at the top, wider at the bottom, to form a triangle. The narrow part, here, they strap to their wolves. The ends trail on the ground. And between the poles, they lash an animal skin to hold whatever they want to bring."

"Why not simply lash items to the wolves?" Durotan asked.

"The weight is better distributed," Draka replied, "and this way the wolf can transport things that might be too awkward to be placed atop a moving creature. And over difficult terrain like stones or snow, this is better."

Orgrim looked at the twig construction, then at the scroll, then at the two females. "Durotan," he said, "If we are both killed in battle, as long as the clan has these two, they won't miss us at all."

"I will not say you are wrong," Durotan said.

Armed with this new information, Durotan went from family to family, helping each of them for a while. He laughed at little jokes some of the children told, offered his advice on which weapons to bring and which were beyond repair and should be left behind, and helped them to begin assembling the carry-poles.

The wolves did not like the feeling of having the poles tied to their bodies, but they grudgingly accepted them. The going was slow at first, particularly since they were all too aware that what seemed to be solid earth might open up and swallow them at any moment.

But that did not happen, and the further they traveled from the poorly named "Haven," the lighter Durotan's heart grew. This felt right to him in a way that the flight from Frostfire Ridge had not. Then, they had been forced to run as fast as possible, able to take only a few precious items. They had lost a home they had never imagined leaving, and the winter had been upon them.

Now, they were choosing to leave a place they had never truly felt was home. They had time to pack carefully, and a new method of taking things with them. The days were hot and long, but that was preferable to the icy darkness. Though the clan's number was reduced and the losses greatly mourned, there were enough wolves so that everyone could ride, with a few left over to, albeit with whimpered protest, pull the carry poles. And most important, Durotan thought, they were going *to* something, not simply *from* something.

As he rode in thoughtful silence beside Draka, Durotan's mind raced with ideas for survival. At the Edge of the World, the true, final north, he had heard there was only snow and ice. Was that where the Seat of the Spirits was? If so, the orcs could not live there, but they could travel there temporarily. Just south of this world of ice and snow, though, was a place called the tundra. There, they could live. There, with the blessing of the Spirits, they could make a home.

As the weeks passed, the Frostwolves watched the forests thin, until there were no trees at all. Pausing at one point, Durotan looked about and observed that there was a clear demarcation where the trees ceased to grow—a line, it seemed, they would not cross. Durotan wondered if orcs, too, should cross it—it seemed like such a clear boundary. But Drek'Thar assured him they should press on.

"If there are no trees, what will we burn in the winter?" Orgrim wanted to know.

"We will discover what can burn and what cannot," Drek'Thar assured him. "The Spirits will guide us." He alone of the Frostwolves had seemed to grow in confidence and even physical vigor as they drew ever closer to the elusive Seat of the Spirits. Though he didn't understand it, Durotan respected it, and many a night as they journeyed it was the only thing that allowed him to drift off to sleep.

They rested at the edge of the forest for a few days, replenishing waterskins, carving new poles or spears or arrow shafts, and snaring small rodents.

The song of the frost wolves' wild brethren was heard as the journey progressed, but the answering response deterred any packs from attacking the orcs. Even so, Durotan ordered that everyone should be in armed groups of at least three when they stopped to find water or food. There had been stories of great bears, as white as the frost wolves, who experienced no fear, but their homes were believed to be even further to the north.

The hunters were sent not just to look for prey, but to discover other things that were wholesome to eat. They learned that the strange, hard moss that grew on stones was nourishing when boiled. They learned to observe the white foxes, and set snares where they hunted.

Then, one day, the sky, which had been very clear and almost painfully blue, began to pale as it met the horizon ahead. As they pushed forward, Durotan noticed the wolves sniffing the air more than usual. He inhaled deeply, but could smell nothing amiss.

A few hours later, Drek'Thar frowned. "Is there a fire?" he asked, worry in his voice.

"Not that I can see," Durotan told him, "though there is a whitish haze on the horizon."

"I smell... smoke, but not of a sort that is familiar to me. And I can taste it. Like metal, somehow. Or soil."

Durotan and Draka exchanged worried glances. Durotan urged Sharptooth over to the finest fighters in the clan, Delgar, Kulzak, and Zarka. "You three," he said. "Ride on ahead and report back. Drek'Thar smells smoke, and I think the wolves do, too."

They nodded. "Red Walkers?" Zarka asked.

"Possibly. Whatever it is, I do not wish to take my people there without knowing what we face. Don't exhaust your wolves. Return before sunset."

He gave them a rough smile. "And if what we face is something good to eat, bring it back with you."

They gave him tired smiles in return. "As my chieftain wills," said Kulzak. He and the others urged their wolves ahead of the pack.

They returned well before sunset. There were no birds or small beasts thrown over their wolves, and Durotan's heart sank at their expressions. He rode out to meet them, anxious to hear their report before telling the rest of the clan.

"What is it?" he asked. "Who created the fire?"

They exchanged glances, and finally Delgar spoke. "I would not have believed it had I not seen it with my own eyes, but..."

"Tell me."

"My chieftain... the soil *itself* is on fire."

23

Durotan wanted to rage. To scream. To kill. But he forced himself to shove the fury down, deep inside, and to breathe slowly even as he clenched his fists. "Do you mean a wildfire?" he asked.

They shook their heads. "The smoke... it's coming up from the ground. There were places where the wolves couldn't even walk," Zarka said.

Draka rode up beside him, saying nothing, just giving him strength with her simple, calm presence. Then, unexpectedly, Drek'Thar moved Wise-ear toward the hushed voices. "Is there a path through this burning ground?"

"I—" Zarka looked unsure. "There were some areas where we could go, yes. But—"

"Then we must continue."

"Drek'Thar," Durotan began, "we use soil to put

out a fire. If the soil itself can burn—"

"This is but more of the same, Durotan," Drek'Thar said. "Fire becomes a river. Water turns hot. Air becomes poison. Earth itself burns or swallows us whole, and plants die at the very root. The elements are sick, and they turn upon one another as well as us in their illness. This danger—and I know that it is danger, we have *seen* that it is—is a symptom of something they are begging us to cure. Would you turn your mother away if, in a fever, she were to strike you or say terrible things?"

"Of course not!"

Drek'Thar smiled. "No, you would never do so. You would know she did not intend for these things to harm you, but she was ill and unable to control herself. So it is now with the elements. They are like our parents, our family. They make it possible for us to survive in this world. I understand now that the darker things become, the more imperative it is that we continue to press forward despite our fears, despite the dangers."

Durotan looked back over the clan. He tried to see them, not as he thought of them, but as they truly were, free from the gentling cloud of his love for them. They were painfully thin, bedraggled. Filthy. Their clothing was poor and nearly worn out. Some had no boots, and had merely wrapped scraps of fur around their feet. The children did not laugh and play, but lay unnaturally quiet on the wolves they rode.

They could go no further. Not without hope.

No.

He had kept holding out hope, both for himself and for his people. *We are Frostwolves*, he had told them. *We will endure.* And they had. His heart swelled with pride in them. They had indeed endured, making new things to replace what was lost, creating songs, loving their children, learning to eat the poorest fare imaginable and pronouncing it good.

They deserved better. They deserved more than hope, they deserved everything that he had promised them.

"Drek'Thar is right," he said, his voice raw. "We must press on. For as long as time, the Spirits have taken care of us. And like good children, when they are ill or weak, we must take care of them."

He turned to look at Draka, Orgrim, and Geyah. "But as chieftain, I am also a father to my people. I must look after their needs, as well. And so, Drek'Thar and I will go to the Seat of the Spirits... alone. The rest of you will stay behind, and protect the Frostwolf clan."

"No." Draka's response was swift and strong. "I swore to be by your side, Durotan, son of Garad, son of Durkosh. I will not leave you."

He smiled at her. "And to our child," he said, "I am also a father. I would not take his life before he has had a chance to live it. This time, you will not sway me. I need you and our child here. Orgrim, you as well."

"But—"

"You are my second-in-command," Durotan

said. "You must stay here, with Draka. I do not know what awaits me."

"You sound like you are not planning to return." Draka's voice was controlled, but he could see her trembling. He reached out and took her hand.

"With a wife like you waiting for me? I most definitely *do* plan on returning," he said, teasing her softly. "But I would know that you are safe. All of you."

"You will not ride alone," Orgrim rumbled. "If you forbid me, then I demand that our finest warriors ride along with you and Drek'Thar."

"And me," Geyah said. All heads turned to regard her. More white streaks had appeared in her hair over the last long months, and hardship had etched lines along her mouth and forehead he had not noticed until now. He recalled how the four of them—he, Geyah, Garad, and Orgrim—would ride as a unified front, to then veer off to chase down their targets. Those were good days. Sweet days.

They were days that had gone, and would never return. Wishing would not make the world right again.

But maybe—just maybe—what he and Drek'Thar were doing would. And all of a sudden he understood why Geyah wanted to come with them.

She was a Lorekeeper, in a world where lore now meant nothing. She had made a lifetime practice of honoring the Spirits, and seeing to it that others knew about them and honored them, too. Drek'Thar did this by sharing his visions. Geyah did so with words: not with the original or new words of a first-sung lok'vadnod, but with ancient words, worn to perfection like supple leather.

"Yes," he said, surprising even himself. "You should be part of this, too, Mother." He saw her relax slightly, and wondered, if she had objected to his quest, if he'd have been able to win that particular argument. He suspected not. "And yes to your request, too, Orgrim. It would not do for the possible saviors of the Spirits to fall short of their goal by running afoul of an angry winter bear."

"It would take a little more than that," Draka said grudgingly.

"It would take a whole legion of bears to keep me from returning to you," Durotan said, and he was not teasing this time. He could not imagine an enemy so fierce that he could not slay it, if it would mean being with Draka and his child.

She saw it in his eyes, and her face softened.

"So," Durotan said. "I, Drek'Thar, Geyah, Delgar, Kulzak, and Zarka will ride over the ground that burns to the Seat of the Spirits."

"Do you want to speak to the clan before you depart?" Orgrim asked.

Durotan looked back at his people, and shook his head. "Speeches are to inspire our people to battle, or to comfort them when disaster strikes. This is neither of these times. Tell them only that we have gone ahead, to see what is there. If we do not return, then you know what to do." He looked from Orgrim to Draka. "Both of you. Orgrim—take them back to where we last found clean water. Let them rest until I return."

"It will be done. When should we look for you?"

That, Durotan did not know. "Drek'Thar? Can you tell us?"

The old shaman cocked his head, as if listening to a distant voice. "Not far, not far," he said, almost humming the words. "They know we approach. They are anxious. We must save them. Half a day's ride, no more, to the Seat of the Spirits."

Durotan thought a moment. He had no idea what awaited them. Surely they would need to stay for at least some time. "Three suns at the utmost," Durotan said. "Someone will come. With luck, we will have found a safe, new home. Without it... in four suns, you will be the Frostwolf chieftain."

"I will protect the Frostwolves as you would," Orgrim said, "but you *will* return. Being chieftain would sorely cut into my drinking time." The two exchanged a laugh, though alcohol had been a luxury abandoned with Frostfire Ridge. Then Orgrim turned to the three warriors who would accompany Durotan. "Come," he said, "let us find you some provisions for the journey."

Draka slipped off Ice and looked up at Durotan, confused that he still sat astride Sharptooth. "Will you not dismount and embrace me, my heart?" she asked.

"No," Durotan said. "I will leave that as further incentive to return."

She reached up to him regardless, and they clasped one another's hands tightly. "I can see you are certain of the rightness of this," Draka said.

"I am," he said. "Draka... I believe that all of the trials, all the losses, all our suffering... they were meant to bring us here, to meet with the Spirits."

"Meet with them, you shall," Draka said, "and then come back to your wife."

He leaned down and pressed his forehead to hers, then he let her go.

24

Something had settled in Durotan's soul. Whatever the outcome of this pilgrimage, for such he realized it was, he was content. He had become chieftain during the worst time in this world's history, and had tried to lead as best he could. Now he, together with two shaman, one the eldest of the clan and one its Lorekeeper, would be going where, if legend was to be believed, only one other orc had ever been. And that orc, too, had been a Frostwolf chieftain.

It felt so right, so appropriate, that he found he could lay aside, at least, for the moment, that which had gnawed at him since his father's death: the question of what would happen if he failed.

It was an odd sensation, given their sinister surroundings. Delgar had not exaggerated: the earth itself—not anything on it—was on fire. Devoid of trees and grasses, the ground emitted wisps of smoke that slithered close to the earth like fog. Here and there, Durotan glimpsed glowing patches and the occasional small flame. Breathing was possible, but difficult. There was no sign of snow or ice to offer water or douse the deeply embedded, sullenly smoking fire. His mind wrestled with the idea: how could earth *burn*?

It did not matter. How could a mountain emit liquid fire, or the ground open up beneath them? How could any of these things happen? Drek'Thar had given him the answer: the Spirits were sick.

As they rode, taking care to avoid the smoldering spots, Durotan glanced from time to time at Geyah and Drek'Thar. They, too, seemed calm, with a strangely youthful eagerness about them. Geyah had suggested that Palkar be left behind. She would guide the elderly shaman, she said. It would be less risk, and if for some reason they did not return, Palkar knew most of what both of them did, and would be able to carry on the Lorekeeper tradition.

"What are we looking for?" Durotan had asked Drek'Thar as they had embarked on the journey.

"We will know," Drek'Thar said, somewhat distantly. It was a frustrating answer, but considering the source—the Spirits themselves—Durotan reasoned that it was likely the best answer the shaman could provide.

He tried another tactic, asking his mother about the story of the Frostwolf chieftain and the Stone Seat that was in the scrolls. "While legends are often based on true events," she told him, "the language used to record them is..." She cocked her head, searching for the word.

"Flowery," Zarka grunted. Durotan laughed, and even Geyah had to smile.

"I would say, either embellished or too sparse," she said. "Too sparse, in this case. It is said 'he went as north as north could be, up to the very Edge of the World, and found there the Seat of the Spirits. And there he entered, and there he sat, for three days and three nights, until the Spirits came unto him.'"

"I had forgotten it was that long," Durotan said. "I told Orgrim we'd be back sooner."

Drek'Thar grunted. "Their situation is dire, so I think it is safe to say the Spirits will come to us sooner rather than later. Their needs, and ours, are urgent."

They pressed on, and the sun made its way across the sky. This far north, night would last only a few hours. Durotan wondered if his eyes were dazzled when he began seeing a line of white along the horizon, but then Kulzak said, "Chieftain... I believe that is snow up ahead."

Durotan licked his parched lips. He had been conservative in his consumption of water, not knowing if there would be a fresh source—indeed, *any* source—awaiting them. To see snow and ice was a relief.

Drek'Thar tensed atop Wise-ear's back. "There," he said, and it gave Durotan a chill to see that the blind shaman was pointing directly at the white line.

"They will be there. Beyond the snow and the ice is the Edge of the World."

No one moved. They sat astride their devoted wolf mounts, faces turned as north as north could be, somehow knowing that if they took one more step, everything would change.

Durotan took a deep breath. "Let us not keep the Spirits waiting," he said, and urged Sharptooth forward.

Soon, the wolves' paws fell on snow instead of burning earth. The group drank from their waterskins freely and filled them with clean snow to melt when they stopped to eat from their rations. Delgar had lashed some fuel to the back of his wolf, and fire was quickly lit. They melted the snow and drank it warm, and the heat in his belly heartened Durotan. They ate quickly and poured the rest of the heated liquid into their waterskins; no one wanted to linger, not with the destination so close.

The white snow that marked the horizon began to develop a blue tinge in the center. Durotan heard a strange noise, almost like rhythmic breathing. The wind picked up, and he shivered, drawing his cloak more tightly around his frame as the chill threatened to knife through him. He sniffed the air.

"Salt," Kulzak said.

"We are close," Drek'Thar said, his voice trembling with excitement.

The wolves pricked up their ears, their black, moist noises working at the strange scents, but moved forward at their masters' urging. The snow seemed to change consistency beneath their feet. Durotan looked down, confused. The earth mixed in with the snow was not brown, but pale. He dropped lightly down to pick some up, sifting it through his hand. It felt rough, like ground nuts.

He looked up. The others were staring, silent, out at the horizon. At first, he couldn't understand what they were looking at. He saw white snow, white earth—

—and blue water. Blue water that stretched as far as the eye could see in every direction save the south, behind them. It moved, creating the soft, breathing sound they had heard, and now he recognized it. He had heard the gentler counterpart of this sound, the lapping of lake water. This vast expanse of water had to be the ocean.

Huge, flat chunks of white ice floated atop it. And beyond these, a mountain of white jutted from the sea. The sun was on its downward arc, but still would not set for some time. Light struck the ice mountain at such an angle it reflected off it with searing brightness, and Durotan found he could not look at it directly. Even an indirect gaze caused spots to dance before his eyes.

He knew at once what it was.

No one said anything. Drek'Thar startled them all when he slipped off Wise-ear and, to Durotan's shock, raced heedlessly down to within an arm's length of the highest reach of the water. He lifted a hand and, blind though he was, pointed straight at the ice mountain.

"There," he said. "They await us *there*. They are in danger. We must hurry!"

Durotan spoke very gently. "Drek'Thar, what lies between us and them is a vast stretch of water. It is too cold for us to swim, and we have no boats. How do we get there?"

Drek'Thar's face grew grey as he listened. His body sagged and he dropped to his knees, his head in his hands. "Please," he begged. "Please, Spirit of Water, help us so that we may help you."

The only answer was the implacable, rhythmic sound of the water lapping on the shore.

This can't be, thought Durotan. *We've come so far, endured so much.* He clenched his fists in fury and turned to Geyah, who looked at him helplessly. Zarka, Delgar, and Kulzak stayed silent.

Durotan threw his head back and roared. The sound carried in the clear air, a cry of pure grief and anger and hopelessness, and when his lungs were empty, he inhaled a great gulp of the frigid air and bellowed, "Spirits! Hear me! Fire, *you* destroyed our village! Earth and Water, *you* swallowed our people! We have marched across dead ground that burns and taste air that we can barely breathe. We see Life dwindling all around us, as our own numbers dwindle. And even so, even with all that you have done to us, you asked us for our aid, and we have come. Where are you, then? *Where are you?*"

The last words echoed and then died, until only the sound of the wind remained. Durotan slumped against Sharptooth's side. Geyah went to him and gently touched his shoulder.

"My son," she said, her voice trembling, "behold."

Durotan lifted his face from the warm, rough comfort of the wolf's fur and gazed with dull eyes. "I see what I have seen before," he sat, flatly. "The blue water, too cold and deep. The ice mountain, out of our reach. The chunks of—" His eyes widened. He stepped away from Sharptooth, staring at the water.

The great, flat pieces of ice were moving. Not simply rocking in the water, but moving purposefully toward the shore, as if they were rafts of logs being steered by an unseen hand. The hairs at the back of his neck prickled as he realized that was exactly what they were.

The Spirits had sent them a way to cross.

Geyah smiled up at her son, looping her arm through his as she guided him, almost in a daze, to the shoreline. Zarka was describing the scene to Drek'Thar, who beamed and stood up straight and tall, lifting his staff in a salute to the Spirits, who had not deserted them after all.

Durotan stared at the natural raft. It bumped up against the shore with each gentle wave, awaiting them. The orcs looked at one another, humbled. Durotan, their chieftain, stepped forward first. He called Sharptooth to him, but the wolf would not come. It looked anxiously at the ice floe, ears unhappily flat, whimpering.

Durotan made a decision. "I dislike leaving you here, but I would dislike it even more if you panicked and we all fell into the water," he said. The other wolves, too, looked more than willing to be left behind. Besides, this might give them a chance to hunt something to eat. They would not travel out of earshot, and would come quickly enough when the orcs returned. Durotan gave his friend a pat, and turned to step onto the ice floe.

It bobbed dangerously, and he froze, letting it settle. He reached out a hand to Geyah. Zarka and Kulzak each took one of Drek'Thar's arms, guiding him carefully. Delgar was the last to step onto the ice.

There were no poles with which to steer the "raft," nor were any poles likely to reach the bottom of this water. But Durotan did not worry. He let his shoulders relax and his heart open as the ice floe now moved against the direction of the waves, borne swiftly on the dark blue toward the glittering, towering mountain that housed the Seat of the Spirits.

Durotan found himself having to crane his neck as the blue-white peaks rose in his field of vision. It was like nothing he had ever seen before. Even Greatfather Mountain, when snow wrapped him in its white blanket, had not looked like this. Durotan wondered if this were truly a mountain at all, or if this entire sacred site were completely carved out of ice.

Their raft slowly came to a halt, and the Frostwolves jumped off onto the snow with great care, lest they capsize their transport. In this environment, to become wet was to become dead. Up ahead, an entrance into the heart of the ice beckoned. Piles of snow, each half as high as an orc, seemed to mark a trail leading up to it. Durotan did not expect to be able to glimpse inside—a cave ought to be dark, after all—but he found to his surprise that this one was not.

A soft gasp of pure awe and reverence escaped him. The Seat of the Spirits was painted in every shade of blue his mind could imagine, and some he had never dreamed of. He saw the faint glow of other colors, and wondered what magic had illuminated it. It pulled at something deep in his bones and his soul.

He realized he had been wrong when he had thought the Frostwolf ancestral home destroyed when the fire-river washed so cruelly over Frostfire Ridge. *This* was their true home.

Durotan dragged his gaze from the beautiful, luminous opening and turned to Drek'Thar, gently placing his hand under the older orc's arm to guide him. Drek'Thar smiled sightlessly at him and began to speak. Then he froze as if he had been turned to stone, his mouth still hanging open.

"Drek'Thar?" Durotan asked anxiously. "What is wrong?"

"They… something is not right." He groaned and pressed the heels of his hands to his temples, grimacing.

"Are they in danger?" Durotan asked. He glanced at Geyah, who shrugged helplessly. The others all drew their weapons, but looked about uncertainly. There was no sound of an enemy, no telltale scent. All was white, and cold, and still, and clean.

"No, no, no," moaned Drek'Thar. "They say… *we* are!"

There was a flurry of motion. Something erupted

from the snow hummocks Durotan had thought were markers, their pristine whiteness now a vile riot of colors: the gray-black of animal-fur cloaks, the blinding yellow-white glint of the sun striking metal, the revolting hue of dark, dried blood covering screaming faces as the Red Walkers—who, Durotan realized with sick horror, had been expecting them—attacked.

25

For a precious and irrecoverable heartbeat, the Frostwolves were so stunned they did not move. It cost them dearly. Delgar was the closest target, and he had barely lifted his axe when a hammer smashed into his skull. Durotan's focus was heightened and he saw every detail—the shape of the hammer's head, the mottled colors of black and red on the Red Walker's hand, how the chunk of stone descended, and the look of shock on Delgar's face before that face was obliterated.

The snow had masked their scent, but now that the Red Walkers had revealed themselves, their stench assaulted Durotan's nostrils like an enemy itself. He choked on the smell, coughing and turning to position Drek'Thar behind him. He heard the shaman calling out to the Spirits for aid, but there was no time to squander waiting to see if the ailing Spirits would help them now. Delgar had already lost his life; his blood was pumping out on the snow, turning it into a puddle of steaming brown fluid.

On instinct, Durotan raised Sever just in time to stop a crashing blow. He let his legs bend slightly, allowing the Red Walker's momentum to carry him a step too far. Stepping away, Durotan used the full force of his turning body, Sever an extension of his massive, powerful arms, as he sliced almost entirely through the Red Walker. Fresh blood poured from the wound, spilling over the dried crust of a victim's blood as the Red Walker stumbled. His hammer fell from his limp hands and his eyes glazed over. He was dead when he hit the snow.

Geyah had brought a spear, and, despite her age, was whirling as deftly as she danced beside the Midsummer bonfire. The length kept her foe's mace away from her, and her smaller frame enabled her to move more swiftly than he could. The Red Walker lunged, trying to smash her weapon as if it were a twig, but before the massive club could shatter the spear, Geyah's weapon had found its mark in his throat. He gurgled, and his body spasmed as Geyah yanked the weapon free and turned back to the fray.

Drek'Thar was still chanting. One of the Red Walkers spotted him and snarled. The gesture cracked the old blood on her face and small flakes of gore fluttered to the snow. She and two other Red Walkers headed straight for Drek'Thar.

"Drek'Thar!" Durotan shouted, but the shaman

ignored him. He stood as if rooted to the earth, his blind face turned toward his enemies. Then, as Durotan watched, fully expecting to see this orc whom he revered above all others cut down before his horrified gaze, Drek'Thar lifted his staff, uttered a string of words Durotan didn't understand, and brought the staff down.

With a groan that sounded like it issued from a living throat, a zigzag crack appeared in the snow. It grew wider and wider, opening like a hungry mouth, and the three Red Walkers toppled into it. Their screams echoed for a long time before they were silenced.

Durotan caught Zarka's and Kulzak's eyes. With one mind, the three of them went after the two remaining Red Walkers, hacking and screaming at them, driving them back until they, too, toppled into the fissure.

"Durotan!" It was Geyah's voice, from inside the entrance to the Seat of the Spirits. "There are more in here! *Hurry!*"

Durotan threw Drek'Thar an agonized glance. "Drek'Thar, the fissure is an arm's length in front of you. I cannot find a way to cross!"

"Kill our enemies! I will be all right out here!" Drek'Thar called back. And after seeing the very earth crack open in response to the shaman's plea, Durotan believed him.

"We will return for you!" he promised, and raced after Kulzak and Zarka into the cavern.

It was heart-stoppingly exquisite, even more so

than the first glimpse had promised, but Durotan could spare no thought for beauty. He was focused on the ugliness, the obscenity of the presence of Red Walkers in this hallowed place. He permitted bloodlust born of righteous fury to fill him, to guide his hand, as he bore down upon them.

He felt blood spatter his face, tasted it in his mouth. His arm seemed to only grow stronger as he swung, parried, struck... *severed*. He heard the sound of battle all around him, the cries of triumph, the death rattle in the throat, the crack of breaking bones and skulls, and the spurt of blood and slither of entrails.

At last, it was done. Durotan whirled, seeking out new enemies, but they all lay stiffening on the icy floor. Panting, he lowered his arms, only now aware that they quivered with exhaustion. Everything was still, so still, in the cavern.

He looked for his comrades. Geyah looked drained, but as her eyes met his, she smiled. Kulzak stood nearby, also taking stock of the situation. Just as Durotan had turned to hasten to Drek'Thar, the old shaman entered, escorted by Zarka.

"How...?" began Durotan.

"The fissure closed when it was no longer needed," said Drek'Thar simply, as if such a thing were not astounding. Then again, this was the Seat of the Spirits.

The wonder of the place struck him all over again. He thought of the tale of that long-ago chieftain's visit. The exploits of the clan's hero had been the focus, and the Spirits themselves portrayed as giving in to the stubborn Frostwolf's will. Durotan now understood that, if that chieftain had been kept waiting for three days and three nights, it would have been an easy thing, with so much beauty to feed the senses.

The cavern they were in was only the beginning. Another entrance at the back of the ice chamber told them where they needed to go, and Durotan once again felt himself called to wander down its softly radiant passages. He could see now that the illumination came not, as he had first assumed, from the stones embedded in the soil, but from the lichen that grew on their surfaces. So much ice gave much reflection, so that each eerily glowing patch lit up a wide area.

And then, Durotan felt pain replace the wonder. The Red Walkers—and the Frostwolves—had shown the ultimate disrespect to the Spirits by shedding blood here.

"How could this have happened?" Geyah asked aloud, pained even more than her son.

"It looks as though they have lived here for a while," Kulzak said, shoving a corpse with the toe end of his boot.

"They came when the Spirits were at their weakest," Durotan said. As he spoke, he felt the outrage gather again in his chest, like some physical thing that sat there, hunched and smoldering. "The Spirits could not defend themselves. Drek'Thar, do you think this was why they called for help?"

Could it have been this simple—yet this brutal? Had the Frostwolves been needed only to remove the ugly stain that was the Red Walkers from this sacred place?

"I do not know," Drek'Thar said, frowning. "They still clamor for us." He cocked his head. "For me... and for Geyah."

Durotan understood. He could not say he wasn't disappointed. But he accepted that the Spirits would need to speak more with their shaman rather than a clan leader. Perhaps this was a rebuke as well, for defiling their Seat with bloodshed.

"Go. We will stay here and do what we can to purify this outer sanctum."

Geyah slipped her arm through Drek'Thar's and led him away, moving slowly so as not to slip on the ice-slicked earth. Durotan watched them go, envious. But he had another task, hopefully one as pleasing to the Spirits. He, Zarka, and Kulzak turned back and looked at the carcasses.

Durotan looked down, his lip curling in disgust, at the filthy, blood-covered bodies of the Red Walkers.

"We have always burned our honored dead, who fell in battle. When we could no longer do so, we mindfully gathered stones to cover their bodies. This is how we show respect. These... *things* do not deserve such treatment. We will feed them to the water's creatures," he said. He could think of nothing more offensive to an orc than to slowly bloat and decay in the water while being nibbled upon by small fish.

"Ha! Fitting," Kulzak said, nodding approvingly. "What about Delgar?"

Durotan grew somber. "He fell outside, his blood pouring onto the snow. It is in the snow that we will bury him. But let us remove these foul things from the Seat of the Spirits."

"At once," Kulzak readily agreed. He reached down and grasped the legs of one of the Red Walkers, preparing to drag it out, but Durotan stopped him.

"No," he said, wishing he could say otherwise but having no choice. "We must carry them out. Their blood must not be allowed to further desecrate this place."

The other two looked as unhappy as he felt, but did not argue. Durotan grimaced as he lifted a body in his arms, bringing the dead flesh within inches of his nose and feeling the blood smear his leather armor. It was vile, *they* were vile, and he was pleased to give them so dishonorable a resting place. He hoped the Spirits would approve.

They moved all the bodies outside, and then, one by one, heaved them into the icy depths. The corpses were wearing mismatched armor, no doubt scavenged from the draenei and orcs they had first butchered and then consumed. Durotan could not help but shudder at the image as he watched the hideous bodies, thus weighted down, sink without a trace.

No one had suggested taking the armor for themselves. A Frostwolf would prefer death to wearing the armor of a Red Walker.

These monsters had met a more honorable end than their dishonorable lives had deserved. Durotan nodded, satisfied. Disposing of the carcasses had been the easy part. Now, he, Zarka, and Kulzak turned their hands toward the task of purifying the area.

They began with the outside area first. They scooped up the blood-touched snow and earth, using items they found inside such as baskets and other containers, and emptied it all into the accepting waters. After this was done, they covered their fallen comrade with clean snow. Here, near the Spirits, Delgar would rest, his grave an oblong mound of pure white.

Solemnly the three moved into the large, ice-embraced chamber, into which the violence had spilled. Durotan took a moment to look around, trying to determine how best to proceed.

He frowned. Something was not right here. For a moment, he was tempted to brush away the feeling. Of course something was not right—the sanctity of this place had been violated. But it wasn't that. It was something else.

The Red Walkers had been hiding here, perhaps because they were feeding, in a way, on the Spirits' energies. The camp was somewhat more orderly than he would have expected from these crazed creatures. It looked, truth be told, like an ordinary orcish encampment. There were sleeping furs, clothing, weapons...

...many weapons.

Many sleeping furs.

Too many.

And suddenly, with all the visceral impact of a blow to the gut, Durotan realized what the Red Walkers' true plan had been.

26

There were steps carved into the layers of first ice, then rock, forming a narrow, winding path. The lichen on the walls provided sufficient illumination as they passed, but up ahead was utter darkness. Drek'Thar's grip on Geyah's arm was strong but trusting. She knew she was not as good a guide as Palkar, who had spent years tending to Drek'Thar, but she was careful and patient, pausing as he felt ahead with his staff for each step.

Geyah was well aware that the shaman was anxious to open himself to the Spirits and give them whatever aid they needed—although she was baffled by the thought that such powerful entities needed anything at all from a small, isolated orc clan. It was humbling… and alarming.

Down they went, through the twists and turns of

their peculiar path, and she felt the air grow warmer. She thought she heard a faint sound, strange after the constant silence.

"Water," Drek'Thar said, his ears identifying it more quickly than hers. "A spring, of some sort, it sounds like." Geyah thought of the melted snow they had drunk, and her mouth was suddenly parched at the thought of a bubbling spring. How cool and clean the water would be, tasting of the minerals of the earth.

They kept going. The air began to feel fresher on their faces, and after another turn, the stairs opened onto a vast underground chamber.

Geyah gasped.

"Tell me," Drek'Thar said, his voice almost, but not quite, begging.

Geyah blinked. The chamber above had been astoundingly beautiful, but what opened up to her here made the ice cavern look like a dark, dingy hut. She began to speak, trying her best, knowing she could not adequately describe the wonder.

The chamber was underground, but not made of ordinary dirt or stone. It had been carved, if such a word could be used, out of what appeared to be solid crystal. It still gave the appearance of ice: blue and white and a thousand shades in between, smooth and cool to the touch. But, impossibly, so far away from the sun, this chamber, this... grotto was still so full of light that her eyes blinked as they grew accustomed to it.

Before her stretched a blanket of healthy, green

grass, dotted here and there with flowers of every color. In the center, the spring which had revealed its presence to them with its cheerful sound splashed and sang. Geyah wondered if she were beholding the last grass and flowers in the world. Beside the spring were apples, berries, pears, cherries, all manner of fruit. She described them to Drek'Thar, but there really was no need: both of them could smell the heavenly scent and Geyah's mouth, parched just a moment ago, now flooded with moisture as hunger stabbed at her. Nestled in a corner was what seemed to be a welcoming hearth fire, but as Geyah looked at it, she saw no smoke rising, nor did the fire seem to require any fuel. Yet the flame flickered and danced cheerfully.

When she had finished speaking, Drek'Thar inhaled swiftly. His hand squeezed her arm. "We must first cleanse our faces and hands of the blood we have shed. Then, we are invited to partake of the food and water offered by Earth and Water, to warm ourselves beside Fire's gift, and breathe deep of the sweet, fresh Air. All these things will nourish us. And then—we must listen."

Moving in a daze, Geyah guided Drek'Thar to the water. She dipped her hands in and then, almost as if driven, frantically scrubbed at her skin until all the blood, all the taint from the Red Walkers, was gone. The water took the old blood and sweat and soil into itself. For a moment, the pool was cloudy and dark, and then all the soil began to disappear until the spring was as clear as if it had never been sullied.

Drek'Thar unwrapped the cloth that hid his eyes

from the world. Geyah had known the shaman when he still had his sight, but since the wolf attack he had been careful not to show his ravaged face to anyone but Palkar. Her heart ached as she saw her friend's face for the first time since that awful battle. She gazed at the puckered scars, the ruination of one eye, the blank gaze of the other, as Drek'Thar bathed his hands, arms, and face. For one breathless, hopeful moment, she wondered if the Spirits would restore Drek'Thar's vision, but all she saw on his face was a gentle easing of tension and a soft smile.

Tears stung her own eyes as she cupped her purified hands and gulped down the water. Cool and sweet, it quenched her thirst and calmed her as she drank, then she reached for the fruit nestled in the grass. Famished though she was, she almost did not wish to eat it, it was so perfect.

Drek'Thar sat back, water streaming from his face. "Give me your hand, old friend," Geyah said, and placed a blood apple, red and round, into his palm. They ate in grateful silence. The apples were juicy and crisp, the berries so ripe they all but burst on the tongue. Geyah did not want to leave. Well could she imagine the Frostwolf chieftain of legend more than happy to sit and wait upon the arrival of the Spirits.

The food sated their hunger more rapidly than was natural, but Geyah did not question that. She took Drek'Thar over to the fire, and they held out their hands to the flames, knowing somehow that even were they to walk into its center, here, in this place, it would never harm them.

"The Spirits..." Drek'Thar began, then frowned as a shadow fell over his naked face. "The... the *Spirit* of Life wishes to speak... to both of us."

He sank down by the fire almost as if his legs had given way. Concerned, Geyah caught his arm, but he waved her off and stretched out on the soft green grass. He reached for her hand, guided it to his heart, then covered it with his other hand.

He opened his mouth. And although it was his voice, Geyah knew instantly that it was not Drek'Thar speaking. A shiver ran through her.

"Once before have the Frostwolves come," said the Spirit of Life. "They came with an arrogance that was endearing in its innocent ignorance of all the complexities of the world. And we, Earth, Air, Fire, Water, and Life, gave a blessing to the Frostwolves. Stubborn and strong, you have honored us ever, even when others used our powers for their own."

Geyah realized that any questions fell to her to ask. She was not prepared, as she had assumed Drek'Thar would be the one speaking to the Spirits. Instead, he spoke *for* them. She desperately hoped her questions were the right ones.

"Spirits, Drek'Thar has said you are in need of our help. We have come. What may we do, to thank you for aiding us for so many generations?"

"You have come, and here, at the end, you have cleansed our sacred place. For that, we are grateful. But you are too late, Lorekeeper," said Drek'Thar's voice, with such a deep sense of sorrow that tears filled Geyah's eyes and spilled down her cheeks.

"The Blooded Ones remembered the old legends, and came to claim our Seat for their own. We were able to defend this, the heart of our Seat, but even though they could not enter here, they drained us greatly. We have been dying, slowly, and now we are all but gone. We reached out to all the Draenor shaman. We begged for aid. Most could not hear us. Some did, but they turned away their faces, unwilling to believe what was truly happening. Still others rejected us outright, choosing to follow Gul'dan and his warlock magic of death instead of us, and our magic of life. You, the Frostwolves, almost heard us in time. Almost," the Spirit of Life said sadly, its borrowed voice trailing off. "But this one, even wise as he is, did not fully understand."

"This can't be true!" Geyah felt her heart cracking in the middle of her chest. "I see Fire, Water, Earth, all here, now—you *cannot* be dead!"

"Not dead," the Spirit of Life assured her. "But weak. Too weak. First Fire, then Earth and Water. Air still holds on, but barely. Life will be the last to let go and surrender."

Surrender? How could a Spirit *surrender*? None of the scrolls had prepared her for this. Not a single legend, or phrase, or teaching, or ritual. Her panicked heart fluttered in her ribcage like a trapped bird. She trembled, clinging to Drek'Thar's limp hand as if to a lifeline.

"You... you are forsaking us? What will we do?" She suddenly recalled Drek'Thar's words on the night of Garad's pyre, the night her son would become chieftain: *Be judged by the Spirits our people have honored since time began, and which will be, even when we are forgotten and no mouths sing our names.*

Anger abruptly replaced fear and she demanded, "If it was too late, then why have you called us here? Just to sit and watch you all *die*?"

Drek'Thar's voice was gentle as it spoke the words of the Spirit of Life. "No, dear one. You have always been strong. Drek'Thar has always been devoted. Your clan will need this. You must be sure to stay with them. We do not die, as you understand the term. But neither can we continue to aid you. You have listened, and come to us, and have purged us of the barbarism that was the Red Walkers. We wished you to know that wherever there is earth, air, fire, water, and life… there also are we, even if we are no more."

"This makes no sense!" shouted Geyah. She realized she was sobbing. "I do not understand!"

"You will," the Spirit of Life promised. "But for now, we must go, and conserve what little is left to us. Your clan will have a final gift from us, and you will need it. Your son needs you now, Geyah. Go to him. Hurry. And… do not forget us."

Drek'Thar's chest fell with an exhalation of breath, and then rose again. But this time, Geyah somehow realized that the Spirit of Life was no longer speaking through him.

"Drek'Thar, did you—"

"Yes," he said, sitting up. "I heard everything.

And I felt..." He shook his head. "I will tell you later. But for now, what I felt was the Spirit's urgency. Durotan needs us—now!"

They went up the steps faster than they had come down. Drek'Thar and Geyah were fueled by fear and urgency. As they neared the top, a hand shot out and seized Drek'Thar's arm, hauling him up the last two steps.

Durotan, who had always, ever, been respectful of his elders, now grabbed Drek'Thar and Geyah both. His eyes were wild, full of fury—and fear.

"This was a trap," he said. "*Dozens* of Red Walkers have been living here. Only a few of them stayed behind to delay us so that the rest of them could go on ahead."

Still reeling from the words of the Spirit of Life, Geyah asked, "Go ahead to where?"

Durotan's face contorted in anguish as he spoke words that nearly broke her.

"To destroy the Frostwolves."

27

"Did they tell you anything that could help us?" Durotan persisted, looking from Drek'Thar to Geyah and back. He tried not to stare at Drek'Thar's face, which he had never seen before. Somehow, despite all logic, he felt the shaman would know.

"The Spirit of Earth said that they would grant us a final gift," Drek'Thar said.

Durotan felt the blood drain from his face. "Final?"

Despite the terrifying implications of his words, Drek'Thar looked curiously placid. He shook his head and said, "There is too much to tell now. And none of it will matter if the clan is exterminated. We must go, right away, and trust in the word of the Spirits, and hope that we are not too late. The Red Walkers have been living here for some time. They have absorbed some of the Spirits' energies."

"They outnumbered us, and yet we defeated them with few injuries," Zarka pointed out. "They fought well enough, but they did not seem so strong to me."

But Durotan understood. "Think, Zarka. They left their weakest behind."

Her eyes widened.

"We will overtake them," Durotan reassured her—and himself. "We have wolves. They do not. Come. Let us spill more of the blood of those who would wear ours."

The ice floe was there, awaiting them. While it still amazed Durotan to be ferried across the water in such complete safety, he was chafing against any restraint. And, as the further shore came into clearer view, he beheld a sight that caused him to drop to his knees in despair. Beside him, Kulzak let out a cry of pain.

Six white shapes could be seen on the white snow; shapes that reminded Durotan of the snow-hidden Red Walkers who had ambushed them. Except these white forms were furred, and far too still.

"What do you see?" asked Drek'Thar.

"Our friends," said Durotan in a broken voice. "The Red Walkers have killed our wolves."

The pain was twofold; first, and most pressing, they now no longer had an advantage over the murderous cannibals who were bearing down on their clan. But more than that, each of them had lost an ally—as Durotan had said, a friend. He had loved Sharptooth.

But Drek'Thar was shaking his head. "No," he said. "Not dead. Not yet. Not all."

How could he tell? Durotan could see no sign of movement from any of the still, white shapes. Then one of them lifted its head weakly before it fell back onto the snow. Hope surged in Durotan, and he leaped onto the bank and rushed to Sharptooth. His old friend whimpered, and Durotan's heart broke as the wolf tried to wag his tail.

Durotan cocked his head as if listening. "One is dead. Two I fear are past saving," Drek'Thar said. "Three yet live that the Spirit of Life will permit me to heal. The Red Walkers do not have mounts, but because of the time they have spent here, they are unnaturally swift. You will not catch them, but you will not be far behind them, either. You will be able to lend your might to the battle."

"But... three wolves cannot carry five," Kulzak said. "Not if they are still recovering, and not for so long a run."

"They will have to," Durotan said shortly.

"No," Drek'Thar said quietly. "I will stay behind, and keep the dying frost wolves company. I will be all right. The Spirit of Life assures me of this."

Durotan was torn. He wanted to order Drek'Thar to accompany them, but knew in his heart that Kulzak was right. "Tell me what you think is best, Drek'Thar, and I will obey. You have spoken with the Spirits, not I."

Drek'Thar moved forward. Wise-ear scented him and made a sad little sound. Drek'Thar placed his hands on his old friend's muzzle, opening it slightly, and gently breathed into the wolf's mouth. Durotan watched, awestruck, as the wounds in the beast's sides closed. A few heartbeats later, Wise-ear leaped up, whining and licking his master's face.

Next, Drek'Thar's hands reached for Sharptooth, and Durotan exhaled in relief as the wolf responded, bounding toward Durotan excitedly. Last was Drift, Zarka's wolf. Sadly, Durotan regarded his mother. She knelt beside Singer, who had been her companion for most of Durotan's life. Now she held the beloved wolf's head between her hands, looked deep into the golden eyes, and murmured, "Thank you." To Drek'Thar, she said, "Ease him into the final sleep," then she rose.

There was no weakness in weeping for one's wolf companion. The bond was strong, true, and lifelong. The weakness, Durotan thought, would be in failing to weep. He vaulted atop Sharptooth's back and extended a hand to Geyah.

"Ride with me, Mother," he said, "and we will use the Spirit of Life's gift to save our clan."

She leaped up behind him. As he crouched low over Sharptooth's neck and said, "Run, my friend," Durotan could only hope that, few as they were, they would be in time, and able to help.

"Do not sulk," Draka told Orgrim.

"I am not sulking," Orgrim said, "I am contemplating."

She folded her arms and regarded him as he rewrapped the shaft of the Doomhammer. "You are sulking. I am, too. We are warriors, and we do not do well when we are not allowed to be such."

"It is not that," Orgrim said. Then he smiled ruefully. "Well, not *just* that. Durotan does not understand how strong a leader he is. He has been what the clan needs in this strange and terrible time. I worry that if anything happens..." He gestured to the Frostwolves around him. Most of them, as he was, were performing tedious chores of maintenance. Some of the children were playing with the wolves, who mock-growled and harmlessly snapped the air around them. "Could I lead them, as he did?"

Draka sat next to Orgrim, still awkward in her changing, larger body. The child would be born within the next two moons. She had been feeling it kick for some time now. The child of Draka and Durotan would be a strong one, she knew. She only hoped that she would not have to raise it alone. Ice was never far, and when he saw his master sit, he plopped down beside her and laid his head on his paws.

"The answer is no. You could not lead as he does." One hand wandered to the swell of her belly. "You are not Durotan. You are Orgrim. Of course you would lead differently. The question becomes: would you lead well?"

He looked at her then. Draka had observed him since she had returned from her Exile, and she knew, as her husband must, that beneath Orgrim's hulking size and bluff attitude, there was a fierce and complicated mind. And a good heart. "And the answer to that question is: yes. I believe you would lead well." She punched his arm. "But not for a long time. Right now, you get to lead a Frostwolf clan that is resting and repairing their armor and clothes. Are you up to that challenge, Orgrim Doomhammer, son of Telkar, son of Ruvash?"

He laughed heartily. "Durotan chose well when he chose you."

"That he did."

"Well," he said, "no one has died yet from mending and sitting, so I believe I am an excellent chieftain." He finished the wrapping and hefted the Doomhammer, feeling the new leather against his callused, thick fingers. "I feel the need to move. To fight. I wish to destroy some terrifying rocks."

"Rocks?" Draka feigned horror. "Truly, you would make an admirable chieftain, to wage battle against so solid an enemy. I promise we will sing a lok'vadnod for—"

A low growl interrupted her. Ice's head was up and his ears were swiveled forward. Draka rose, shielding her eyes from the glare of the sun, and looked where the wolf was staring. She could glimpse a blur on the horizon.

It could not be Durotan's return. The wolves would know his scent, and if they reacted at all it would be to go greet the party.

It seemed as if Orgrim was about to discover how well he could lead the Frostwolves after all.

28

By now, others had noticed the distant figures as well. They were all on their feet, calling their agitated wolves to them. Draka fully expected Orgrim to attack immediately, without identifying who—or what—was approaching, but he did not.

"Lugar," he shouted, "Krogan—ride with me!" He shouted for Biter, and the wolf appeared, snarling and seemingly eager for a fight. Draka turned to mount Ice, but Orgrim's voice halted her. "Draka, you stay here," he ordered. "Protect yourself and your child."

She whirled on him. "I am a Frostwolf! It is an honor to fight for my clan, and die if I must!"

"Durotan does not think so, nor do I. I will face whatever is out there before I tell him I let his wife and child rush out to battle. I will *never* let harm come to you or the baby, Draka, not if I can prevent it. Know that as truth. Stay and defend yourself, as I know you can, but leave this first line of attack to others!"

She roared in frustrated fury, but she had to admit he was right. While every clan member would lay down his or her life to protect Draka's unborn child, she could not make that sacrifice herself. Cursing, she sought her bow and arrow. She spied a small round shield and an idea flashed into her head. Seizing the shield, she strapped it around her swollen belly.

"There, little one," she said, "protection." She leaped onto Ice and, using only her muscular legs, steered him indirectly toward the approaching threat, veering slightly off to the side. At that moment, Orgrim shouted something that froze her to her bones.

"*Red Walkers!*"

For a moment, she couldn't breathe. In the back of her mind, Draka had always known the Red Walkers would come for them. In her dreams, she would relive the memory of coming across Nokrar's mutilated body. The sight was branded into her brain. She would never have wished for them to descend upon the encampment, but now that they had, she saw her opportunity to expunge that memory once and for all. *We will put an end to them,* Draka thought fiercely, and channeled the frisson of fear into hot, gleeful bloodlust.

A cursory glance told her that the Red Walkers outnumbered the Frostwolves at least three to one, perhaps more. But they had no wolves, and they were attacking the last bastion of a clan that had nothing to lose. Her lips curved around her tusks with a smile. With Ice at a dead run, Draka nocked the arrow, raised her bow, and fired.

The first arrow caught a Red Walker in his eye, and he dropped. The second caught one in her unprotected throat. She fell to her knees, clawing at the wound, then toppled. Draka noticed how heavily muscled these Red Walkers were, compared to the ones they had encountered earlier, and to their own hunger-worn bodies. They moved quickly, easily, without tiring. Had their horrifying choice of sustenance proven so abundant?

Draka heard an arrow whizz past her with the sound of an angry insect and cursed herself. She had been so angry, she had lost focus. If they had archers as well, she would need to be more careful—and she would do her best to take them out first.

She ceased firing, bringing Ice around in a broad sweep to assess the situation. She was not surprised to see Orgrim Doomhammer more than holding his own. Draka knew that to fight with a hammer, one had to attune oneself to it, to maximize the arcs. It was almost like a dance as Orgrim let his body follow where the Doomhammer went. He had to keep moving, or else he would stumble over the corpses he piled up.

Some of the Frostwolves were down. A quick count told Draka that no fewer than three of the great wolves had been killed, their crimson blood staining their white fur. Their riders, though, were alive, albeit injured. Draka frowned, even as she lifted her bow again and sought another target.

One Red Walker was fighting his way directly toward Orgrim. He stood almost a full head taller than any of the others, and moved with an implacable sense of purpose. His head was shaved bald save for a single swinging braid, stiff with blood. He wore only the barest scraps of armor, choosing instead to reveal a broad chest and powerful arms that, like the braid, had been coated in blood. It was as if, Draka thought, he did not care who attacked him. *Does he think himself invincible?* Draka wondered. *If so, Orgrim or I will soon teach him otherwise.*

The chieftain of the abominable clan, for so Draka suspected him to be, carried two axes. He hacked left and right, his head swiveling back again and again to check Orgrim's location. In the swirl of close-quarters combat, Draka couldn't get a clear shot at him and growled in frustration.

The Red Walker slashed—swiftly, violently, almost casually, and a Frostwolf screamed. She clutched her sword arm, blood flowing between her fingers. She was easy prey, but the Red Walker did not press his advantage. Instead, he kicked out, catching the injured female in the stomach. Draka's body tightened in sympathy, thinking of the tiny life she housed. The Frostwolf stumbled backwards, falling.

But still alive.

Why—

She heard her mate's voice in her mind. *The Red Walkers needed to kill the wolves outright, and swiftly. That was the greatest threat...*

For an instant, Draka felt as cold as winter.

Chills chased each other around her skin, then anger surged through her, a rage so hot she began to sweat. "You monsters," she muttered. "Spirits, guard my baby!" And Draka turned Ice toward the fray.

"Orgrim!" she shouted. "Orgrim!" He turned briefly, caught her eyes, and scowled.

"Get *back*, Draka!"

Orcs could be overcome, subdued, and made to walk under their own power...

"They're trying to wound us, not kill us!" Draka persisted. Orgrim's scowl deepened. She understood his confusion. It made no sense at all. Why wound an enemy when you could kill them?

The others, including the children, they have taken prisoner.

Food for later.

Draka saw comprehension flow over Orgrim's face like water. His features contorted into a mask of absolute fury. "Kill them, Frostwolves!" Orgrim shouted. *"Kill them all!"*

And then Draka heard a sound that made her heart leap and tears sting her eyes. It was the glorious sound of frost wolves howling—from the north.

The Spirit of Life's gift had been manifold. The Frostwolves felt as refreshed as if they had slept deeply for days. As strong as if they had feasted upon nourishing food their entire lives. Their senses grew almost as sharp as the newly energized wolves upon which they rode. Even as he felt calmness and focus descend upon him, Durotan wondered if this was how the members of the despised Red Walker clan felt with their stolen strength. But he chose to let the thought intensify his resolve, rather than cause him despair. The latter would not help him save his clan—his wife—his child.

The gift will not last, the Spirit told Drek'Thar. *But it may last long enough. Go, and save your people.*

The wolves ran as never before: smoothly, steadily, without tiring. Their riders did not speak to one another. There was no need to. The Spirit of Life had entered them for a short while, and though they could not read one another's thoughts, they were in harmony.

They had arrived too late to prevent the battle, but a quick glance showed Durotan that, while his clan was outnumbered, they seemed to be holding their own. The returning Frostwolves did not slow their pace, charging into the thick of the fight with weapons swinging and war cries bursting from their lips.

Never in his life had Durotan felt more righteous than he did at this moment. The Red Walkers were things that should never have been, and wiping them from the face of Draenor would be like cutting out rotting tissue. He leaped off of Sharptooth, freeing the wolf to attack separately, and grinned fiercely at the luckless Red Walker who charged him. She bore two small axes. One she swung high, at his face, and she brought the second across her body in a horizontal sweep.

Sever flashed, and chopped, and both her arms—their hands still gripping the axes—fell to the ground.

She stared at the spurting stubs in astonishment before her head joined them.

Durotan sensed another behind him and whirled, driving Sever into the Red Walker's chest. A bellow of rage alerted him to a third, and he drew back the axe to strike again. But before he could do so, an arrow suddenly sprouted from the Red Walker's eye, and he tumbled down.

Durotan recognized the fletching, and a moment later, his heart called out to him.

"Durotan!" Draka shouted. "Orgrim fights their chieftain!"

Durotan glanced around. He saw Zarka and Kulzak fighting almost lazily, yet Red Walkers were tumbling to the earth left and right. Geyah fought like one half her age, leaping and dancing, wielding the spear as if it were nothing at all. Even the Frostwolves who had not received the Spirit's blessing were heartened to see their chieftain's return and were fighting with renewed vigor.

But where was Orgrim, and the Red Walkers' chieftain?

And then he saw them: Orgrim, massive, bald, determined, wielding the enormous Doomhammer as calmly as if it were a child's toy; and the chieftain—bigger than Orgrim, as densely muscled, wielding two axes so swiftly they were blurs. Durotan was torn. He did not want to deprive Orgrim of the honor of killing the leader of this monstrous clan, but neither did he wish his friend dead—and the chieftain alive.

He would go to the aid of his second-in-command, and intervene if necessary. Another Red Walker, wielding a morning star with blooded barbs, leaped into his path. Durotan ducked as the morning star whirred harmlessly over his head, and swung Sever upward. The Red Walker opened his mouth as if to protest. Blood gushed forward. Disgusted, Durotan yanked his blade free, and pressed on.

He was close now. The two were evenly matched. Durotan realized that his intervention would not be needed. Though Orgrim was tiring, as he had received no blessing, he was holding his own.

Senses alert for any attack, Durotan let his gaze roam the battlefield. Many Frostwolves were down, but he could see they were only wounded. The Red Walkers, however, did not move, and he saw two more fall before his eyes—one slain by another arrow, perhaps Draka's, perhaps not, and another one gasped out his life at the end of Geyah's spear. Unable to believe it, Durotan turned in a tight circle. Only a handful of Red Walkers remained alive! His heart full, he sent a grateful prayer to the Spirits.

Durotan turned to look at the battle between his second-in-command and the Red Walker chieftain. It was almost over, he realized. The Red Walker's left arm dangled, completely useless. Durotan could see that his hand was pulverized. He still fought with the one axe; a single-bladed weapon that looked small against the Doomhammer. Brave, but futile.

Orgrim bellowed, and lifted the Doomhammer. Durotan smiled.

Once Orgrim killed the chieftain, then—

Killed the chieftain.

"No," Durotan whispered. "No. Orgrim! *Orgrim!* Take him alive! Do you hear me? *We must take him alive*!"

29

The chieftain of the Red Walker Clan struggled against Orgrim and Kulzak, but they had him pinned to the earth. "Give me the honor of separating his ugly head from his shoulders, my chieftain," Orgrim grunted.

"No," Durotan said, "Not yet. Take him away and bind him, for now. We need to tend to the wounded. Then I will speak with him. " He could feel the gift of the Spirit ebbing from him, and he was suddenly unspeakably weary. Sever hung abruptly heavy in his hands. He, like every Frostwolf, burned to slay this creature that now lay before him, pinned and helpless if not yet broken.

He would do so. But Durotan wanted answers first. Grudgingly, Orgrim and Kulzak obeyed their chieftain's order, trussing the last living Red Walker up like the animal he was. Even so, the blood-covered monster met Durotan's gaze impudently as he was led away ungently.

"My heart," came Draka's voice. Turning, Durotan embraced her tightly. He held her for a long moment, then released her. "Tell me what happened."

"There is much to say, and much I have yet to hear," Durotan said. "For now, tell me what happened with our clan." He listened as Draka explained how their attackers had descended like a foul-smelling wave, and how she had noticed that they were injuring the Frostwolves, not killing them outright.

"They thought to enslave us, then feed upon us," she snarled, "but they did not understand that we must be dead in order to not be a threat!" The tactic, in the end, had doomed the Red Walkers.

Most of the injured could walk, and soon the shaman were busy stitching wounds closed, preparing drafts, and applying poultices to injuries. Durotan called for Zarka, ordering her to return to the Seat of the Spirits, and bring back Drek'Thar and whatever wolves had survived.

His clan was being tended to.

It was time to speak to the Red Walker chieftain.

Orgrim stood guard over the captive. Not to make certain he didn't escape; it was clear that Orgrim had ensured that would not happen. No, Durotan suspected it was to keep the chieftain alive. Every Frostwolf in the camp doubtless wished him dead.

The Red Walker glanced up as Durotan's shadow fell over him, and smiled. Durotan glared at him, Thunderstrike in his hand, searching for the orc inside the monster.

He couldn't find it.

"You violated the Seat of the Spirits," Durotan said.

"You Frostwolves are not the only ones with stories," the chieftain replied.

"And you knew we would come."

"Eventually, yes, you would. After our failure, when you killed our hunting party, we went to the north to wait for you. This time, you would come to us. We had scouts to keep an eye on you, and simply waited." He smiled. It was a hideous sight. "We took our strength from the Spirits while you wandered right to us."

I must not kill him. Not yet.

"I want to understand how this happened," Durotan said at last. "The Red Walkers were an orc clan, like the rest of us. You faced the same challenges we did. Gul'dan says you refused to join him, as we did. What happened to you? How did you descend into—into this collective madness? Commit such atrocities?" He shook his head, almost pityingly. "Your clan," he said, "went insane."

The chieftain stared at him for a moment, then began to laugh. It was a dreadful sound, starting low, deep in the throat, and then rising to a full belly laugh before at last it subsided. Tears of mirth moistened the orc's eyes.

"Insane," he said, his voice deep and rich and compelling. "Crazy. Mad. Devoid of reason. I assure you, Frostwolf, I am none of these things. Nor are those who follow me."

"You hunt draenei—you hunt your own kind—and call us prey. You slaughter us and carve us up and roast us on a spit! These are not the actions of sane orcs!"

"We are far from insane," the Red Walker continued. His calmness threatened to drive Durotan to a near-madness of his own, but he restrained himself. "We are saner, more rational, than you Frostwolves."

Durotan could no longer control himself. He backhanded the orc and did not curb the force of his blow. The Red Walker's head jerked to the side, but then he merely chuckled again. Blood dripped down his chin, mingling with that of murdered and devoured orcs.

"We are more alike than you think, Durotan, son of Garad," he said, and Durotan froze at the mention of his name and that of his father. "We are both intelligent enough to know that casting in our clan's lot with Gul'dan would be a foolish and dangerous choice. And so, we made another choice altogether. We decided that we would survive on our own. We would not be talbuks. We would be orcs. You have made that same choice—to *stay orcs*. You are not of the soft south. You would not become one of Gul'dan's creatures. The only difference between us is that you have survived—thus far—by moving from place to place, each spot a poorer landing than the next, trying to eke out an existence on what little is there."

"I will silence your insulting—" Orgrim began, lifting the Doomhammer. But Durotan's hand shot out, forestalling the blow. His eyes bored into those of the other chieftain. They were light brown... and clear.

"Go on," Durotan said. His voice was devoid of emotion.

The other smiled. "How has this choice served your clan, Durotan?" He gestured with his shattered hand. It had to have been painful, but he gave no sign of it. "Do you prosper? Do you thrive? Is this life something to be savored? Or do you just exist, stumbling forward aimlessly?" He shook his head. "Did you know, we all secretly admired you?"

That startled Durotan. Although, had not Gul'dan said as much?

"I had thought better of the Frostwolves. What a disappointment you turned out to be."

The words sounded mad—and yet, there was a terrible sort of reason to it. He was fascinated and repelled by what this orc was saying... but Durotan needed to know more.

"I know why we chose as we did," Durotan said. "But why did you choose to become..." He couldn't even speak the word.

Those unnervingly rational eyes searched his, and then the chieftain spoke. His voice was calm, almost bored, as if he were reciting a well-known story. "We, like you, refused the call to join the Horde. We, like you, struggled with finding enough food to survive. We took to covering ourselves with the blood of animals to frighten other orcs from stealing what was ours."

So simple a beginning for something so atrocious. A tactic—nothing more.

"We tracked some draenei encroaching on our territory. They frightened the talbuk herd, and in a rage, we slew them all. As was our habit by then, we covered ourselves with the blood." He mimed the gesture, touching his face. "And some of it got into our mouths."

His tongue crept out to lick his large lower lip. "And it was sweet."

Durotan thought of the gentle, smiling faces of the draenei who had shared his fire. Of how they had risked their own lives to save the children of the orcs, placing themselves in potential danger by bringing those children home. He felt sick in body and soul as the memories played across his mind.

"They chased away our rightful food. And so they *became* our rightful food." The chieftain shrugged. "When next we won a battle against orcs, it was not much different. Flesh is flesh. You will discover that."

Durotan jerked as if struck. "What did you say?"

"It is your only choice, if you wish to stay a true orc. We are predators, Frostwolf. There are predators, and there is prey. There are victors, and there are the defeated. There are orcs, and there are talbuks. We scorned the aid of others, and became the stronger for it."

He lifted his face closer. The reek of old blood filled Durotan's nostrils. "The bodies of my Red

Walkers lie strewn about. Your people need not go hungry tonight. Let us build a new clan. We will grow strong, while others weaken."

He smiled. Durotan could smell blood on his breath. "Take the step, Durotan, son of Garad, son of Durkosh. Become the chieftain of the Red *Wolves*. Be a true orc!"

The words exploded from Durotan like the fire-river from Greatfather Mountain, as violent and as hot.

"We will *never* be like you!"

The chieftain laughed. "Won't you? Look around. There's nothing left here but dust and bones. You will eat—or you will die."

"Eat *him*, then!" It was Kagra. Durotan had not realized that, as he had spoken with the Red Walker, his clan had quietly come to listen. Kagra shouldered her way through the press of Frostwolves, snarling in her rage.

"Kill him, Durotan! He deserves to die a thousand times over for what he and his kind have done. Give him the death that he gave my Nokrar! Better yet, let him suffer! *Devour him piece by piece!*"

As if her words had burst a dam, it seemed as though all the rage and fear and desperation that had been building up was suddenly released. Howls of fury, threats, promises, filled the air.

"Kill him! Eat his flesh! Remember what they have done!" came the cries.

Durotan heard them all. He knew they were grieving, and vengeful in this moment. But still he stood, his gaze locked with the Red Walker chieftain. The other's wet, bloody mouth curved in a knowing grin as he listened to the Frostwolves clamoring for his blood.

The raging cries fell away. Durotan thought of his father's initial refusal of Gul'dan's summons. He had wanted to keep the Frostwolves' proud, independent identity. He had not wished for the Frostwolves to leave their ancestral lands, or to abandon the old ways. He wanted them to stay in the north, and endure.

He thought of his child, yet unborn, who might have perished today. He thought of that precious little life entering a world where insane behavior, like that of the Red Walkers, might well be the only sane option for survival. Where the earth was dead, nothing grew, the water and air were tainted, and even the ground caught fire.

His clan was angry now, yes. But they were not Red Walkers. They would never become Red Wolves.

Some orc clans are cruel, his father had said, so long ago. *They enjoy tormenting and torturing their prey… and their enemies. A Frostwolf takes no joy in suffering.*

Not even in the suffering of our enemies.

"We are Frostwolves," Durotan said simply, and—quickly, cleanly—he drove Thunderstrike home.

30

"We have no ocean into which to toss the remains," Kulzak said, "but at least we can leave the Red Walkers to rot."

But his chieftain shook his head. "No," he said. "I have come to believe our treatment of them was wrong, at the Seat of the Spirits. I… understand them a little better. Whatever they did, they were orcs. We will treat them with the respect they did not show others. And by doing so, remind ourselves of what we will never become."

His clan did not like the decision, but they obeyed. Durotan understood their reluctance. He hoped, with time, they would understand what had been behind his change of heart, and he himself helped to gather the rocks for the task.

Everyone's spirits lifted when the Zarka returned

with not only Drek'Thar, but a limping frost wolf who had managed to survive. The elderly shaman joined his brethren in tending the wounded.

Night approached at last. There was only lichen soup to be eaten, but no one seemed to care. There was a steadiness about the Frostwolves that had not been there before.

Now, at last, there had come a moment for Durotan to sit with his council. As they partook of the simple meal, Drek'Thar spoke of his experience in the Seat of the Spirits. Durotan's chest tightened with sorrow as Drek'Thar described the slow decline of the Spirits and shared with them the Spirit of Life's words of comfort and sadness both. He tried to comprehend the idea of something that was death, but not death, and what that would mean for Draenor, and for his clan.

For a long time, they sat in silence, finishing their meager meal. Durotan reflected on all that had happened that had led to this moment: Gul'dan's visit, his father's death, Draka's return from Exile, and the journey the clan had been forced to undertake since Greatfather Mountain had destroyed Frostfire Ridge. The Red Walkers, Garona's warning, the hungry earth, the dead grasses and trees, the haunting, unforgettable beauty of the Seat of the Spirits. And the final words of the Red Walker chieftain.

He put his bowl down and regarded those around him: Draka, Drek'Thar, Geyah, and Orgrim. Friends and family who had never failed him. He had been blessed, he realized, even through all the dark things that had happened. And his heart, which had been so full of pain for so long, was suddenly at peace.

Durotan finally understood what he needed to do.

"Come with me," he said simply. Without question, they rose and followed him as he strode to the center of the encampment. The rest of the clan, clustered in small family groups, fell silent at their chieftain's approach.

He looked at the gathered Frostwolves. So few left, now. Each one of them was precious. He would behave as a chieftain should, and make the best choice to protect them.

"The Red Walker chieftain was right," he said. He spoke clearly and quietly, but his voice was heard in the expectant silence. "He and his clan were not insane. They faced the same challenges we did, and made the same choice we made: to stay here, in Draenor, and somehow find a way to survive. Their way was monstrous, but it was successful. Successful in a world where, we now know, the Spirits will no longer be truly present."

Concerned murmuring rippled through the crowd. Durotan held up a hand and continued.

"Our shaman Drek'Thar spoke with the voice of the Spirit of Life. It gave us the strength to overcome our enemy, and it gave us the reassurance that wherever there was earth, air, fire, water, and life... there, also, would they be.

"My father and I both refused to join Gul'dan. We felt that he was wrong. That there would be danger to our clan if we followed him. The slave Garona even warned us about him. So, what is a chieftain to do?"

He spread his hands. "Whatever the lore says about what was done in the past, whatever the rituals stipulate, whatever rules or laws or traditions there may be—there is one law, one tradition, which must not be violated. And that is that a chieftain must do whatever is truly best for the clan."

Durotan watched Geyah as he spoke. Her eyes widened briefly, then grew sad.

"Our world is all but dead, and it will never recover. We know this now—we have heard it from the Spirit of Life itself. The Red Walkers chose to feed upon their own kind. Their chieftain said we would do the same. He was wrong. We will *never* become like them. But neither will we become Gul'dan's creatures."

He surveyed them, looking each member of the Frostwolf clan in the eyes. "We will journey to this new land Gul'dan's magics have discovered. We will find earth, air, water, fire, and life there, and they will know us. We will survive... *as Frostwolves*!"

"My chieftain!" It was Geyah, and Durotan tensed. He had thought she had accepted his decision, but perhaps not. "May I speak?"

He nodded, bracing himself. Geyah got to her feet, standing straight and proud, as was her right as wife and mother of chieftains, as a shaman, as Lorekeeper. "You know I follow our traditions. They are important to us. Our actions make us who we are, not our words, but the words have bonded to the actions down through time."

She turned to look at her son. "I loved Garad, and I know he was wise. He honored the traditions, and he led us well until the day he died." Her breath caught for a moment, but she continued. "I saw his son part with tradition again, and again, and again. And now, he wishes us to leave our home for a strange new land. This was not the way of Garad."

Her voice softened. "But Durotan is not Garad, and Durotan has led us well. I held on to the decisions, the choices of my husband, because it was all he had left to us—to me. But Durotan, son of Garad, son of Durkosh—like the Spirits, Garad is gone, but not yet gone. He lives in you. And he would be proud of the choices you have made—and are making now."

Durotan thought, but was not sure, he saw the glitter of tears in her eyes. Geyah made a fist of one hand and thumped it on her chest. "I will follow my chieftain!"

"And I!" Orgrim bellowed, imitating Geyah.

"You are my husband," Draka said quietly to Durotan, for his ears, "whatever happens."

One by one, all the Frostwolves, even those who had once rebelled against Durotan, followed suit. The cold night air was filled with a rhythmic sound, as of the beating of a hundred hearts.

No chieftain, Durotan thought, *has ever led a finer clan than this.*

He raised Thunderstrike. "Tomorrow, the sun

will show its face on the first steps of our next journey. A new homeland awaits."

Durotan took a deep breath.

"Tomorrow—the Frostwolves march to join the Horde!"

ACKNOWLEDGMENTS

Many chefs participated in this dish, and I value them all. At Blizzard, thanks to James Waugh, my friend and touchstone for this project, Cate Gary, and Sean Copeland. At Titan, much appreciation for my excellent editor, Natalie Laverick. And at Legendary, shout-outs to Jamie Kampel for her enthusiasm and patience with script queries, Anna Nettle for cheerfully supplying research photos no matter how often I asked, and Barnaby Legg for his game-changer of an idea and his no-holds-barred enthusiasm for my work. Truly a pleasure to work with you all. I'll do it again any time, anywhere, any project.

Special thanks go to Tyler Kerr, for educating me on how environments can die, and to my fellow authors, William H. Kirby and Mark Anthony, for a writing retreat and suggestions that resulted in all kinds of (literary) destruction. I couldn't have ruined Draenor quite so effectively without you, guys.

Finally, heartfelt gratitude to the readers, who have supported my writing since that fateful day when *Lord of the Clans* hit the bookshelves.

Strength and honor!

ABOUT THE AUTHOR

Award-winning and eight-time *New York Times* bestselling author Christie Golden has written nearly fifty novels and several short stories in the fields of science fiction, fantasy, and horror. Among her many projects are over a dozen *Star Trek* novels, nearly a dozen for gaming giant Blizzard's *World of Warcraft* and *StarCraft* novels, and three books in the nine-book *Star Wars* series, *Fate of the Jedi*, which she co-wrote with authors Aaron Allston and Troy Denning.

Born in Georgia with stints in Michigan and Colorado, Golden has returned to Virginia for a spell.

Follow Christie on Twitter @ChristieGolden or visit her website: www.christiegolden.com.